THE NINE-TAILED FOX

Also by Martin Limón

Jade Lady Burning
Slicky Boys
Buddha's Money
The Door to Bitterness
The Wandering Ghost
G.I. Bones
Mr. Kill
The Joy Brigade
The Iron Sickle
The Ville Rat
Ping-Pong Heart

Nightmare Range

THE NINE-TAILED FOX

Martin Limón

Published by
Soho Press, Inc.
853 Broadway
New York, NY 10003

Limón, Martin.
The nine-tailed fox / Martin Limón.
A Sergeants Sueño and Bascom novel ; 12

ISBN 978-1-61695-823-7
eISBN 978-1-61695-824-4

1. Sueño, George (Fictitious character)—Fiction. 2. Bascom,
Ernie (Fictitious character)—Fiction. 3. United States Army
Criminal Investigation Command—Fiction. 4. Americans—Korea—
Fiction. 5. Korea (South)—History—1960–1988—Fiction. I. Title

PS3562.I465 N56 2017 813'.54—dc23 2017011746

Interior design by Janine Agro, Soho Press, Inc.

Printed in the United States of America

10 9 8 7 6 5 4 3 2 1

To my dad, Peter T. Limón, World War II veteran and survivor of the attack on Pearl Harbor.

THE NINE-
TAILED FOX

-1-

Brigadier General Hubert N. Frankenton, Chief of Staff of the 8th United States Army, frowned as he stared at a wall-sized map of the Korean Peninsula. After pondering it for a minute, he slapped his pointer at a red dot and said, "The first soldier disappeared here, from Camp Kyle near Uijongbu." He turned toward his aide, a captain, and asked, "What was his name?"

She checked her notes. "Werkowski." She then recited his rank and unit as everyone at the conference table dutifully scribbled it down.

"Quartermaster unit," the Chief of Staff murmured, as if to himself. "The next disappearance," he continued, "happened here, at a supply-and-maintenance outfit of the Nineteenth Support Group."

He pointed to an area closer to the Yellow Sea: a compound known as ASCOM, the Army Support Command near Bupyong.

"And the most recent disappearance happened way the hell

down south in the village just outside of Hialeah Compound, near Pusan." The largest port city in South Korea, about two hundred miles from Seoul.

The Chief of Staff pulled up his khaki pants and paced the room. The only person with the bravery—or rank—to venture a comment was my boss, Colonel Walter P. Brace, Provost Marshal of the 8th United States Army.

"These disappearances," Colonel Brace said, clearing his throat and lowering the timbre of his voice, "might not be related, sir. It's possible these fellows have gone AWOL and will turn up eventually, drunk and broke and begging to be taken back."

General Frankenton nodded his head, still pacing, his hands clasped behind his back.

"It's possible, Walt," he agreed. "I hope that's what happened. But none of the facts in these cases jibe with your typical AWOL. None of the soldiers involved took anything with them. Their overnight bags were found in their lockers. Only one of them disappeared just after end-of-month payday, when most soldiers go AWOL. According to Data Processing, none of them have used their ration control plates to buy anything out of the PX since they left, which they would normally do in order to raise a little money on the black market." He waved his pointer in a circle in the air as if it were a divining rod. "And most importantly, the shrinks tell me none of the missing men appeared to be under any particular stress from personal problems or an important upcoming inspection. In fact, in all three cases, these men's commanders couldn't say enough good things about them. Ideal troops, they were called. Reliable and dedicated to their units. Top soldiers. And yet they disappeared without a trace, and apparently with no advance planning."

The general sat down heavily at the head of the table. "And I don't need to tell you," he said with a sigh, "that we're catching holy hell from their families and their congressmen back home."

After a respectful silence, one of the officers ventured an inquiry. "Do we suspect North Korean activity?"

General Frankenton winced.

In the more than twenty years since the Korean War, the warring nation had been divided along the DMZ; the Communist North Korean regime on one side and the authoritarian Park Chung-hee military regime on the other. Just thirty miles north of Seoul, 700,000 Red soldiers waited impatiently for the order to invade, just as they did in 1950. On the southern side, 450,000 Republic of Korea soldiers stood guard, resolutely prepared to repel any foolhardy aggression. Meanwhile, North Korean commando units made the occasional clandestine foray into South Korea, spreading death to the unwary, and spy activity was a regular feature of life in this intense corner of the Cold War.

The Chief of Staff pondered the question about North

Korea, lacing his fingers in front of his belly. "It's always possible," he said. "But North Korean spies usually go after well-thought-out targets. Ones with access to classified information, most often. These three fellows, while good soldiers, worked in nothing of a sensitive nature and had no hand in anything the Communists are likely to want."

The officers lining the mahogany conference table grew quiet. The Chief of Staff stood again and paced the length of the room, though his highly polished low quarters made no sound on the plush wall-to-wall carpet.

My name is George Sueño. I'm an agent for the Criminal Investigation Division of the 8th United States Army, stationed at 8th Army headquarters in Seoul. My investigative partner Ernie Bascom and I sat in two straight-backed chairs against the outer wall of the conference room. Why we'd been ordered to stand by, I wasn't quite sure. These classified briefings were usually for brass only, not lower-level enlisted scum like us. Ernie was more nervous than I was. He avoided headquarters when he could, and suspected that we were about to be railroaded into something we wouldn't like.

The Chief of Staff stopped pacing and seemed to jump out of his reverie. His eyes searched the room and eventually focused on me.

"Agent Sueño," he said, pronouncing my name correctly, with the "ñ" like the "ny" in "canyon."

"Yes, sir," I said, sitting up straighter.

"You know the ville," he stated—the GI villages, red-light districts packed with bars and nightclubs and whorehouses, that sat outside each of the over fifty US military compounds in South Korea. "Very well, from what your boss tells me." He glanced over at Colonel Brace. "What do you think would make young troopers like these disappear without a trace?"

All heads at the conference table turned to stare at me. Ernie fidgeted in his seat.

"A woman," I replied.

The conference room broke into laughter. Smiling, the Chief of Staff turned away. After the laughter died down, he turned back to me and said, "I think you're right. I think that should be the first avenue of approach. I'm told you and your partner here, Agent Bascom, are both pretty good at blending in out in the ville."

Ernie clicked his ginseng gum but didn't answer.

"We manage, sir," I replied.

"More than manage," the Chief of Staff said. "You can speak, read, and write Korean, and your partner here seems to have a knack for communing with the underclass of whatever group you encounter. That's why I invited you two here." He hiked up his pants again. "From what I'm told, you're the two best damn investigators we have in-country."

I didn't answer.

The conference room had gone deathly silent, every head still turned toward us. Some of them with blank, wide-eyed stares, waiting greedily for me to make a fool of myself. Others with frowns, annoyance that someone so low in the hierarchy should be anointed with the Chief of Staff's attention. There are few things officers hate more than enlisted men being praised above them, and on the rare occasion when it happens, they plot their revenge carefully. I was more than just comic relief. I was a pig being fattened for a luau.

Oblivious to the pique bubbling about him, the Chief of Staff swiveled to study the map, then turned abruptly back to me. "Given what we know so far, Agent Sueño, where would you start your investigation?"

"Pusan," I said without hesitation.

"Why?"

"The disappearance from Hialeah Compound was the most recent, sir. Just two days ago. We're most likely to find people there who saw something and, more importantly, still remember what they saw."

The Chief of Staff nodded. "How much time do you need to get down there?" he asked.

"If you give us a chopper," I told him, "we can leave now."

He grinned slightly at the answer, then said, "Better change out of those monkey suits," nodding at our dress-green uniforms.

"Yes, sir."

He turned to his assistant, the female captain. "Call the One-Oh-Five Aviation Unit and schedule these two men a chopper. I want them in Pusan before noon chow."

"Yes, sir," she said, rising to her feet. A nice-looking woman with reddish-brown hair knotted tightly atop her head and a name tag that said RETZLEFF. "Come with me."

Ernie and I followed her out of the conference room. Without being told, another of the officers had stood and was handing out sheaves of paperwork. Each thin stack was topped with a light blue cover sheet stamped TOP SECRET.

All the eyes that had been studying us before now completely ignored us. Behind us, the door shut silently.

In Captain Retzleff's office, we were issued FOR OFFICIAL USE ONLY reports that had been generated by 8th Army Personnel, containing the backgrounds of the three missing GIs as well as the MP blotter reports of their disappearances. She lifted her telephone.

"How soon can you be at the helipad?" she asked.

"Thirty minutes," I told her.

She started to dial. After a brief conversation, she hung up the phone and turned to us. "General Frankenton may seem calm, but in reality, he's very upset. Soldiers don't just disappear like this. Not in his command."

"Not until now," Ernie said.

Her eyes narrowed. "Everyone says you're a wise guy, Bascom."

"Everyone's right," Ernie replied.

"The only question is," she continued, "can you find the three missing men?"

"If anybody can find them, me and my partner can."

Generous lips turned up in a half-smile. "Do you agree?"

"Guaranteed," I replied.

"You two are pretty cocksure of yourselves, aren't you?"

"We haven't failed yet," Ernie said, exaggerating perhaps a tad.

The grin faded, and Captain Retzleff paused. In the end, she decided to say nothing except: "You're dismissed." She turned her back on us and strode toward the conference room. As he watched her leave, Ernie clicked his ginseng gum more rapidly than usual.

We exited through the main doors and hurried toward the jeep.

"Why'd you mess with her?" I asked.

Ernie shrugged. "Those officers in the conference room were laughing at us. I wanted to show her that we couldn't be pushed around. Besides, I wanted to spend more time looking at her."

"You're going to get your low-ranking butt in trouble one of these days."

"She'd be worth it."

Fraternization between officers and enlisted personnel was a court-martial offense—a fact that I knew only too well, given my most recent relationship with military psychiatrist Leah Prevault. Ernie hopped into the jeep and switched on the ignition. I slid into the passenger seat.

"Colonel Brace ain't going to like it," Ernie said, "having the Chief of Staff assign two of his men to an investigation."

"Why not?"

Ernie turned and studied me. "Are you *dingy dingy*? It makes him look incompetent, like the Chief of Staff has to reach down and do his job for him."

I shrugged. "I think you're making too much of it."

"You'll see." He backed the jeep out of its parking spot. Then he asked, "Why'd you pick Pusan? That bit about finding witnesses to the last disappearance was a bunch of bull."

"Simple," I told him. "Pusan is farthest from the flagpole."

As we drove past the two-story brick 8th Army headquarters building, off to our left sat a seventy-five-millimeter howitzer used for ceremonial purposes and three flagpoles with the banners of the United States, the Republic of Korea, and the United Nations Command waving against an overcast backdrop.

"You should've asked for per diem," Ernie said.

"I can't think of *everything*. Why didn't you speak up?"

"Too many honchos."

"You afraid?" I asked.

"Very. Afraid I'll strangle one of them." Ernie's fingers tightened on the steering wheel. "We've got to find these guys."

"Why?"

"To prove we're not the bozos the brass thinks we are."

We drove to the barracks. Twenty minutes later, in our

running-the-ville outfits—blue jeans, sneakers, sports shirts with a collar, and nylon jackets with fire-breathing dragons embroidered on the back—we were on our way to the 105th Aviation Unit helipad. The chopper was already there when we arrived, engine whining, enormous metal blades swirling in an ever-accelerating gyre.

We climbed aboard.

The crew chief shouted something I couldn't hear, fitted headsets over our ears, and strapped us into the canvas seats. When he was satisfied that we were secure, he slid the large metal door shut and said something into the small mic in front of his mouth. The blades above revved faster, the chopper shuddered, and with a great, whooshing insult to gravity, the giant whirlybird lifted into an endless gray sky.

-2-

Hialeah Compound had once been a racetrack, as indicated by its name. It was christened as such by the first American troops stationed here after the end of World War II. The Japanese Imperial Army had colonized Korea from 1910 until liberation in 1945, and the Japanese officers had apparently enjoyed the sport of kings. They'd set up a track here on this flat plain some four or five miles inland from the Port of Pusan proper.

A brightly painted helipad sat in the center of a huge expanse of grass that had once been the infield of the track. At the outer rail sat an oddly shaped circular building with a sign that read HIALEAH COMPOUND OFFICERS CLUB. People had once lined up there to buy admission tickets and place their bets. There were no longer thoroughbreds here, but I could almost hear their hooves pounding on the dirt.

When the chopper landed, the crew chief hopped onto the tarmac and made big waving hand gestures to ensure that

Ernie and I departed the chopper through the side door and proceeded away from it with our heads down. As the blades slowed, we waved at him and the pilot and copilot, then moved across the lawn toward the side of the field opposite the Officers Club.

We'd been here before, some months ago, and knew what our first stop was. The Hialeah Compound Military Police Station sat astride the cement-barbed-wire-and-sandbagged edifice that composed the front gate. We pushed through the big double door and approached the front counter. A bored corporal studied us briefly and shouted over his shoulder. "LT, they're here!"

A small man emerged from the back office. He wore freshly pressed fatigues. His rank was First Lieutenant. His name tag was stenciled with the name Messler.

"You're back," he said, not seeming particularly happy about it.

"Don't bother with the ceremony," Ernie told him. "Just a brass band will do."

"Sign in," he said, pushing a legal pad–sized ledger toward us.

"Since when?"

"Since the new Hialeah Compound Provost Marshal ordered that all visiting law enforcement personnel sign in. Signature, printed name, date and time of arrival, and purpose of visit."

Ernie shoved the ledger back at him. "Tell the Hialeah Compound Provost Marshal to grease this and use it as a suppository."

An officer wearing the gold maple leaves of a major walked out from the back hallway. His name tag said Wilson. "You having a problem signing my ledger?" he asked, staring at Ernie. He was a husky man, and neat, with a wrinkle-free khaki uniform and wire-rimmed glasses. His short black hair lay back on his skull, combed as if with a metal brush.

"We're here to find one of your little lost troopers," Ernie said. "Not sign bullshit ledgers."

The major glared at Ernie for a while, but apparently the wheels were turning. He knew we'd been ordered down here by the 8th Army Chief of Staff, General Frankenton himself, and causing a fuss over local procedure wasn't going to endear him to the honchos at HQ. Not when they had Congress breathing down their necks.

That was Ernie. When he knew he held the high hand, he went all in. The problem with this was that in the Army, you didn't hold the high hand forever. Somehow, someplace, they always got you back. Major Wilson shoved the ledger aside. His face impassive, he began to speak.

"Specialist Shirkey was last seen at the Heitei Lounge, just a few yards outside the front gate. Some say he left with a girl. Others say he caught a cab to Texas Street. None of the testimony is reliable, since the last sighting was less than an hour before the midnight curfew, and everyone in the club had been drinking since getting off duty at seventeen hundred hours. According to our sign-out/sign-in register, Shirkey signed out on pass at seventeen fifteen hours but never returned to compound and never signed back in off pass. The houseboy who works in his barracks arrived at work before dawn, but he swears Shirkey's bunk wasn't disturbed. The man you're looking for was out there drinking, and then he wasn't. If you can find a lead off that, more power to you."

With that, Major Wilson turned and walked back into the hallway.

Ernie sniffed. "We read all that in the damn report."

We made all the usual stops: inspecting the sign-out/sign-in register ourselves, talking to the houseboy, whose name was Mr. Ko, and even searching Shirkey's wall locker, but we found nothing unusual, just personal effects and uniforms. Shirkey worked at the Hialeah Cold Storage Facility. Enormous boxes full of frozen beef and pork were ferried by forklift to the backs of eighteen-wheelers that would run them from here up to Seoul and beyond, catering to the carnivorous instincts of the fifty-thousand-some GIs who protected South Korea from the ravenous Commies up north.

The reception we received in the cold storage facility was anything but indifferent. Every one of Shirkey's coworkers had a theory. Some said he just got fed up with the Army, two or three thought he'd been kidnapped by the North Koreans, and one even claimed he'd been abducted by aliens from Jupiter. What they did agree on was that Specialist Shirkey accompanied the entire work crew off compound to the Heitei Lounge that night, and they'd all gotten very drunk. But no one remembered exactly when, or under what conditions, Shirkey had left.

The only odd thing that happened while we were at the facility was that somebody dropped a fifty-pound box of frozen pork chops off the back of a truck. It landed with a loud thud, like a muffled implosion. Everyone jumped. Instead of apologizing for the mishap, the three GIs in the back of the truck just stared at us, hungry for a reaction.

Even though it only missed Ernie by about ten feet, he remained calm. "You lose something?" he asked them. When they didn't reply, he kicked the busted box and said, "You should watch your cholesterol. This stuff can give you a heart attack."

Outside of the warehouse, he said, "Shitheads."

"They don't like CID," I replied. "That makes 'em pretty normal."

"It makes them jerks. One of their own is missing, and they still have to act like they're tough."

"Makes 'em feel good," I replied. "Like they're in charge of something."

"They're not in charge of squat."

■ ■ ■

The Heitei Lounge sat in the center of a short strip of bars, nightclubs, and chophouses that ran directly out of the front gate of Hialeah Compound. It was still early, about an hour before the seventeen hundred close-of-business cannon went off, so the barmaids and hostesses had plenty of time to talk. Some of them were working on their hair and makeup. Others filed their nails.

"Long time ago," Miss Roh, the head waitress, told us, "Shirkey have girlfriend."

"How long ago?"

"Maybe when he first come from States."

"What was this woman's name?" Ernie asked.

"Soon-hui," she told us. "She never work here. She work somewhere on Texas Street."

Texas Street, or *Teik-sas kolmok* as it was known by the local Korean population, was the notorious nightclub and bar district that ran along the waterfront, catering to the sailors and merchant marines who visited the bustling Port of Pusan. They called it Texas because in their minds, it was like the Wild West.

I searched the MP report. "There's nothing in here about her."

Miss Roh shrugged and sawed industriously at a recalcitrant cuticle. "They leave out."

"Why?"

"Shirkey, he knuckle-sandwich with her. Lot of trouble. He get SOFA charge."

SOFA. The Status of Forces Agreement between the United States and the Republic of Korea. It regulated all formal disputes between American forces and Korean civilians, including allegations of assault.

"So the Hialeah Compound MPs were protecting Shirkey?" Ernie asked.

Miss Roh shrugged again. "All GI same-same."

"Was she hurt bad, this Soon-hui?" I asked.

"Somebody say she gonna have baby. Shirkey baby. After he knuckle-sandwich her, no more baby."

Ernie and I glanced at each other. I continued with the questions.

"Do you know where Soon-hui works?"

"Somewhere on Texas Street."

There were maybe a hundred barrooms scattered in the ten-by-six-block area known as Texas Street. The girls conferred amongst themselves, speaking Korean rapidly. I couldn't understand it all; when Koreans speak quickly, their words often slur together, sounding nothing like the idioms in the textbook for my night class back on 8th Army compound.

Finally, Miss Roh turned to me and said, "Sea Dragon Club we think, maybe. Anyway, she have three boyfriend, all work submarine. Come in different times."

US attack submarines patrolled the arctic regions north of Siberia, ready to take on the Soviet Union on a moment's notice. The convenient part, from this Soon-hui's point of view, must have been that only one of the subs was allowed in port for repairs and maintenance at a time. Which meant that she only had to deal with one boyfriend at a time.

I slapped three thousand *won* on the bar, about six bucks, and told the girls to buy themselves some refreshments. Miss Roh sneered at the money but said nothing.

Outside, Ernie said, "You embarrassed me."

"*I* embarrassed *you*?"

"Yeah. You didn't tip enough."

"I didn't see you reaching in *your* pocket."

"I don't need to tip."

"Why not?"

"Charm," he said, grinning.

Ernie waved down a taxi. Or a kimchi cab, as GIs call the box-like little sedans. Fifteen minutes later, after rolling through the suburbs of the vast city of Pusan, we disembarked in the neon-spangled environs of the red-light district known as Texas Street.

The Sea Dragon Nightclub was a utilitarian enough place for what it had to accomplish, which was the efficient extraction of money from lonely sailors far from home. The walls were lined with high-backed booths, convenient for intimate snuggling with Korean business girls. In the back of the large room sat a short bar, and in the center was a lowered dance floor maybe big enough for a half-dozen couples. Speakers for the sound system were elevated just out of reach on small platforms, and right now the volume was turned down, which was merciful, because a Korean female singer was warbling out a saccharine song of heartache and regret.

The woman behind the bar wasn't happy to see us. "You GI," she said. "Not sailor."

Our short haircuts and Korean-made nylon jackets gave us away. Not to mention that there were few ships in port, and the sailors on them hadn't been granted liberty yet. The bargirl began a brief tirade. "Girl in Sea Dragon Club no talk to GI," she said. "Too Cheap Charley. No can make money."

"The sailors," Ernie said, "and the merchant marines, they spend a lot of money?"

"American sailors spend a lot of money. Maybe two, three months they on submarine, no can spend money. They come Texas Street, spend lots of money. Merchant marine, most Cheap Charley just like GI. Maybe captain spend money, officers, that's it."

"So you make money on the American sailors," I said.

"Especially submarine sailor." She shook her head. "They *taaksan* crazy." Very crazy.

I leaned across the bar. "Why are submarine sailors crazier than regular sailors?"

Her eyes widened. "Because they under*water*," she said, as if it were the most obvious thing in the world.

I had no bona fides to argue with her analysis. Instead I asked, "Will you sell us a drink?"

"What you want?"

"OB," I said. "How much is it?"

"OB one thousand *won*," she said.

"For a beer?" Ernie said. "In Seoul it's half that. Five hundred *won*."

She shrugged. "Then you go Seoul."

We finally realized that we had no choice, since they had nothing cheaper than a bottle of OB beer. We ordered two.

"How about Soon-hui?" I asked. "Is she here?"

"Most tick she come," the bartender said.

"When?" I asked, trying to narrow the time frame down from "most tick," which was GI slang for "pretty soon."

"She come." The woman walked away from us and busied herself restocking beer and soft drinks in the cooler.

A door to the right of the bar opened onto a cement stairway. Women's voices drifted down from upstairs. In many of these places, especially near seaports like Pusan and Inchon, the barrooms provided food and lodging to the women who worked for them. It might be easy to look down on these young women for their sordid careers, but the Korean economy, though growing, still couldn't provide enough jobs for the entire female population. Not every woman could marry, especially when all able-bodied Korean males served in the military from ages twenty through twenty-three; after military service, these young men had trouble finding jobs themselves. Even though new factories were providing jobs, there still wasn't enough opportunity to go around. Poor farm families eked out a precarious existence, and most of them couldn't afford to feed an unmarried adult daughter. At this time in the early '70s, the average per capita income in Korea was less than eight hundred dollars per year. Even that was distributed without any consideration of the lives and futures of poor Korean country girls. As such, both the draw and dangers of Texas Street were more than many young women could resist. I'd seen too many whose lives had ended in tragedy.

Carrying our beers, Ernie and I climbed the cement stairwell without waiting for permission. A skinny boy of about ten or eleven sat midway up the steps, busy shining ladies' footwear. Even though the heat hadn't been turned on yet and the Sea Dragon Nightclub was frigid, he wore only cheap plastic sandals, loose-fitting shorts, and a T-shirt. He stopped his industrious brushing and stared at us, wide-eyed. Quickly he packed up his polish and rag and scurried downstairs.

Ernie looked after him. "Why'd you frighten him off?"

"I didn't do anything."

Seconds later, from out behind the bar, a back door slammed.

The voices of the women became clearer as we approached the second floor. Someone said, *"Migun wayo."* GIs are here.

Just like that, they'd pinpointed us as Cheap Charley soldiers stationed in-country instead of sailors on liberty with a wad of cash sizzling in our pockets.

"Anyonghaseiyo?" I greeted them. "I've heard that at the Sea Dragon Club there are many beautiful ladies. Is that so?"

One of the women replied, *"Choa hani?"* Which roughly meant, "You'd like that, wouldn't you?"

She stood in the central cement aisle, hands on her hips, wearing a T-shirt and beige shorts. Ernie approached her and took her by the arm and sang in a falsetto voice, *"Yobo. Yobo. I love you, yobo!"*

Faces peered out of the half dozen doorways that stretched down the hallway. They were smiling, and some of them laughed. It was boring in the late afternoon after everyone had taken their trip to the bathhouse, and they were waiting for the rice-and-bean-curd soup and kimchi they'd be served for dinner before the start of the evening's work. And Ernie and I were young, and we knew a lot more about Korea than some fresh-off-the-boat sailor. I offered one of the girls my beer. She grabbed the bottle and tilted it back, but apparently some of the suds caught in her throat. She coughed and sputtered as the other girls laughed at her discomfort.

"Yonsup pilliyo!" one of them shouted. You need practice!

I was about to ask around for Soon-hui when the bartender ran up the stairs.

"Weikurei nonun?" she shouted at me. What's the matter with you? And then to the girls, "These are GIs. They're useless. Put on your makeup. Get dressed. Get ready for work."

One of the younger girls whined, "What about the rice?"

"You don't work, you don't eat," the bartender shouted. "Hurry up!" She turned and stormed down the steps.

I noticed one woman squatting forlornly in the hallway, her arms folded across her knees. She was the only one who hadn't joined in the festivities. She stared straight ahead, her face unmoving. I walked toward her and took a gamble.

"Soon-hui?" I asked.

She looked up at me. "How you know?"

I shrugged. From what I'd been told had happened to her, it figured that she might not be too interested in interacting with GIs. "Shirkey," I said. "We're looking for him."

Slowly she rose to her feet and stepped back into her room. There were four small bunks there, about the right size for children. Metal wires were strung above from wall to wall, and a tiny rain forest of women's clothing and underwear hung from them. She stopped beneath a bright red brassiere and swiveled. "Why you bother me?" she asked.

Her face was a long oval. Defensive eyes peered out at the world above a round-tipped nose. Shapely lips pursed tightly, trying desperately to hang on to her last tattered remnants of dignity.

"Shirkey's disappeared," I told her.

She looked puzzled and then asked, "What's it mean? Disappeared?"

In Korean, I explained. And then I asked her when she'd last seen him.

"When he punch me," she said, clutching her stomach. "Before I lose baby."

"You didn't see him after that?"

"No," she replied, looking away.

Ernie was outside talking to the girls in a subdued voice, doing his best to keep them occupied while I interviewed Soon-hui. From downstairs the bartender's voice bellowed, *"Bali!"* Hurry! Other women walked into the room, staring at me and Soon-hui curiously. As they started to get dressed, we returned to the hallway.

"So you haven't seen him or talked to him," I said, "since you lost the baby?"

"No," she replied vehemently, shaking her head.

"Do you know anyone who *has* seen him?"

She continued shaking her head. "GI don't come Sea Dragon Club," she said. "Not many."

"But he did come out here when you first met him?"

"Yes. No sailors that night. Hialeah Compound GIs know when ships all gone."

"Out to sea."

She nodded.

"You liked him?"

"Yes. He very nice. I thought maybe he take me to States. We stay together sometimes. I run away from Sea Dragon Club with him, maybe three days. When I come back, bartender, she *taaksan* angry. I don't care. I like Shirkey."

"And he liked you?"

She nodded.

"But you became pregnant." I used the Korean term *imshin*.

"Yes. My stomach grow big, he become angry. He told me to see doctor, take out baby, but I don't want."

"Until he beat you," I said. "And he punched you in the stomach."

"Yes," she said, staring into space as if suddenly puzzled. "I don't know."

"You don't know what?"

She looked up at me. "I don't know man can be so mean."

"But now you do."

She nodded her head. "Now I know. Baby gone. Baby know, too."

"The baby knows?"

"Yes. I go temple. Pray. Sometimes baby talk to me."

I paused, using perhaps the most effective interrogation technique: silence.

"He mad at daddy," she continued. "Someday Shirkey be . . ." She switched back to Korean. "*Chobol hei.*"

"Punished," I said.

"Yes. Baby say that someday Shirkey be punished."

I handed her some money, more than I'd coughed up at the Heitei Lounge. She looked at the small wad of bills as if it were a dead creature. Without a word, she stuck the bills in the loose folds of her skirt.

-3-

"She's a damn *suspect*," Ernie said, as we rode a kimchi cab back to Hialeah Compound.

"Nah," I replied. "How could she kidnap a grown man?"

"Maybe she killed him and dumped his body in the port." He pointed toward the inlet, lined now with ships on our side and sparkling lights on the far shore. "For all we know, Specialist Shirkey is out there right now. Floating."

"That wouldn't explain the other guys who disappeared."

"Maybe they're not related. Maybe it's all just a big coincidence."

"Maybe. But Soon-hui's a Korean civilian, anyway. We don't have any jurisdiction over her."

"So call Mr. Kill," Ernie replied.

Gil Kwon-up was the Chief Homicide Inspector of the Korean National Police—a big shot with a fancy office at the KNP headquarters in Seoul. The guys in American law enforcement, of course, distorted his name from Gil to Mr.

Kill. Which fit by a bizarre logic, given his role as a homicide investigator. We'd worked with him on a few cases, mostly involving GI-on-Korean crime, and there was a strong rapport there. I knew that if I called him and asked him to have Soon-hui picked up and questioned by the Pusan KNP office, he'd do it. Still, I was reluctant. The KNPs were far from gentle when conducting their interrogations. I figured Soon-hui'd been through enough.

When I hesitated, Ernie said, "You're too softhearted, Sueño. That's your problem."

"There's no rush," I said. "She's not going anywhere."

"How do you know?"

"She's practically a slave there. No money. No family to go back to. What's she going to do? Apply to Harvard?"

Ernie turned and stared at me. "What the hell's gotten into you?"

"I don't like it," I said, crossing my arms.

"Like what?"

"It really is like slavery. They're not there by choice," I said.

"At the Sea Dragon Club? They're not slaves."

"Close to it."

Apparently, we'd agreed to disagree, because we were both silent for the rest of the trip.

When we arrived at the front gate of Hialeah Compound, it was my turn to pay the driver. At the pedestrian entrance, we showed a bored MP our military IDs. After winding through a narrow hallway, we exited the MP station and strode along a sidewalk toward the Hialeah Compound Enlisted Club. Using admirable restraint, we bypassed the enticing restaurant and bar operation and kept going about a quarter mile toward the Hialeah Compound Sports and Recreation Center, which was nothing more than two enormous Quonset huts hooked together. We checked out towels, sweatpants, and shirts, went to change, and stopped by the weight room to pump some iron. After the workout came a steam bath and a shower, and thus refreshed, we returned to the Enlisted Club. In the dining room, we ate a square meal accompanied by only ice water and hot coffee.

"This teetotal business sucks," Ernie said.

"It'll pay off tonight around midnight."

Ernie checked his watch. "Three more hours. I don't care what you say. At eleven, I'm having a drink."

"You mean twenty-three hundred hours."

"Yeah. I've synchronized my watch."

By eleven P.M., one hour before the midnight-to-four curfew, Ernie and I stood in the shadows of the main drag of the strip right outside Hialeah Compound sipping on an open bottle of *soju*, the fiery rice liquor manufactured in Korea from time immemorial.

The twelve-to-four curfew had been established by the South Korean government shortly after the war. Everyone except authorized personnel had to be off the streets. The reason was supposedly that this made it easier for the ROK Army to apprehend North Korean intruders. The real reason, I believed, was for the Park Chung-hee dictatorship to flex its muscles with a constant reminder to its populace of who was boss. A citizen caught out after curfew was subject to a fine at best, and being shot on sight at worst. As a result, kimchi cabs were lined up in front of the bars and nightclubs, waiting to whisk last-minute customers home before the midnight bell tolled.

"What do you expect to find, Sueño?"

"I don't know. I just know that Shirkey left the Heitei Lounge just before curfew hit. By himself, apparently. I want to see what the ville looks like at that time of night."

"And maybe find a witness?"

"It's worth a try."

"One thing I know," Ernie said, "is that the MPs who wrote that blotter report didn't stay out here at night until all hours."

"Probably not," I admitted.

"But you're thorough, huh, Sueño?"

I looked at him. "Drink some more *soju*."

He did. Then he wiped the rim of the bottle and handed it to me. I popped back a glug, grimaced, and handed it back to him.

"You don't like it?" he asked.

"It does the job."

Ernie took a long swig. "Truer words were never spoken."

An old woman pushed a cart down the sidewalk. Set on rubber wheels, it held a stove in the center with a flaming charcoal briquette heating up a pan of sizzling oil. The aroma of batter-fried sweet potatoes and fish wafted tantalizingly through the air.

"Let's buy some mackerel," I told Ernie.

He grabbed his stomach. "That stuff gives me the runs."

"Come on."

He followed me to the cart. An oil lamp illuminated not only the stove atop the cart, but the wrinkled face of its stout proprietor. She wore a scarf over her gray hair and enough layered wool sweaters to fight off the night's chill.

"*Olmayo?*" I asked. How much?

She responded in English. "One dollar, big bag. You take barracks, anybody eat." She waved her hands, indicating all my buddies.

While she was still hoping I'd spend some money, I discovered that her name was Suh Ajjima—Auntie Suh—and she was out here every night selling snacks to half-drunk GIs. I asked her about what she'd seen three nights ago. She stared at me blankly. I mentioned the name Shirkey. This time, in addition to the blank look, she shook her head slowly.

"He came out of the Heitei Lounge," I told her, pointing at the Heitei's neon sign. "From there we think he walked away from the compound. He was alone, still wearing his fatigue uniform. Did you see him?"

"I no see," she said quickly. Too quickly. "You want small bag, hundred *won*." About twenty cents.

"Small bag," I said.

She grabbed a loose sheet of newspaper, plopped greasy slices of sweet potato and breaded fish flesh onto it, and folded it into a neat package. Grabbing another sheet of paper to help absorb the grease, she wrapped it again and handed it to me. I pulled a hundred-*won* coin out of my pocket and dropped it into her open palm.

"You were here that night," I said.

She looked up at me, worried, but didn't deny it. She grabbed a fresh sweet potato and began to slice it, though she already had more than enough bobbing in the hot grease. I placed my hand atop hers and held it steady. With my free hand, I reached inside my coat pocket and pulled out my badge. I showed it to her and switched to Korean. I told her I wanted her to tell us what she saw that night. When she hesitated, I told her that if Shirkey wasn't found, the post commander would restrict all GIs to compound.

"For their safety," I told her. "Too dangerous for them to come out here. You'll lose business."

Worried eyes crinkled even more tightly. Like so many people, her economic prosperity—even her ability to eat regularly—was probably measured day-by-day.

I waved my arm to indicate the entire block. "Not just you,

everybody. No more GIs at the tailor shop. No more GIs at the brassware emporium. No more GIs at the Heitei Lounge."

She glanced at the businesses around us. A few GIs emerged from one of the bars and, spotting her, headed straight for her cart. Ernie and I backed off and observed. The transaction didn't take long. All the GIs seemed to know her, and within seconds, they had large, grease-stained parcels under their arms and were heading for the pedestrian entrance to Hialeah Compound. When they were gone, Ernie and I once again approached Auntie Suh.

Apparently, my argument had swayed her. Without looking up at me, she said, "She pretty lady."

I had no idea who she was talking about, but as long as she was talking, I knew better than to interrupt. Ernie moved away. I stood in front of the cart, my hands in my pockets and my face impassive.

"She wear, how you say, something come out here." She plucked at the upper front of her chest.

"Frills?" I said.

"Yes. Long time ago woman wear. Not now."

"A blouse with frills," I said. "What else?"

"Black coat." She mimicked shrugging it on. "Skirt, down to shoes."

"How long was the coat?"

"Here," she said, slicing her hand along the broad expanse of her waistline.

"What about her hair? Face?"

"Hair stand up high." She motioned at about six inches above the top of her skull. "Face pretty. Soft. Round eyes. But she not young."

"How old?"

Auntie Suh pondered this, pursing her lips. "Maybe forty. Most tick." Soon.

"What'd she do?"

"One GI, who I don't know. He come out of Heitei Lounge." She pronounced the word with an accent: *loun-gee*. "He *taaksan* stinko." Very drunk. "He see woman stand there." She pointed to the corner beneath one of the few streetlamps. "That night lot of, how you say, *angei*."

"Fog," I said.

"Yes. Fog. No can see. But he see her. Go talk to her."

"What happened then?"

"They talk, not too long. Then together they walk back that way." She indicated the street that ran perpendicular to the strip. There were fewer lights back there.

"Did you see where they went?"

"No. After that, I no see. Many GI come out of Heitei Lounge. Come out of other clubs. Most tick curfew. They all hungry. Buy a lot of fish."

I asked to see her Korean National Identity card, and when she hesitated, I reminded her again of how important it was that we find Shirkey. She pulled out her ID card and showed it to me. I jotted down her full name, address, and National Identity card serial number and handed the card back to her. I knew better than to ask for a phone number. Telephones were expensive in Korea; businesses had them, but only the rich could afford to keep one in their home.

I thanked her for her cooperation, and Ernie and I went to explore the cross street. When we rounded the corner, I handed the small parcel of deep-fried sweet potato and mackerel to him. He opened it, sniffed, and his face twisted in disgust. He tossed the parcel into the gutter.

"That's wasteful," I told him.

"The cats'll find it."

Only one neon sign glistened in the shadow of the side street: the Number One Inn. Beneath the English, in smaller *hangul* script, it read CHEIL YOGUAN, which meant exactly the same thing. It was a three-story building that stood about a hundred yards from the bar district.

"You think they went there?" Ernie asked.

"Maybe. Auntie Suh didn't recognize the woman, which meant she was new in town. Maybe a streetwalker from nearby, looking to make a quick buck. Where else would they go?"

The other buildings were closed and shuttered businesses: a bicycle repair shop, a bulk grain storage. Behind that were residences for the working poor of the city of Pusan.

"They could've gone back in one of those alleys," Ernie said. "Tried it standing up."

"Yeah. But if they'd done that, Shirkey probably wouldn't have disappeared. Or even if she'd killed him, she would've left the body there."

Ernie didn't reply. We reached the cement steps leading up to the double-doored entrance of the *yoguan*. I pushed through and heard a bell ring. A woman slid open an oil-papered door and scurried out of a side room. At the entranceway, more than a dozen pairs of shoes sat beneath a two-foot-high raised floor. The hallway was varnished a dark brown and immaculately clean.

"Anyonghaseiyo," I said to the woman.

She stood with both hands in front of her waist and bowed slightly. She wore a long house dress and, like Auntie Suh, too many sweaters.

Just to make conversation, I started with, *"Bang issoyo?"* Do you have a room?

She nodded.

"Olmayo?"

She told me. Ten thousand *won*. Twenty bucks.

That seemed sort of steep, but I wasn't here to bargain. I showed her my badge. Immediately, she frowned in worry.

We slipped off our shoes and stepped up onto the slick wooden flooring. We walked forward to look down the perpendicular hallway, and saw nothing but a long row of closed wooden doors. I figured that up the wooden staircase was more of the same.

I didn't ask for a guest register, since these small mom-and-pop operations weren't required to formally check in their customers. It was a cash-only business, and if Shirkey and the woman with the frilly blouse had stopped here, they easily could've gotten a room anonymously. But I also knew that a woman who ran a place like this could be counted on to have an excellent memory. Her welfare and that of her family depended on running a tight ship and making a profit, so she wouldn't miss a trick. I considered backing off and waiting for the KNPs to question her. The pressure they could put on a local business owner was enormous, but I hoped she might be more open to an informal approach, as was Auntie Suh at the fried food cart.

"My friend," I said in Korean, "a GI named Shirkey, he came in here two nights ago with an older Korean woman." I mimicked frills on the chest. "She was wearing a nice blouse, a black vest, and a long skirt. Do you remember them?"

The woman eyed me warily.

I tried the restricted-to-compound routine. I told her that if we didn't locate Shirkey, GIs wouldn't be allowed off Hialeah Compound and her business would suffer. Still, she was unmoved, and told me that if I didn't want a room, I should leave. I considered calling the KNPs to ask for their help, but I didn't like the thought of how long that might take.

Ernie sauntered toward a closet door, pulled it open, and fumbled through shelving stacked with wooden trays and small plastic thermoses. At a Korean inn, it was traditional to pro-vide guests with barley tea and warm hand towels to wipe their faces. Without looking back, Ernie took one of the thermoses and tossed it over his shoulder. Barley tea flew everywhere.

Startled, the woman turned and rushed toward him.

Ernie tossed another thermos.

The woman reached him in time to pull a third thermos out of his hand. She clutched it to her bosom and backed away from him as if he were mad. He held her gaze and nodded toward me. A middle-aged Korean man, wearing only pajama bottoms and a T-shirt, appeared out of the same door she'd emerged from. His eyes were wide, and he held a short cudgel in his hands.

"*Yobo,*" he said, addressing her. "*I nomu sikki weikurei?*" Wife, what are these SOBs doing?

"*Kyongchal,*" I said—police—waving my badge toward him. He continued to clutch his cudgel like Hank Aaron waiting for a pitch. I turned back to the woman and repeated the ques-tion. "Do you remember them?"

"Yes," she said, keeping her eyes on Ernie and clutching the plastic thermos as if it were a precious thirteenth-century celadon vase. Her husband started to move toward us, but she motioned for him to stop. He did, his face red, but it didn't seem like he had much patience left. The woman's thoughts seemed to catch up with her, and she said, "He brought her in."

"The GI," I repeated, "he brought the older woman in?"

"Yes. She didn't want to come inside, but he was drunk, almost dragging her. She fought back, and they were both screaming and upsetting the other customers. I told them to leave. She managed to pull him outside, and I locked them out."

"So they didn't get a room?"

"No. I don't want their kind in here."

"Their kind?" I asked. "But you must get plenty of GIs and business girls."

"Yes. But she wasn't a business girl."

"What was she?"

The woman's forehead crinkled. "There was something strange about her," she said. "Too old for him. And more than that. Too proper."

"Proper?" I repeated.

"Yes. It made no sense." Now she ignored Ernie and stared straight at me. "She shouldn't have been with an American. She was a respectable woman."

Merely being seen with an American was enough to throw an honest Korean woman's name into disrepute.

"What happened after you locked them out?"

"They left," she said simply.

"Where did they go?"

"I don't know."

"Toward the compound or away from it?"

"Away from it. That way." She pointed down the street.

"What's down there?"

"Nothing. Just more houses."

"No bars, restaurants, hotels?"

"No. For that, you have to go downtown."

"And they were walking?"

"Yes. I didn't hear a car."

I asked for her Korean national identity card. Her husband protested, telling her not to show it to me. I turned to him and raised the specter of the KNPs. After discussing it with him, she finally complied. I quickly jotted down her information and returned her card to her, keeping a wary eye on her husband and his cudgel.

Before we left, I bowed and thanked them.

As the front door swung shut, I looked back and saw her husband, still glaring at me with weapon in hand. She had already grabbed a large rag and was kneeling on the floor, wiping up puddles of barley tea.

Outside, I turned to Ernie. "Did you have to be so rude?"

"We don't have all *freaking* night. For all we know, Shirkey's life is in danger. We're supposed to be solving a crime, not spreading joy and laughter." Ernie checked his watch. "Besides, there's only twenty minutes left until curfew."

"That guy was about to bash my head in."

"Not to worry. I have these." Ernie showed me the set of brass knuckles he usually kept in his back pocket.

"I'm sure that would've eased the pain of my split skull."

"Always glad to help," Ernie said.

We walked along the dark street, away from the Number One Inn and Hialeah Compound. Ahead stretched nothing but a narrow two-lane road lined with walls of brick and stone.

"There's nothing down this way," Ernie said.

"But this is where they went."

"Somebody must've been waiting for them. Somebody in a vehicle."

"Maybe a taxi."

"Probably not. Not just before curfew. Cab drivers go where the people are. Like back there in the bar district."

It didn't make sense. Shirkey had tried to drag some decent woman into a hot bed operation, she'd refused, and then they'd walked out into the night on a road to nowhere. Then I spotted something about twenty yards ahead. An indentation in the unbroken line of walls.

Ernie spotted it, too. We hurried forward.

In seconds, we stood in front of what appeared to be a collection spot for residential trash. There was a large wooden bin and several of the two-wheeled carts used by city-contracted trash collectors.

"You could park a car here," I said.

"Yeah," Ernie agreed. "But why?"

We studied the area as best we could in the dim light. Neither of us had thought to bring our flashlights. There was clear evidence of tire tracks, but that could've been from someone using the space to turn around. I pulled myself up the side of the bin until I hooked my nose over the edge. Ernie grabbed the soles of my feet and pushed me up farther. I teetered forward, almost falling in, but managed to maintain my balance. The bin was empty, only a few stray newspapers and broken bottles.

I lowered myself back down and dusted off my shirt. "Nothing. They must've made a trash pickup recently."

We checked around and behind the bin. No bodies or shoes or belt buckles. No indication that a human being had ever been dumped here.

"So maybe they kept walking?" Ernie said.

"Maybe."

We looked down the road. There didn't appear to be another cross street for a half mile.

"Maybe she lives down there somewhere," Ernie said.

"Maybe. But we don't know shit."

Ernie didn't argue with that. Double-timing it, we trotted back past the Number One Inn, turned onto the main drag, and headed toward the front gate of Hialeah Compound. One by one, the neon signs of the bar district clicked off. Ten yards in front of the gate, a gaggle of GIs stood around, smoking and mumbling to one another. When we approached, I heard one of them say, "Are those the guys?"

Another said yes, and a brick whistled out of the night.

-4-

We dodged the brick, but the next thing we knew, the small mob was moving toward us. Angry, drunk faces stepped into the glare of the streetlamp. One of the GIs pointed his forefinger at us. I remembered him—the shift leader from the Hialeah Compound Cold Storage Facility.

"You're not gonna start making us look bad," he said. "It's a lie. Shirkey didn't beat up that business girl from the Sea Dragon Nightclub."

"She was just trying to get SOFA money," another GI said.

Ernie knew what to do with a hostile group: head straight into it, which he did. He stepped right at the first guy speaking and shouted, "Nobody gives a *shit* about whether he beat up some business girl!" When he was close enough, he shoved the guy in the chest with both hands.

The GI reeled backward.

"Out of my *way*!" Ernie shouted, starting to bull his way through the crowd. I followed, ready to fight if I had to, but hoping we could make it to the pedestrian entrance before these guys regrouped. No such luck. Some guy in the crowd grabbed Ernie by the neck, and then they were wrestling. I leapt forward and popped the attacker upside his head. Soon everybody was shouting and jostling and trying to throw punches in close quarters. I shoved forward, keeping my head down, as did Ernie.

We were making headway when a whistle shrilled at the pedestrian entrance. A door burst open, and a squad of helmeted MPs brandishing nightsticks charged out. Swinging wildly, they broke up the mob. Ernie and I backed away, too, since the MPs clearly didn't care who they hit.

I pulled out my badge and held it up as I stepped into the light. Ernie did the same, and one of the MPs stopped swinging and waved us toward the compound. We flashed our badges at any of the helmeted MPs that glanced our way, like priests with a crucifix at a gathering of vampires. Finally, we reached the open door and stepped inside.

Lieutenant Messler stood there, hands on hips, his head looking small in his giant visored helmet.

"Do these Hialeah boys always play so rough?" Ernie asked, wiping sweat from his eyes.

"Only when Criminal Investigation stops by for a visit."

"Thanks for saving us," I said.

"It wasn't you," he replied. "It's midnight. Every GI out there is committing a curfew violation."

"So if this had happened earlier," I said, "you would've just let them beat the hell out of us?"

He shrugged. "You have a hundred percent medical."

We stepped past him and collapsed in the waiting room.

We could've gone over to the Hialeah Compound Billeting Office to see if they had a room. If they did, we'd have to sign for linen and blankets, and in the morning we'd have to turn them back in and wait for the NCO in charge to inventory not only the linen, but also the quarters to make sure we hadn't damaged any of the cheap furniture. That seemed like too much of a hassle, so instead, we rolled up our jackets like pillows and made ourselves as comfortable as possible on the hard wooden office benches.

In the middle of the night, I got up to use the latrine, but when I returned to my bench and tried to sleep again, I couldn't. All I could think about was the woman in old-fashioned clothing with frills, the young GI who'd pushed her around, and the long, narrow roadway that led away from the Number One Inn. The more I thought about it, the more I was convinced that someone else—someone with transportation—must've been involved. But why? Who would want to kidnap an American GI? It wasn't like we were worth anything.

The next morning at six A.M., Ernie and I were up, faces scrubbed, standing tall at the Hialeah Compound helipad. The chopper still sat there, one of its blades tilted toward the ground and secured by a metal hook. The crew chief and the two pilots, wearing their flight uniforms and carrying their helmets crooked under their arms, strode across the grassy field.

The crew chief gazed at us, amused. "Up all night?" he asked.

"You could say that," Ernie replied.

"Okay, I will." The crew chief slid the side door of the helicopter open and motioned with his right arm. "Hop aboard."

We did. Gratefully.

In a few minutes, the engine was revved up, and we lifted off the ground. The flight was uneventful, with very little turbulence. For once, Korea was living up to its ancient name of Chosun, the Land of the Morning Calm.

When we landed in Seoul, a female officer stood on the tarmac. She wore a loose-fitting fatigue uniform and held onto her cap with one hand as the wind from the chopper blades swept her backward. Ernie and I hopped off and, still crouching, ran forward until we realized she was Captain Retzleff, Assistant to the Chief of Staff.

"Your presence is requested," she said.

Which is the military's ironic way of saying your presence is *required* and you'd better get your butt in gear. Normally Ernie would've mouthed off, but apparently there was something about Captain Retzleff that threw him off his regular game. He looked her up and down—boldly, as if formulating some sort of plan. She avoided his gaze, ignoring him, but as we walked toward her green army staff car, she glanced back at Ernie, who was now nonchalantly unwrapping another stick of ginseng gum.

Not again, I thought. Ernie Bascom complicating an investigation with a romance. This time with a military officer, and therefore strictly prohibited by the Uniform Code of Military Justice.

We climbed into the car, Captain Retzleff behind the wheel, me in the passenger seat and Ernie in the back. I asked, "Where are we going?"

Captain Retzleff adjusted her rearview mirror, stared into it just a little too long, and then said, "To see a body."

"A dead one?" I asked.

"So they tell me."

A half hour later, our sedan was being waved through the front gate of a small military compound. A ROK marine with an M16 rifle stood beneath an archway plastered in Korean lettering.

"What's it say?" Captain Retzleff asked.

"Coastal Defense Unit Number 1082," I told her.

The Korean military had so many small bases—Army, Navy, Marine Corps, and Air Force—scattered throughout the peninsula that most of them didn't have names like the US military installations did, just numbers.

We passed a short row of camouflage-painted Quonset huts before another marine waved us to a halt. Captain

Retzleff parked the car. As we climbed out, a dapper lieutenant approached us, saluted Captain Retzleff, and introduced himself in broken English as Lieutenant Chon. We followed him along a dirt trail past sandbagged gun emplacements until a string of small islands emerged from the morning mist.

The Korean War had never officially ended. Only an armistice had been signed, not a peace treaty. The South Koreans never knew when or where the Communist North Korean government might attempt an invasion again. For the last twenty years, they'd been watching, waiting.

We'd almost reached the end of the promontory when Lieutenant Chon stopped and motioned toward the water below. He passed Captain Retzleff his heavy-duty flashlight, which she then handed to me as if it were radioactive. Ernie and I studied the area and stepped carefully down the rocky slope. Seawater sloshed through looped concertina wire.

"There," Ernie said, pointing.

Something dark, tangled in seaweed.

I stepped into the shallow water and played the flashlight's beam across it. Open-mouthed, a face gaped toward the sky. Beneath it, a fatigue uniform, faded and tattered but still recognizable. Now we were close enough to wince at the odor.

"How long's he been here?" Ernie asked.

"We need to get the body out in order to tell," I said.

We did our best to part the concertina wire in order to wade forward, but the coiled metal warped and twisted as we attempted to make headway. On the path above, Lieutenant Chon barked an order, and two marines with plier-like cutters rapidly descended the incline and began expertly snipping and pulling back on the webbed barricade. Soon, I was able to wade in almost up to my hips. I grabbed the corpse beneath its arms. To my relief, the body held together as I pulled it away from the clinging barbs. The two marines closed in and used their cutters to release the torso, then the legs. Shivering, I dragged the body toward the shore, and Ernie helped me hoist it onto the pebble-strewn beach.

Their job complete, the two marines retreated.

As I caught my breath, I handed the flashlight to Ernie. He played it slowly along the body, reaching out as he did so to pull seaweed away from the face and limbs.

"Buck sergeant insignia," Ernie said. He spoke in short bursts, trying not to breathe. Now that the body had been exposed to air, its stench was becoming powerful. Ernie leaned forward and shined the light on an embroidered name tag. "Werkowski."

"The guy from Camp Kyle," I said.

"Yeah. The first one who disappeared."

"How in the hell did he end up here?"

Ernie ignored my question and continued to study the body. "Everything seems intact. No boots or socks, but they might've fallen off in the water. Both legs and arms okay." He turned one of the hands palm-up. "Defensive wounds."

"From what?"

"Not gunshots, that's for sure. Some kind of blade. A sharp one. Penetrated right past the bone and came out the other side."

He then zeroed in on the center of Werkowski's chest. There was a large tear in the thick material.

"Entrance wound looks deep," Ernie said.

"The same knife?"

"Probably." We didn't have a ruler, but Ernie gingerly unbuttoned the shirt and used his thumb to estimate the length of the wound. "About an inch and a half."

"How wide?"

"Narrow. Pretty thin blade. Definitely not a butcher knife." He leaned forward. "Hard to tell out here, but it doesn't even seem as wide as a bayonet."

Ernie leaned back, turned his head away for a moment, then slowly exhaled and inhaled. Facing the body again, he said, "Help me turn him over."

The 8th US Army didn't have a forensics team. In the minds of the honchos, that was an undue expense. They didn't believe there was enough crime in their ranks to justify hiring technicians, setting up a lab, and providing transportation, plus everything else that would be required. The nearest forensics lab was at Camp Zama in Japan, and the Army thought that shipping samples, photographs, and other evidence there was good enough.

Ernie and I knew from hard experience that the techs in Japan didn't place 8th Army requests on high priority; results could easily take two weeks, sometimes a month. So we often examined evidence on our own, though technically, we weren't supposed to. The 8th Army coroner was designated as the person to gather evidence and ship it to Camp Zama.

But if we abided by every military regulation, we'd never get anything done. Ernie and I followed the ones we agreed with and ignored the rest.

I stepped closer and knelt, and on the count of three, Ernie and I rolled the remains of Sergeant Werkowski over onto his belly. He landed with a moist thump.

Behind us, a vehicle rolled up and turned off its engine. There was a loud commotion with yelling in both English and Korean. Finally, footsteps approached.

"The coroner's here," Captain Retzleff called from the pathway above.

In a few seconds, they would take possession of the body. Ernie shined the flashlight on the back of Werkowski's skull. "Look at this." In the center, hair had been pulled off and the skin rubbed raw, forming an egg-shaped oval. "Like somebody took a Brillo pad to his head."

"Or rubbed it against blacktop." I involuntarily recalled some particularly cruel incidents from my third-grade year in the LA City School District.

Ernie played the light a foot below Werkowski's shoulder

blades toward the wound we'd both noticed when we first turned him over. "Exit wound. Too close to the wound on the front to be separate."

"A little higher," I said.

Ernie measured it with his thumb. "Not as long. Only about an inch. But the width is the same."

"The blade was long," I said, "and curved upward."

Ernie stood up. Boots clattered against pebbles, and rocks rolled downhill.

"Stand away from that body!" somebody shouted.

"Says who?" challenged Ernie.

"Says the Eighth Army Coroner's Office."

We pushed past the three officious-looking medics and trudged uphill until we reached Captain Retzleff. Ernie tossed the flashlight to Lieutenant Chon.

The coroner, a snide civilian named Wasson, hurried past us and halted when he saw the slippery rocks. "Bring him up here," he commanded his subordinates, waving a pudgy hand.

When we stepped away, Captain Retzleff lowered her voice and asked, "Who is it?"

"One of our boys," Ernie replied.

"Which one?"

"Werkowski. The one from Camp Kyle."

She stared downhill, stricken. "General Frankenton will be furious."

"Not as furious as me," Ernie replied.

"You're wet," she said.

"Thanks for noticing."

She almost reached out to him, but then thought better of it and held her hand poised in midair. Ernie grinned and patted her on the back. We walked over to the sedan.

On the drive to Seoul, Retzleff was silent. I wasn't sure if she was in shock after seeing Werkowski pulled from the frigid Yellow Sea, concerned about the impact of this murder on her military career, or just thinking about Ernie.

Maybe all of the above.

When Retzleff dropped us at the 105th Aviation Unit, we retrieved Ernie's jeep and drove straight to the barracks. After showering, shaving, and changing into the coat and tie required of all 8th Army CID agents, we returned to the CID Admin Office.

"Where in the hell you been?" Staff Sergeant Riley growled.

Ernie didn't bother to answer, instead marching straight toward the still-perking coffee urn in the back. I plopped down into a straight-backed chair upholstered in government gray.

"Where's your report?" Riley asked.

"Take it easy," I told him. "I'll type it up after I get a cup of java."

"No time," Riley replied. "You should've done it last night. The Provost Marshal has a job for you this morning."

"We're already on a job," I told him. "Assigned to us by the Eighth Army Chief of Staff, in case you forgot."

"Don't be a name-dropper, Sueño. The Provost Marshal is still your immediate supervisor."

I rolled my eyes. That was the Army for you. Always pulling you in two different directions, then blaming you if you complained about it. "What?"

"What do you mean, what?"

"What the hell does Brace want us to do?"

"That's *Colonel* Brace to you."

Ernie approached with two cups of coffee. He handed me one, and I sipped it gratefully.

"Where's mine?" Riley asked.

"Up your tight little rectum. Ain't you checked on it lately? Everybody else has."

Miss Kim, the statuesque admin assistant, stopped typing. She grabbed a tissue from the box on her desk, stood up, and glided out the door and down the hallway in her high heels.

"Now you've done it," Riley said. "Upset Miss Kim again." He made a big show of checking his watch. "How long did it take you? Not even ten minutes."

On the edge of Riley's desk, Ernie found the day's issue of the *Pacific Stars & Stripes* and thumbed through it until he spotted the sports page.

Ernie and Miss Kim had once been a couple. Anyone on the outside looking in might've thought that they'd been developing a serious relationship. But those closest to Ernie Bascom knew better. I wasn't happy about him two-timing her, but I didn't believe it was my place to interfere. It took a while for Miss Kim to find out about his assignations, but her response was immediate. She dropped him like a bad habit. Even when we'd pulled her out of a serious jam recently—one could say we saved her life—she made a point of thanking me but ignoring him.

Whenever I talked to Ernie about Miss Kim, he shrugged. "Stuff happens."

I'd never known anyone who cared less about the opinions of others. Ernie claimed it hit him during his second tour in Vietnam. "I thought I was dead," he'd told me. "A load of high-explosive ammo in my truck, the VC closing in. Instead of praying to God to save me, I promised that if I survived, I'd never deny myself anything again. I'd do what I wanted to do, when I wanted to do it, and I wouldn't give a damn what anyone else thought."

As far as I could tell, he'd stuck religiously to that pledge.

"So what happened?" I'd asked. "You managed to evade the VC?"

"No. They decided to ambush another truck in the convoy. The one with C-rations."

"Wouldn't it make more sense to go after the truck with the ammo?"

Ernie had thought it over. "I guess they were hungry."

I put aside such reminiscences and set down my coffee. "So what is it, Riley? What does the Colonel want us to do?"

"Nice of you to ask," Riley said. He shuffled through some paperwork. "Here it is. A copy of both the invoice and shipping order. Should be out there waiting for you now."

"What the hell are you talking about?" Ernie asked.

"Black market is what I'm talking about. Big-ticket item. Burrows and Slabem uncovered it."

Jake Burrows and Felix Slabem were fellow CID agents. Brown-nosers to the max.

"Why don't *they* take care of it?"

"It's downtown," Riley replied, as if that explained everything. "At this cockamamie Korean address. Burrows and Slabem would never be able to find it."

"Not our fault they're morons."

"Hey, they haven't gone native like you two. Provost Marshal's orders. He wants you to check out a pickup at the motor pool, drive downtown, and confiscate the item."

"What item?"

"A refrigerator."

Ernie groaned. "Those suckers are heavy."

Riley ignored him. "According to this invoice, the PX delivered it out there yesterday."

"So it must've been on somebody's ration control plate. What makes it illegal?"

"Where it's being delivered. Not an authorized PX user's

home. That makes it a violation of Eighth Army regulations. An unauthorized transfer of duty-free goods."

The words "Eighth Army regulations" and "unauthorized transfer" were tenderly caressed as they rolled off Riley's tongue. He loved that kind of talk. Especially the word *unauthorized*. He made it sound obscene.

"Tell Burrows and Slabem to do it," Ernie said. "How many years they been here, and they're still afraid to leave the compound?"

"They can't read the signs," Riley said.

In the Army, ignorance could be a huge asset.

"But we have three GIs who disappeared," Ernie told him. "One of them's dead. Two more are still out there."

"*Dead?*"

"Yeah."

"Why didn't you report that?"

"Because you've been busy jacking your jaw."

"Does the Provost Marshal know?"

"He will. Captain Retzleff is probably briefing the Chief of Staff right now."

Riley thought about it, scratching his head. "Okay, I'll take care of that and make sure Colonel Brace isn't blindsided. Meanwhile, you two take care of this. And I mean *pronto*. Shouldn't take you more than a half hour or so."

"A half hour?"

"Yeah, if you quit dicking around."

Ernie ignored him and continued to read the sports section.

We knew we had to complete this detail. When Colonel Brace specified an errand, he was a stickler to make sure we got it done. He probably wanted to save face after the Chief of Staff assigned us to the missing GIs case in front of God and everyone else. Crossing him under these conditions wouldn't be wise. To save some face of our own, we took our time finishing our coffee.

Ernie and I drove over to the 21st Transportation Company (Car), better known as "Twenty-One T Car," the motor pool that supports 8th Army headquarters. We parked his jeep and checked out a three-quarter-ton truck. Ernie sat behind the steering wheel, and I directed him, occasionally referring to my map of Seoul, through busy traffic to a district known as Hyochang-dong.

Burrows and Slabem weren't the only GIs who couldn't find an address in this massive city. The system isn't set up like it is in the States, with streets and numbers, but instead based on an old Chinese land-lot system. Seoul has a number of districts known as *ku*, which are further broken down into villages or neighborhoods called *dong*. The final entry in every address is *ho*, which means "house" or "door." Since the city has grown so much since the end of the Korean War, these *ho* are often not in numerical order, and one has to wander around a neighborhood asking directions to find it. Still, there was no reason that Burrows and Slabem couldn't have earned their pay and done the job. Maybe they would've learned something.

We cruised past a whitewashed three-story building with the Korean flag fluttering out front: the Yongsan District police station. About a half mile past that, using my map and dead reckoning, I told Ernie to turn left. We wound through the narrow lanes past television repair shops and tiny wooden stationary stores until finally I told him to stop at an open-fronted *kagei*, a store with discs of puffed rice interspersed with dried cuttlefish hanging from the front rafter. Ernie locked the truck and joined me inside the *kagei* to replenish his supply of ginseng gum. Though we were only about two miles as the crow flies from 8th Army headquarters, this was light-years away culturally. GIs had no reason to stop out here. Normally, kids from the neighborhood would've crowded around the truck, gawking at the presence of real soldiers, but today they were in school.

The old lady behind the counter grinned at us, and I asked for her help, reading off the address. She took the sheet of paper from my hands, then reached into a cabinet and pulled out a pair of reading glasses that made her eyes appear twice their original size. She studied the address.

"Not too far," she said in Korean, pointing down the road. "Past the herbalist's shop, maybe twenty meters and then turn left."

When she handed the paper back, she stared at me to see if I understood.

"*Allasoyo,*" I told her. I understand. I thanked her, and we left.

Ernie was already chomping on two fresh sticks of gum when he started the truck. I pointed to a sign ahead slashed with Chinese characters. "Go past that herbalist shop," I told him, "and after twenty meters, turn left."

Twenty yards past the turn, a wooden sign leaned out from above sliding glass doors. I pointed and said, "Slow down." He did. I checked the numbers etched onto the doorframe and compared them to the address on the invoice.

"This is it," I said.

Ernie parked the three-quarter-ton directly in front. As I climbed out the passenger door, I read the sign, which read YOSONG GUONRYOK YONHAP. And beneath that, in smaller but neatly stenciled English: WOMEN'S POWER COALITION.

"Since when did women get power?" Ernie asked.

I shrugged. "Looks like they're taking it."

"Smart." Then he thought about it. "How soon do you think it'll be till they get stomped on?"

"Not long," I said.

"Yeah," Ernie replied. "Hope they enjoy it while it lasts."

The ladies of the Women's Power Coalition weren't happy to see us. In fact, they were outraged. Especially when I showed them the paperwork and Ernie set to work unscrewing the refrigerator from a Korean-made electrical transformer buzzing on the floor. In short order, he'd disabled the refrigerator, unplugged it, and slid it away from the wall in the tiny service area where it sat. There was also a stainless steel hot water urn that looked like PX property to me, not to mention the freeze-dried coffee crystals and the soluble creamer and the individual tea bags. It was all prime Stateside product, but our only official concern was the refrigerator, which we'd specifically been assigned to pick up. Apparently, someone made a call after our arrival, because within five minutes, a tall, square-faced Korean woman stormed in through the front door.

"*Wei kurei nonun?*" she said. What are you doing?

She was a big woman, buxom, and the sharp planes of her enraged visage made her look like a warrior goddess. She wore a plain blue cotton dress that fell past her knees, a brown belt cinched tightly at her waist, and, as protection against the November cold, a thick brown wool cardigan that she'd failed to button. The way the other women deferred to her, I took her for the head honcho.

I showed her the paperwork.

"PX item," I said, pointing at the line on the form. "Can't be out here." Then I used Riley's term. "Not authorized."

She backhanded the air as if to slap the invoice away. "Katie donated that to us," she said in English. "Katie! Do you know her? The Officers' Wives Club?"

I shook my head, startled by her rapid switch from Korean to fluent English. "Doesn't matter," I replied. "Katie, whoever she is, is not allowed to bring a refrigerator out here."

The regulation stated that PX-purchased goods could not be transferred to non-PX users unless they were de minimis items, valued at less than twenty-five dollars.

She tightened her fists and glowered at me. For a moment I thought she might start hitting me, and I was glad that she didn't have a weapon stuck beneath her broad leather belt. We had to get the damn refrigerator out of here as quickly as possible. I joined Ernie in removing items from the fridge. Mostly open containers of Yogulut, a liquid yogurt product; a few tins of apple cider; bunches of fresh fruit. Pretty much the opposite of every fridge I'd seen on base—no beer, no hot dogs. On the lower shelf were several prescription drugs and suppositories, even baby formula and what looked like small bottles of mother's milk.

So someone here was nursing. These items would go bad in a number of hours, but there was nothing Ernie or I could do about that. We pulled everything and laid it out as neatly as we could on the counter.

As we worked, I asked Ernie, "You checked the serial number?"

"Yeah, this is the right refrigerator."

Some of the women were crying now. The tall woman was speaking on the phone in English, trying to get through to someone on the American compound. She was frowning, and her imposing form quivered with anger. I realized I was staring at her, and that I found it pleasant to do so. Her hair was long, straight, and jet-black, and she had a nice jawline, despite the twisted scowl she was aiming at me. Despite myself, I admired her strength. Then I remembered we had a job to complete.

Ernie and I each took an end of the refrigerator, hoisted it up, and carried it outside. Just as we were about to load it into the back of the three-quarter-ton, the de facto leader of the Women's Power Coalition appeared at the door, slipped on her sandals, and rushed outside.

"You!" she shouted, pointing to me. "Katie is on the phone. Talk to her!"

I knew what would happen. The woman on the phone, whoever she was, would explain the many reasons why the refrigerator was needed very badly by the Woman's Power Coalition and try to talk us out of taking it. But it wasn't our decision to make. The Provost Marshal had reviewed the case and decided he wanted this refrigerator back on compound. He certainly hadn't asked for our opinion, and even if Katie made me sympathetic to her cause, it could only stir up trouble. There was no point in talking to her.

Without answering, Ernie and I tilted the refrigerator up and slid it onto the truck. Ernie closed the back and dropped the hooks at the end of two short chains into their respective slots to secure the gate. He hurried around to the driver's side, and I made my move toward the passenger's seat. The leader of the Women's Power Coalition blocked my way. As I was about to maneuver around her, she slapped me. Hard. She was as strong as she looked. I held my cheek and gazed at her in shock. Her entire face burned red, tears forming in the corners of her almond-shaped eyes.

"You hurt women," she said. "You don't even care. You *hurt* women."

Then she stepped away from me. Regally, as if dismissing a servant. I climbed into the front passenger seat, eager for this business to be over. When she reached the porch leading inside, the woman bent toward the ground as if searching for something. She apparently found whatever it was she was looking for, because she then stood upright, staring us down. Ernie started the engine, pulled forward a few yards, and then made a three-point turn in the narrow lane. As we started back toward the storefront office that housed the Women's Power Coalition, the tall woman strode into the road. Her long hair waved in the morning breeze. Using her full height and weight, she flung a rock directly at us. Reflexively, Ernie and I ducked, and at the same time we heard a loud *thwunk*. When I looked back up, the truck's windshield had shattered.

Ernie swerved around the woman and kept driving, squinting through a thousand kaleidoscopic shards of glass. "She took it sort of hard," he said.

"Yeah, sort of," I said, still breathing heavily. "I wonder what her name is."

"The big one?"

"Yeah."

"Sandy Koufax," Ernie said, "judging by her fastball."

-5-

Back on compound, we stored the refrigerator in the CID evidence room. In the admin office, Miss Kim handed me a phone message on pink paper. "Very urgent," she told me. "Chief Homicide Inspector Gil Kwon-up wants to talk to you."

Mr. Kill. He'd probably gotten wind of our activities in Pusan—and the discovery of Sergeant Werkowski's body. I showed the message to Ernie.

"Our next stop is Camp Kyle," he said. "Right?"

"Yes," I replied. "Where Werkowski was assigned, and the first place a GI disappeared."

"So KNP headquarters is on our way."

I frowned. "Maybe we should skip it this time."

"Why?" Ernie asked. And then he got it. "You're afraid of what they might do to Soon-hui and that food cart lady Auntie Suh once they find out they have information about Shirkey's disappearance."

I nodded.

Ernie thought about it. "They might disappear, too," he said, "if their role in this embarrasses the Korean government in any way."

"Mr. Kill wouldn't do that," I said. "Would he?"

"I don't know."

Mr. Kill dealt with those at the highest levels of the Korean power structure. He was well-connected, dangerous, and, most importantly, secretive.

We thought it over, but ultimately decided that going straight up to Camp Kyle to continue our investigation would probably be worse than meeting with Mr. Kill. We might be able to figure out what the KNPs were thinking if we stopped at their headquarters, maybe even influence that thinking.

I returned the refrigerator invoice to Riley. He grabbed it and said, "Where is it?"

"In the evidence storage room."

"Have you turned in your report on the trip to Pusan yet?"

"You know I haven't," I told him. "You didn't give me time."

"*Time?* All you've got is time, trooper. You're on duty twenty-four hours a day, seven days a week."

"You'll get your report," I said.

Before he could give me a deadline, Ernie and I walked out of the CID office.

It wasn't our day. When we dropped the truck off at Twenty-One T Car, the Operations Officer, Chief Warrant Peters, said he planned to file a Report of Survey for the broken windshield, which most likely meant we would end up paying for it. Unless, that is, we could convince the Report of Survey officer that it had been damaged in the line of duty. But nobody I knew had ever won one of those. A meteorite could land on your officially dispatched military vehicle, and you'd still be held liable.

Ernie retrieved his jeep. After stopping at the barracks and changing into our running-the-ville outfits, we drove to downtown Seoul.

On the way there, we were quiet. Ernie made his way through midmorning traffic, easily maneuvering the finely tuned vehicle while we both tried to ignore the fact that we had lost control of our lives and this investigation.

"All they do is mess with us," Ernie said.

"That's the Army."

"Maybe we should talk to the Chief of Staff, tell him to order everyone off our backs."

I glanced at Ernie skeptically. Blowing the whistle up the chain of command might give us temporary relief and the space we needed to thoroughly conduct our investigation, but Colonel Brace, Staff Sergeant Riley, and Chief Warrant Officer Peters would certainly make our lives hell in the months to follow. This was simply a GI's life. And we'd have to put up with it, even with the lives of two missing soldiers at stake.

Ernie's grip on the steering wheel loosened. "Fine," he said. "Maybe not."

Officer Oh, Mr. Kill's assistant, met us in the lobby. As usual, she looked sharp in her dark blue skirt, light blue blouse, and the KNP cap pinned to her curly black hair. But her face betrayed worry, which was unusual. She usually sported the same grim expression, which I suspected was to ward off Ernie's attention. She escorted us into the elevator and up to the top floor of KNP headquarters, where Mr. Kill's newly remodeled office sat.

He was hunched over a stack of paperwork on his desk as another dark-suited officer hovered over him. Mr. Kill looked up, nodded, and motioned for us to be seated. It was a small office, considering his rank, but with accoutrements like a goose-necked lamp and a celadon vase filled with artificial cloth flowers. I thought of the *ajjimas*—the middle-aged women—who'd spent hours deftly crafting them. Ernie and I sat on the edge of a low divan in front of a mahogany coffee table. When Kill finished whatever he was working on, the other officer bowed and retreated from the office. Officer Oh stepped outside. After she shut the door, Mr. Kill scribbled a few last notes, rose to his feet, buttoned his jacket over his flat stomach, and joined us at the coffee table.

"You were in Pusan last night," he said. Not a question, a statement of fact. We didn't bother to ask how he knew—the

KNPs had forces stationed in every town, village, and hamlet in the country, not to mention their liaison office at 8th Army headquarters. Because the Park Chung-hee regime wanted to maintain a tight hold on power, the Korean National Police was the only official body of law enforcement; local police forces weren't allowed. So the KNPs were charged with both preventing local crime and protecting the nation from North Korean incursions.

"GIs disappearing," he continued. "No trace. This is bad."

"Really bad," I repeated.

"And now one has turned up dead." He studied us for a reaction, not getting one. "But you didn't ask for our help."

"It's not up to us," I said. "We were ordered to go to Pusan, so we went."

"Yes," he said. "Good soldiers."

Ernie fidgeted in his seat.

"I'll get to the point," Mr. Kill said. "We've been looking into these disappearances, too. But our investigators weren't able to get much information from the women who work in the GI bars. In previous interviews, none of the women at the Heitei Lounge told my men about Soon-hui on Texas Street. But they told you."

Both Ernie and I hid our surprise. Apparently, without realizing it, we had been shadowed by the KNPs in Pusan.

"The women at the Heitei Lounge," Ernie said, "aren't scared of us."

"No. It's ironic; they trust Americans, but not their own countrymen."

Mr. Kill was one of the few Koreans I knew whose English proficiency was high enough that he could use a word like "ironic" so accurately. He'd not only graduated from a top Korean university, but years ago he'd been selected to attend an Ivy League school in the States. At the time, the US government was focused on building a cadre of loyal, anti-communist law enforcement officers throughout our allied nations. Mr. Kill had been one of the chosen. How anticommunist he was and how loyal to the Park Chung-hee regime, I'd never been able to ascertain. He kept his personal opinions hidden very well.

"Where's your next stop?" he asked.

I hesitated, then said, "Camp Kyle. Where the first GI went missing."

"Outside Uijongbu?"

I nodded.

"You know you can ask for our assistance anytime."

I nodded again.

He leaned back in his seat. "We're worried about this one," he said.

"Why?" Ernie asked. "Three GIs go AWOL. One of them ran into some trouble. Maybe it was an accident. Maybe he was drunk. Maybe he slipped and fell into the Yellow Sea. What's the big deal?"

Ernie neglected to mention the stab wound—hoping, I figured, to keep at least one secret from the KNPs.

"We don't think they went AWOL," Mr. Kill replied. "We're worried about them, just as your commander is. This could cause huge trouble with the American government."

The authoritarian Park Chung-hee government receives millions of dollars in economic and military aid from the US every year. And our land, sea, and air forces are committed by written agreement to the defense of South Korea. Many observers believe that this close relationship with the Americans is the only thing preventing North Korea from attacking again in their never-ending pursuit to reunify Korea under the red flag of Communism. If word got out about the missing GIs, the negative publicity back in the States could threaten the arrangement between the US and the ROK—the system that paid Mr. Kill's salary.

"So if you don't think they went AWOL," Ernie said, "what do you suppose happened to them?"

Mr. Kill shrugged. "We're not sure. Usually, when someone disappears so abruptly, it's because they ran into serious trouble, and we find their bodies in short order. This was the case with Werkowski, but he was found in an odd place: on the shore of the Yellow Sea, far from his home compound. It appears he was stabbed by someone, or possibly impaled by some sort of machinery." So much for keeping secrets from Mr. Kill. "But the other two are still missing. And these were strong, fully grown men, trained to protect themselves. It is very strange."

If it was strange to Mr. Kill, who had over two decades of experience as a homicide investigator, it was sure as hell strange to me. I thought about telling him what Auntie Suh had said—her description of the old-fashioned woman in the fog who'd accompanied Specialist Shirkey—but I figured he'd find out on his own, if he hadn't already.

Mr. Kill slapped his knees, stood suddenly, and said, "Okay, let's go."

"Go where?"

"I have something to show you."

He marched toward the door, and when he opened it, Officer Oh was standing just a few feet away outside. She snapped to attention.

"*Kaja!*" he said. Let's go.

Officer Oh led the way, clearly having been briefed on where we were going. The four of us entered the elevator and rode quietly downward until we passed the lobby and descended into basement level three. The door hissed open, and we stepped into a hallway illuminated dimly by yellow lights overhead. The air was different down here, with the tart smell of chemicals and something else hovering around us like a clammy hand.

Ernie sniffed. "The meat locker," he said.

A double door at the end of the hallway was stenciled with the word *bopuihak*. Forensics.

Officer Oh held the door open as we entered. A technician was standing by: a white-coated man with plastic gloves next to a gurney. A long white sheet covered what appeared to be a body. The man stood back and bowed as Inspector Kill approached.

"We wanted you to take a look before we sent this one to the morgue," Mr. Kill said, grabbing the edge of the sheet. He whipped it back.

Laying naked on the cold metal was the body of a young woman, strands of seaweed laced through her tangled black hair. I studied her from head to toe, then focused on the face. It was puffed and distorted, teeth showing beneath puckered lips as if grimacing in agony. Ernie said it first.

"Soon-hui."

I turned to Kill. "What happened to her?"

"Drowning. Our boys went back to talk to her late last night, after following you back to Hialeah Compound, but she'd already disappeared. They interviewed the other women at the Sea Dragon Nightclub, pieced things together, and found her floating off a pier about a half mile away."

"How'd she get up here so fast?" Ernie asked.

"This case," Mr. Kill replied, "is top priority to us. We flew her here by chopper."

"Do we know who did this?" I asked.

He shook his head. "Not yet. Not sure. But our best investigators in Pusan are working on it."

"We need to go down there," I said. "Find her killer."

"*No!*" Mr. Kill shouted, giving us an order for the first time since we'd known him. "You continue with what you're doing. Our men in Pusan will handle this."

"But we're the ones who talked to her. This is our fault."

"You have no way of knowing that. Besides, we don't have jurisdiction on American compounds. Only you do. You have to keep working that side of the case. It's likely we don't have much time."

He was right. We had two other GIs out there in the wind, and for all we knew, they were still alive. It was up to us to look into activity in the US compounds. Still, I wasn't happy about being left out of the investigation in Pusan. I wanted to atone somehow for the death of this innocent woman.

Ernie said, "So it wasn't just the KNPs following us that night in Pusan."

"Our men saw no one else following you," Mr. Kill replied. "Whoever targeted Soon-hui tailed her after you left."

I remembered the shoeshine boy whom I'd startled, and who ran off so quickly. Maybe he'd gone to alert someone. And then I thought of something else.

"How did you know that Ernie and I were on our way to Pusan?"

"We have our contacts," Mr. Kill replied.

And plenty of them. Korean civilians worked in clerical jobs at 8th Army headquarters, as air traffic controllers at the 105th Aviation helipad, and even as translators at the Hialeah

Compound MP Station. Any—or all—of them could be on the KNP payroll.

"As we speak," Mr. Kill said, interrupting my thoughts, "my men in Pusan are asking questions out at the Sea Dragon Nightclub."

"Do you expect the bar girls to cooperate?" Ernie asked.

"Yes," Mr. Kill replied. "This time, they will." He lightly tapped a knotted fist into his open palm.

I studied Soon-hui's face again, thinking of the child she'd lost; of her trips to the Buddhist temple; of Shirkey, the GI who'd betrayed her; and her cruel death—trapped, maybe held, underwater as she struggled to breathe. I forced myself to shove the thoughts from my mind. As I did so, the muscles around her mouth and eyes seemed to relax. Eventually her grimace disappeared.

The change in expression from a frantic murder victim to a woman at peace, I realized, was all in my imagination.

Ernie grabbed my arm and pulled me away from the corpse.

We wound our way out of the busy downtown Seoul traffic and reached the Main Supply Route leading north from Seoul toward the city of Uijongbu. At the beginning of the Korean War, Uijongbu had briefly become famous when the North Korean Army poured across the 38th Parallel and steamrolled down the Eastern Corridor, the ROK Army fleeing in its path. A few ROK units regrouped and made a stand on the outskirts of Uijongbu. For a brief moment, the citizenry of Seoul was heartened, hoping their brave soldiers would hold the line. In the end, they did buy more time for refugees to escape south across the Han River, but eventually the South Korean Army was overrun. After that, Seoul was taken, and the North Korean Army of Kim Il-sung continued south. It was then that President Harry Truman made the decision to send US troops over from Japan to stop their advance. Uijongbu is still considered a strategic strongpoint, surrounded by both ROK and US military bases.

Ernie's voice snapped me back to reality. "I've been thinking."

"Uh-oh," I said.

"Shirkey might not be dead."

"Let's hope not."

"When that old broad wouldn't get a room with him at the Number One Inn, maybe he raped her."

"What? Where?"

"Near that trash bin."

"Then what?"

"Then he had to get rid of her."

"You think he killed her?"

"Could be." Ernie slowed behind a convoy of five-ton ROK Army trucks, each towing a 155-millimeter howitzer. When he spotted an opening, he stepped on the gas and sped past the trucks one at a time, pulling in front of each one in turn to avoid oncoming traffic. Bored ROK Army soldiers with M16 rifles between their knees peered out of the canvas-covered backs of the trucks.

"What would he have done with the body?" I asked.

"Could've thrown it in the trash bin."

"And somebody collected it without noticing her?"

"There's a lot of trash in there."

"Okay. And then?"

"He would've had nowhere to go," Ernie said. "There are only two ways to get out of the country: across the DMZ, which is suicide, or through one of the points of international embarkation, which would be impossible to get through without a passport and a visa."

"Right," I agreed. GIs enter Korea with only their military identification cards and aren't allowed to leave until they receive official departure orders.

"And the Koreans have him on a list now. They're looking for him," Ernie said.

"So what would he do?" I asked. "No money. No family. No help. No way out of the country."

"Soon-hui," Ernie said. "Maybe he went back to her and asked her to help him out. Meanwhile, he's using connections to get a phony military ID and ration control plate. Once he has that, he can go on compounds where he's not known and purchase stuff in the PX. Set himself up in the black market."

"And when Soon-hui talked to us," I said, "that shoeshine

boy told Shirkey we were there, and he went back that night and offed her."

"Could be."

"But why? No matter what she told us, she couldn't have hurt him much. He knows the Army's looking for him, anyway."

"Maybe they had a fight."

"Maybe. Or maybe somebody else murdered Soon-hui."

"Like who?"

"I don't have any freaking idea."

"So we leave it up to the Pusan KNPs?"

"Do we have a choice?"

"Not right now," Ernie replied, pumping the breaks to slow for a truck piled high with Napa cabbage. He sped up and passed the truck. "The Chief of Staff expects us to look into all three disappearances. Werkowski from Camp Kyle, the floater, how long was he missing?"

I thumbed through the reports Captain Retzleff had given us. "Over two weeks."

"How long you figure he was in the water?"

"Not long. The body was in good shape."

"Stunk, though. And he was young, like the other two," Ernie said.

I checked his date of birth. Not all buck sergeants were young. I'd seen forty-somethings who'd been in the Army twenty years and still hadn't made sergeant stripes. But that was unusual, and becoming more atypical in the Army now that personnel operations were being centralized in Washington, DC. It was becoming difficult for a below-par soldier to find a place to hide. But Werkowski was in his twenties, and on track to be promoted quickly through the ranks.

We were now on the outskirts of Uijongbu. A sign said HUANYONG! Welcome! Beneath that were two Chinese characters that I didn't have time to decipher because Ernie had hit the gas.

"Slow down!" I said.

He laughed, assuming I was joking.

We drove past a sign that said SOKYU, or gasoline, then past a truck repair yard and a taxicab wash before entering Uijongbu proper. The city had been flattened by Commie artillery during the war, but more and more three- and four-story buildings were now popping up in the city center. There was even midafternoon congestion as Ernie drove us to the central traffic circle.

"Which way?" he asked.

"Right. Toward DivArty." The US Second Infantry Division Artillery Headquarters at Camp Stanley.

After traveling about a mile east, just before reaching Camp Stanley, I asked Ernie to slow down again. This time he did. Acres of rice paddies stretched across the valley to our left.

"There it is," I said, pointing. On our right, a white-washed sign was stenciled with black letters: CAMP KYLE,

HEADQUARTERS AND COMPANY A, 4TH MAINTENANCE
BATTALION.

He turned right onto the narrow two-lane blacktop. At the
front gate, we showed the MP our dispatch. He stared at us
curiously, not accustomed to strangers, but waved us through.
We parked near a circle of whitewashed stones surrounding
three flagpoles—those of the United States, the Republic of
Korea, and the United Nations Command—and as we climbed
out of the jeep, dull faces gawked. We waded through what
seemed like an entire battalion of open-mouthed confusion
before we finally found someone who actually knew something about the late Sergeant Werkowski.

-6-

"I'm a whoremonger from way back."

Master Sergeant Orville "Pug" Grayson stared at me with moist blue eyes and took a long drag on his cigarette, followed by a coughing jag that shook the loose, closely shaved flesh beneath his chin so badly, I thought his tonsils might pop out. When his throat cleared, he turned back to us and said, "I've seen 'em all."

Ernie and I sat in a tiny barroom called the Kimchi Club, tucked away in a narrow lane some ten twists and turns outside the front gate of Camp Kyle.

During our inquiries on base, everyone told us to talk to Pug Grayson. He was known as king of the ville rats in these parts, and after the cannon went off at seventeen hundred hours, we found him right where people told us he'd be. At a table in the Kimchi Club, in the corner opposite the jukebox.

"Did you see Werkowski with her?" Ernie asked.

"Did I," Grayson replied. "They must've spent tens of hours together, talking like they were long-lost friends."

"Every night?"

"Damn near. She was chatting him up. Having him buy her drinks. Probably borrowing a little money from him every night before he went back to the compound. Getting him ready for the big one."

"The big hustle?"

"That's what I thought," Grayson said. "That she wanted a nice camera out of the PX. Or stereo equipment. Something he'd get in trouble for, but not until his DEROS." Date of Estimated Return from Overseas. "Meanwhile, she'd be long gone."

Just before GIs left Korea, their personal goods were inventoried to make sure they hadn't sold any of the high-value rationed items they'd purchased out of the PX. If they'd sold something as expensive as a television or an imported wristwatch, or even given it away as a gift, they would be guilty of a ration control violation and could face non-judicial punishment or court-martial.

"But you were wrong," I said.

"*Was* I." Grayson shook his head. "She wanted way more than some expensive gift."

"What'd she want?" Ernie asked.

"She was out for blood," Grayson said.

He raised his hand and ordered us another round of drinks. A bored Korean barmaid brought them over, keeping her face impassive in an attempt to avoid conversation. As she set her tray down and served the drinks, Grayson patted her hand as if she were his granddaughter. Ernie paid the tab. Grayson tossed back his straight double shot of bourbon before starting on the beer.

"I like it here," Grayson said, waving his cigarette at the small tables and short bar and half dozen booths that lined the far wall. "They don't play the music too loud, and most of the business girls are old, like me. Well, not *so* old, but not youngsters, either. That's one of the things that made Werkowski unusual— here, anyway. He was young. Only been in the army for two or three years. Most of the young troops hit the Miniskirt Club up the road, where they play all that hard rock crap, or worse, the Soul Train Club around the corner for the black troops. Me, I like it here. The music is quiet, the girls don't wear hot pants, and if you don't feel like talking, they leave you alone."

"A place for lifers," Ernie said.

Grayson nodded, stubbing his cigarette out in a tin ashtray. "That's right," he said, "a place for lifers like me. And the girls here don't try to hustle me, mainly because they know they couldn't even if they tried. Like I say, I've seen it all. Stuttgart, Saigon, Bangkok, you name it, I've been there. If I decide to spend time with one of the girls, I give her money. Treat her fair. But I never let any of them hustle me."

"And this woman was hustling Werkowski?"

He nodded. "No doubt in my military mind."

"Did you talk to him about it?" I asked.

He shook his head wearily. "You can't tell nothing to a young troop like that, especially once he's developed a hard-on."

"So you just came in every night and observed."

Grayson shrugged. "I didn't figure she would do him any harm. She'd get a little money, which I figured she needed to survive, and he'd get in a little trouble just before he went home. That's the name of the game. Hustle or be hustled. I figured Werkowski would learn—what do they call it these days?—a *valuable life lesson*. We used to call them hard knocks."

I asked him to describe the woman.

He did, in detail. The description almost exactly matched the one Auntie Suh had given us earlier. But Grayson was able to recall more specifics. She was at least ten years older than Werkowski, maybe fifteen, but she had a pretty, heart-shaped face.

I raised my eyebrow at Ernie. Looked like his theory about Shirkey murdering some random older woman was a miss. This woman was a concrete link between the disappearances of Specialist Shirkey in Pusan and Sergeant Werkowski in Uijongbu.

"Her most distinctive feature," Grayson continued, "was her nose. Very pointed. Almost tilted up at the end."

"That's unusual. Do you think she might not be Korean?" I asked.

"It's possible."

"Did she look like she'd had work done?"

"Surgery? How the hell would I know?"

Although Grayson hadn't eavesdropped on the couple, he was sure she spoke English. And, just once, she'd worn something other than her austere black skirt and vest. The last night he'd seen her, she'd been wearing a patterned blue silk dress.

"That's how I knew she was making her move," Grayson told us. "Her tits were hanging out."

"And Werkowski was looking?"

"You better believe he was."

"Did you see them leave?"

"Nah. By then it was late, and I'd already had a few double bourbons."

"Where do you figure they went?" Ernie asked.

"There's only one *yoguan* in this village," he told us. "If they didn't go there, they have to have taken a cab to downtown Uijongbu."

"And after that night," I said, "you never saw Werkowski again?"

"No. It wasn't until a couple days later that I heard he'd gone AWOL."

"What'd you think when you found out?"

"I figured he'd taken off with her. I didn't blame him; she wasn't bad-looking. But I also figured he'd be back with his tail between his legs as soon as his money ran out."

"He left after end-of-month payday?"

"Yeah. That's why nobody was surprised after the third or fourth day. But after a week, the rumor started swirling."

"What rumor?"

"That the old broad might have been what the Korean girls call a gummy whore."

"A *what*?" This was a new one on me. And to Ernie, too.

Grayson waved his cigarette. "No, that's not right. Let me ask Kimmi." He waved the barmaid over. "What do they call that, Kimmi? A gummy whore or something like that?"

She frowned, looking slightly offended.

"You know," he said, waving his cigarette again. "A woman who used to be a fox."

"*Gumiho*," she said.

"See?" Grayson said. "I was right. A gummy whore."

Kimmi rolled her eyes and returned to the bar.

Wood creaked beneath our feet as we ascended the three-story building, the tallest in the vicinity of Camp Kyle. The black *hangul* lettering on the wooden sign outside read MOBOM YOGUAN, or Exemplary Inn. Beneath that, in neatly stenciled English lettering, it said BEST HOTEL. Commercial establishments in Korea often had Korean and English signs with slightly or even completely different meanings. Sometimes through simple mistranslation, but usually because what was said in English wasn't as important to the proprietor as the fact that English had been employed to lend a cosmopolitan air to the enterprise.

On the top floor, we turned right and stood before a short check-in counter.

The manager had heard us climbing the steps and emerged from the small sliding door that led to her living quarters. I showed her my badge. She crossed her arms and reluctantly provided her ID information, then answered our questions carefully. I described the woman that Master Sergeant Grayson called a "gummy whore," as well as Werkowski.

No, the manager hadn't seen a couple who matched that description. Most of the business girls who checked in here were regulars, and at least as young as the American GIs, usually younger. I explained that if she didn't level with me, I'd ask the KNPs to pay the inn a visit, but she held to her story. No couple like the one I'd described had come in. No woman of any age in an austere black vest and skirt, nor one in a low-cut blue silk dress.

"Miniskirt," she told us. "All miniskirt."

"And black boots?" Ernie asked, smiling.

"Yes," she replied, looking at him oddly.

I elbowed him to shut up.

I asked if there was anywhere nearby they might've stayed, but she said hers was the only *yoguan* between here and downtown Uijongbu.

We were about to leave when she said, "Two weeks ago?"

"Yes." She had a small standing calendar on the counter, and I pointed at the date of Werkowski's disappearance.

"About that time," she told me in English, "man come. Big man. Not tall, but strong," she said, holding her arms out to the side. "He driver."

Interesting. We listened patiently.

"No place to park in this area." She had a short driveway in front of the *yoguan*, and when the man had asked to use it to park his vehicle, she'd charged him a thousand *won*. About two bucks.

"He pay," she told me, sounding surprised.

"What'd he do then?"

"He wait."

"Inside the vehicle?"

"Yes."

"How long was he there?"

She told us that she'd heard him start the engine and drive away about an hour before curfew. About the same time Grayson claimed that Werkowski and the *gumiho* had left the Kimchi Club.

"Did the driver have any passengers?"

"I no see."

"What'd he look like?"

She shuddered and hugged herself, rubbing her upper arms. "Mean. He look mean. Face twisted and burned. He look like a man we used to see in Korea a long time ago. When

I was a little girl." Then she said the word in Korean. I didn't understand it, and asked her to explain. She tried, something about fire and heat, but it still made no sense to me.

I pulled out my notebook, handed her my pen, and asked her to write the word in *hangul*.

She did. *Daejang jang-i*. I had no idea what it meant.

According to her, his vehicle was your typical dark, box-shaped domestic sedan, likely a Hyundai. The type that traveled in swarms all over Korea. She didn't remember anything distinctive about it, and hadn't bothered to write down the license plate number. Still, this was the first real lead we had. If this driver did work for our alleged kidnapper, that would explain how she managed to pop up all over Korea. The *gumiho* had wheels.

We thanked the proprietor and left. On the drive back to Seoul, Ernie and I discussed our theory.

"She's a pickup artist," he said. "Seduces young GIs and whisks them away in her Hyundai sedan, chauffeured by some guy with a mangled face."

"Why GIs?"

"Like everyone says, she's a respectable woman. If she gets it on with a foreigner, there's less of a chance anyone in her circle will hear about it."

"Wouldn't she be worried about the clap?" I asked. The incidence of venereal disease is much higher amongst American GIs than it is in Korea's general population.

"So she takes precautions," Ernie said. "Or maybe she gets off on the danger. You know, forbidden fruit and all that."

"Okay," I said. "That jibes with what we know—or think we do—except for one thing."

"What's that?"

"The GIs never come back. And one of them is dead. Skewered through the heart."

"Yeah," Ernie replied. "I'm working on that."

We'd already passed through the high-rise area of downtown Seoul, and now the huge entrance to Namsan Tunnel Number Three loomed in front of us. Ernie zoomed straight into the darkness. About twenty yards in, he honked his horn.

"What'd you do that for?"

"Just to wake people up."

It worked. About a half dozen kimchi cabs had started honking, too.

I studied Ernie. "You're happy," I said.

His grin broadened. "What's not to be happy about?"

Then I got it. "You have a date," I told him. When he didn't deny it, I continued. "With Captain Retzleff."

His expression didn't falter, but he said, "Hey, you shouldn't spread rumors like that."

I crossed my arms. "You're going to get your low-ranking butt in a serious ringer."

"Isn't that where it usually is?"

I wondered how they'd even managed to set up a rendezvous,

but I knew with Ernie it was sometimes as simple as a woman handing him a slip of paper.

When we emerged from the still-reverberating tunnel, I studied the accompanying traffic. Other than the taxicabs, privately owned Hyundai sedans were possibly the most common on the road. Most had tinted windows, and a few even had short white curtains to provide privacy in the back seat. Almost all were chauffeur-driven. Under the Park Chung-hee regime, the tax on privately owned vehicles was so prohibitively high—fifty percent or more of the price of the car—that most people couldn't afford to buy one. But if you were rich enough to afford that, then hiring a chauffeur was de rigueur. A full-time driver's annual salary was less than half what the car cost, and the Korean elite had to keep up appearances, for which a chauffeur was required.

So this respectable woman in the back seat of her chauffeured Hyundai sedan would attract little, if any, law enforcement notice. She would be virtually invisible as she traveled the country at will. But a GI in her car? That would attract a *lot* of attention. In fact, it would almost certainly be reported up the line. And if they'd traveled far, they could easily run into one of the random ROK Army roadblocks set up at all hours. If the ROK Army caught her with an American GI, she would be pulled over and questioned.

How would she have handled that?

Ernie dropped me off at the barracks, and instead of asking him more questions, I waggled my finger at him.

"Who are you to talk?" he said, laughing as he took off with a screech of his tires.

I walked inside the plain stucco walls of the foyer past the CQ desk and stopped at the beer machine. I inserted the requisite thirty-five cents, and out popped a cold can of Falstaff. Like magic. The snack machine was depleted, except for one wrinkled bag of cheese-flavored crackers. Thus fortified, I repaired to my room. Alone in the dark, I thought of Leah Prevault. Apparently, the honchos at the 121st Evac Hospital had gotten wind of the fact that she and I had been seeing each other. They'd said nothing—no formal reprimand was forthcoming—but when her two-year tour was up, her request for extension was denied. Leah Prevault had been quietly shipped off to Tripler Army Hospital in Honolulu. "Budget cuts," they'd told her, but she didn't believe a word of it.

"They're trying to keep us apart," she'd told me.

"It won't work," I'd replied.

It had been almost three months now since I'd escorted her to Osan Air Force Base and watched her board a C-130 to Hawaii. Now I wished I'd given her a gift of some sort. Maybe a ring.

-7-

When we arrived at the CID office the next morning, Riley sat silently at his desk, his face buried in paperwork. Miss Kim stared resolutely at her keyboard, typing rhythmically like someone who'd been hypnotized. They were both intently ignoring the screams emerging from the Provost Marshal's office.

Apparently, from twenty yards down the hall, Colonel Brace somehow sensed our arrival. "Bascom! Sueño! Get in here!"

We got in there.

"Why are you wearing *those*?" he asked.

He glared at the jackets and ties we were required to wear as 8th Army CID agents.

"Eighth Army supplement to Department of the Army regulation one ninety-five dash one point three thirty-seven, *sir*!" Ernie explained, doing his best to sound like a military automaton while he was at it.

"Get changed," the Provost Marshal said, ignoring Ernie's attempt at satire. "Into fatigues. You have a work detail to take care of."

The woman standing beside his desk, who'd done most of the hollering, crossed her arms and let out a satisfied *humph*.

"Work detail?" I asked, thinking of the missing persons investigation.

"Yes," he replied. "Get that refrigerator out of the evidence room and transport it back to where you found it."

"Take it *back*?" Ernie asked.

Colonel Brace looked up at him. "Do I have to tell you twice?"

In the Army, arguing with a colonel is never a wise idea for an enlisted man. But Ernie wasn't your average enlisted man. He didn't give a Flying Funghini.

"What was the big fuss about it being against regulation?" Ernie asked. "About the Women's Power Coalition not being *authorized* to possess duty-free PX goods?"

"We have an LOA," the woman said. A Letter of Authorization.

I looked at her for the first time. She was about five foot four, with dirty blonde hair cut in a bob at just about shoulder length. She wore a purple dress beneath her long beige coat.

"I signed it myself," she said, "while Mrs. Frankenton was in Tokyo, and I was the Acting President of the OWC." The Officers' Wives Club.

Ernie and I both turned to Colonel Brace, awaiting an explanation. He didn't have to give us one, of course. We enlisted men were just supposed to follow orders. On the other hand, we were currently handling the biggest missing persons case to hit US Forces Korea in months, possibly years, which had apparently just turned into a murder investigation, and he was sending us to shuttle a refrigerator back and forth. He cleared his throat and spoke.

"When Mrs. Frankenton returned from Tokyo," Colonel Brace told us, "she rescinded all LOAs issued by Mrs. Allsworthy here. She said that the Acting President didn't have the authority to sign them."

When a field grade officer or higher signs an LOA, that transcends ration control regulations. Theoretically, it's for things like a unit party, when more than the allowed two-cases-per-purchase amount of beer or soda is needed. Or on big-ticket items when, for example, a unit takes donations and purchases a water heater or stove for a local orphanage. Sometimes LOAs are abused, but there's a thorough record kept of them in the 8th Army Ration Control Office. Since we often worked black market cases, Ernie and I had seen more than a few LOAs, but I'd never heard of one being rescinded.

"Mrs. Frankenton," I asked, "the Chief of Staff's wife?"

Colonel Brace nodded.

Now I knew how she'd managed to rescind the LOA. In the

Army, the wives of high-ranking officers have almost as much power as their husbands. Sometimes more.

I turned to the lady in the beige coat. "You must be Katie."

"Are you the one who refused to talk to me on the phone?"

I nodded.

"That was a damned rude thing to do," she said.

Her cheeks were red. She was in her early thirties, which would likely make her husband a mid-ranking officer. A major, maybe, or a lieutenant colonel. Like most officers' wives, it was clear she considered the enlisted men who worked for her husband to be her employees, too.

"We were only doing our job," Ernie said.

She glared at him.

"Who is that woman?" I asked. "The tall one who runs things out there?"

"Ok-ja," she said.

"That's her whole name?" I asked. "Just Ok-ja?"

"Wang Ok-ja," she told me.

There are many homophones in Korean, but *wang* is most often translated as king. And that was certainly befitting for the regal Wang Ok-ja.

"Why?"

I rubbed my cheek. "Just curious."

"She threw a rock," Ernie added, "that shattered our windshield."

"Good for her," she said.

"What's your business out there, ma'am?" Ernie asked.

"What is this, an interrogation? Are you planning to arrest me?" She looked at Colonel Brace. He pretended to be busy lighting his pipe, apparently not minding us digging around a little.

"No," Ernie replied. "We'd just like to know what we're dealing with."

"You're dealing with the women of the United States and Korea who are taking their power back. And now we want our *refrigerator*." She checked her watch and we glanced at Colonel Brace. Instead of asking if we had any other irons in the fire, he turned to her and said, "Mrs. Allsworthy, they'll have it back before noon."

So it was Katie Allsworthy, firebrand of the OWC, versus Mrs. Frankenton, wife of the Chief of Staff, 8th United States Army.

How had we gotten into the middle of this?

Before we left, I stopped at Miss Kim's desk. When I sat down, she stopped typing, looked up, and smiled. I asked if I could borrow her Korean-English dictionary. She pulled it out of her desk drawer, laid it atop her immaculate desk, and slid it toward me.

I looked up *daejang jang-i* and discovered that it meant "blacksmith." I should've known. Heat and flames, just like the manager of the *yoguan* had tried to explain. She'd even made some hammering motions, but I hadn't picked up on them. If he was a smithy who used traditional Korean methods, that might explain why his face was burnt and mangled. Especially if he'd ever splashed molten iron on himself.

For the next word, I needed Miss Kim's help. I slid the dictionary back to her.

"*Gumiho*," I said, not "gummy whore," as Pug Grayson had said it.

Miss Kim's eyes widened. "Who teach you?" she asked.

I shrugged. "Somebody. What's it mean?"

She shuddered and rubbed her bare arms. "Not good," she said.

I waited.

"From Chinese," she told me. "Japan have, too."

Then she opened the dictionary, thumbing through it rapidly with her slender fingers. Finally, she stopped and pointed.

It was definitely a word derived from Chinese. There were three characters following the printed *hangul*. I pulled out my notebook and jotted them down. The first one was easy, the character for the number nine. The second two were more complicated—each with more than a half dozen strokes—and when I was done, I turned my notebook to Miss Kim, and she checked them and made a couple of minor corrections.

Now I knew how to write the word *gumiho* in both Korean and Chinese. The literal translation of it was "nine-tailed fox." The dictionary said "a cunning person." But Miss Kim told me there was more to it than that. She lowered her voice and spoke in Korean.

"Some people believe," she said, "that the *gumiho* is not human, but a fox that has managed to survive for centuries. Once it reaches the age of one thousand years, the gods smile upon it, and it is allowed to transform itself. Then it is no longer a fox, but a woman with magical powers."

"What kind of woman?" I asked.

"Very lustful," she said. "Like an animal." She blushed, snatched a tissue out of her box, and held it to her nose. "Some people believe that the *gumiho* can disappear and reappear in another spot, and even change its shape."

"Do you believe this?" I asked.

"Of course not." Then she said, *"Mishin."* Superstition.

I thanked her and stood up. As I walked away, she once again hugged herself and rubbed her arms. Though the steam heater clanged away merrily, it still seemed like she was freezing.

Ernie and I drove to the motor pool, hoping to retrieve the three-quarter-ton truck we'd used to pick up the refrigerator in the first place. Chief Warrant Peters told us that it was "dead-lined" due to its shattered windshield. Which meant that, because of safety issues, it couldn't be moved or dispatched by anyone. We asked him for a different one.

"They're all out right now," he said. "Maybe at close of business." Five P.M.

"Don't you have another truck?" Ernie asked. "Maybe a deuce-and-a-half?"

"Nothing. Everything's out."

"We don't have time for this shit," Ernie told him. "We're trying to find three missing GIs. The clock is ticking." He didn't bother to mention that one of them was already dead.

"Missing?" Peters asked. "Maybe they ought to be big boys and find their own way home."

"This case is top priority," Ernie told him.

"Well, la-di-da," Peters said. "You look just like a couple of enlisted pukes to me."

Ernie was about to pop him in the jaw, but I pulled Ernie back.

"Asshole," Ernie said as we walked away.

"You don't talk to a warrant officer that way!" Peters called after us.

"I just did," Ernie replied.

Back at the barracks, we changed into our running-the-ville outfits. It was almost noontime, and we'd skipped breakfast, so we decided to have some chow before making our next move. We headed to the 8th Army Snack Bar.

Strange was in his usual spot at a two-person table next to the wall. Ernie sat down opposite him as I pulled up a free chair. His real name was Harvey, his rank was Sergeant First Class, and he was the NCO in charge of the Classified

Documents Distribution Center at 8th Army headquarters. He was a pervert, but also an invaluable source of information, so Ernie and I catered to him.

"Heard about your escapade at that Commie stronghold," Strange told us as soon as we sat down.

"What Commie stronghold?" Ernie asked.

"Whatchamacallit. Broads with a Hard-On Committee, or something like that."

"The Women's Power Coalition," I said.

"Yeah, that one. You really walked into it."

"Walked into what?" Ernie asked.

Strange raised one eyebrow above his shades. "They're jerking you around," he said, waggling his empty cigarette holder with thin lips. "You have no idea how big this catfight is that you've gotten tangled up in."

"You mean Mrs. Frankenton?" The president of the Officers' Wives Club.

"Yeah. She hates that young broad. The blonde one."

"Katie Allsworthy."

"Right. Old Lady Frankenton thinks sweet young Katie is putting the moves on her husband."

"The Chief of Staff?"

"Who else is her husband?"

Ernie and I glanced at each other. Finally, Ernie asked, "Do you think it's true? Is Mrs. Allsworthy seducing General Frankenton?"

"Well," Strange said, "she's doing what she has to do to convince him to help her support Commies."

"So they've been in the sack together?"

"Are you kidding? She's just stringing the old goat along, trying to control him. She'd no more spread her legs for him than she would for a couple of enlisted pukes like you."

"Wanna bet?" Ernie said.

I waved him off. "So Mrs. Frankenton feels insecure about her marriage."

"You'd understand why," Strange said, "if you saw her."

Gossip is a vicious thing. But Mrs. Frankenton's worries weren't uncommon for Army wives. As a military couple ages, both the husband and wife become less physically attractive to the opposite sex, but the husband often gains in rank and therefore in power. Power, the ultimate aphrodisiac, attracts people who need something, and the husband, after years of being just a low-ranking officer, becomes the most popular guy in town. Naturally, the wife feels left behind, alone and worried. Some women shrug it off and get on with their lives; others withdraw into themselves. A few become vindictive.

Apparently, Mrs. Frankenton was the vindictive type.

"And she hates Commies," Strange added.

"What makes you think the Women's Power Coalition is Communist?" I asked.

"It's not me. It's every counterintelligence agency in Korea. They're all monitoring it."

"Just because they want women to get a fair shake?" Ernie said.

Strange turned and looked at him. "You ever heard of anything more Communist than *that*?"

A group of men loudly entered the snack bar, led by a dapper-looking man with greased-back hair, pressed slacks, thick-soled shoes, and an expensive-looking blue windbreaker. Strange glared at him.

"Who's that?" I asked.

"Don 'Fancy Pants' Yancey," Strange replied. "I hate that guy."

"Why?"

"He works at Special Services. In charge of the gyms and the arts and crafts center and stuff like that. So he has access to all the dependent wives." Strange's cigarette holder waggled. "And their teenage daughters. He's a smooth talker. Everybody loves him."

"You haven't said why you hate him."

"That's not enough?" Strange swiveled and looked right at me. "And now they say he's opening a swanky new joint in Itaewon called the Harbor Lights Club."

"GIs can't open businesses," I said.

"*He* can. His wife is a tall piece of work named Agnes. She used to be the 'publicity coordinator' for some casino out in Inchon. Which means she was spreading her legs for the rich and famous from Hong Kong to Tokyo."

"How do you know all this?" Ernie asked.

"How do I know anything?" Strange replied.

Sergeant First Class Harvey not only had access to all the classified information that flowed through 8th Army headquarters, but he was also a notorious gossip with studiously cultivated contacts throughout the military community in Seoul. Still, much of what he told us was either fantasy or outright wrong.

When Ernie and I didn't seem all that interested in Yancey, Strange asked, "Any leads on the Three Stooges?"

"The Three Stooges?"

"Yeah, the three GIs who disappeared. Everybody's talking about it. General Frankenton is getting daily phone calls from the Pentagon. Apparently, one of the Congressmen is raising hell. Asking how in God's name Eighth Army could lose three GIs in a row."

"We didn't lose them," Ernie said. "They walked away."

Strange spread his arms at the Quonset hut. "Why would they want to leave this paradise?" When we didn't answer, he said, "A woman. That's it, isn't it? They sniffed something they liked, and they followed it out."

"We don't know yet," I replied.

"Couldn't just be your routine business girl," Strange said, "must've been something special. Something any GI would trade a month's pay for."

He continued to study us, looking for a hint of reaction.

We didn't give him one. Ernie slapped his knees and said, "I'm gonna get some chow."

"Me, too." I followed him to the chow line. Ernie ordered a cheeseburger with fries, and I ordered a BLT and coffee. When we returned with our trays, Strange had left. But he'd spread a thin layer of sugar in the center of the table. In it, he'd traced two words: *gummy whore.*

-8-

The third GI who'd gone missing was named Holdren. He was a Private First Class, and the youngest of the trio that both Ernie and I had adopted Strange's term for—the Three Stooges.

"Strange has that effect on you," Ernie said. "He worms his way into your mind."

We ran west along the Han River Road, Ernie maneuvering his jeep through kimchi cab traffic and past a long line of birch trees sitting on a bank that led down to the ancient River Han. Our destination was ASCOM, the large logistical base located just outside of the city of Bupyong. In the distance, toward the Han River Estuary, a dark bank of fog sat on its haunches, glowering like a hungry dragon.

I turned back to business, reciting the particulars from the MP report Captain Retzleff had given us after the Chief of Staff's briefing, which seemed so long ago now.

"Holdren was a tow truck driver assigned to the Forty-Fourth

Engineer Battalion," I said. "He'd been in-country almost ten months."

"Not a newbie," Ernie said.

"No," I replied. "He knew the ropes."

"And out in the ville?"

"According to the MP report, his buddies claim he was constantly out there. A real ville rat."

Ernie pondered that for a moment and I thought he was going to ask me about the case, but instead he said, "How did Strange know about the gummy whore?"

I shrugged. "Don't worry about him. He's just trying to show off, prove he's smarter than us."

"Still, Pug Grayson swore that the MPs never interviewed him, so we were the first ones he talked to."

"But he also said all the business girls in town were talking about it. So somebody found out. After all, the term 'gummy whore' is sort of hard to forget. It must've appeared in one of the reports that Strange has access to."

"Or someone was gossiping about it."

"Yeah, maybe."

"So why didn't the MPs pursue the lead?"

"It sounds too farfetched. No MP wants to sign off on a report talking about a nine-tailed, thousand-year-old fox called a 'gummy whore.'"

"How about us?" Ernie asked. "Did you put it in our report?"

"Haven't had time to type one up yet," I told him. "With our refrigerator deliveries and running all over the damn country."

"Riley will be pissed."

"He's always pissed."

"In this crazy, mixed-up world," Ernie said, "he's the one person we can count on."

We rolled through the town of Bupyong and finally arrived at ASCOM. A huge, whitewashed wooden arch loomed over the front gate. In large black letters it said, WELCOME TO THE UNITED STATES ARMY SUPPORT COMMAND (ASCOM). The MP at the gate checked our dispatch. "Purpose of visit?" he asked.

"I need some support for my command," Ernie said.

The man studied us warily. "Identification?"

We handed him our military ID cards. He jotted the information down on his clipboard, then returned them to us and waved us through.

Ernie rolled slowly onto the compound. "You think he knows we're CID?"

"Of course he does," I replied. "We're wearing civilian clothes, and besides, nobody drives all the way out here from Seoul just for the hell of it."

"What was Holdren's unit again?"

I told him. At the first crossroads was a white information board with the names of various units and functions and their corresponding directional arrows. The arrow that pointed left said, 44TH ENGINEER BATTALION (CONSTRUCTION). We followed the narrow strip of blacktop.

In a gravel-strewn parking lot in front of battalion headquarters, Ernie pulled over and parked. We didn't spend much time at the 44th Engineers because the initial MP report had covered most of that ground. According to his unit commander, Corporal Holdren had been a hard-working soldier with no blemishes on his record. If we had reason to, we'd reevaluate this information later, but for now we accepted it. The only thing we needed to find out was who his best buddy in the unit was. While we were told that Holdren was a loner and kept mostly to himself, the company clerk did confide to us that to the best of his knowledge, Holdren had spent virtually all his spare time out in the ville at the Wild Lady Nightclub.

"Did he have a girlfriend out there?" I asked.

The bespectacled young man shook his head. "I don't know. I take night classes."

"What are you majoring in?" I asked.

"Accounting."

"So you'll be rich one day."

He grinned. "I hope so."

"Go to Wall Street," Ernie told him, pointing his forefinger at him like a pistol. "That's where the action is."

"I'll keep that in mind."

We thanked him and headed outside. Ernie pulled a stick of ginseng gum out of his pocket and stuck it in his mouth.

"He can have Wall Street," Ernie said. "I'll keep the ville."

"And business girls and dried cuttlefish and *soju*?" I added.

"Those, too," Ernie replied. "Eat your heart out, Manhattan."

We drove over to the ASCOM PX, left the jeep in the parking lot, and hoofed it to the gate. At the pedestrian exit, another guard checked our identification. Outside, after crossing the two-lane street and stepping over the railroad tracks, we were in the ville. A few square acres that the Korean map had no special name for, but the GIs hailed as ASCOM City.

It was midafternoon, and though the sky was dark and overcast, none of the clubs had switched on their neon. Still, the place looked exciting. Narrow lanes, barely wide enough for a single kimchi cab, all with mazes of tiny pedestrian alleys branching off from them—wooden signs jutting from walls, touting the names of chophouses, beauty shops, and brassware emporiums. The unlit neon signs on the main stretch were made of plastic; I guessed what the colors might be for the Red Dragon Nightclub, the Kiss Kiss Lounge, the Yobo Bar, and the Suzy Wong Dance Hall, just a small cross-section of the bars and clubs here. The whole of this debauched tumult was crammed into a tiny area currently full of women with laundry atop their heads, men hauling charcoal briquette-laden A-frames on their backs, and business girls with their hair clasped up, parading in shorts and T-shirts to and from the Golden Mermaid Bathhouse. The occasional uniformed Korean national policeman strolled slowly through the maze, swinging his gleaming wooden nightstick like the pendulum of a clock.

Ernie breathed in deeply. I inhaled, too, closing my eyes and attempting to identify every molecule swirling through the afternoon breeze. The outhouses were close by. Mercifully, the air was also laced with the bite of charcoal gas and the tart aroma of anchovies boiling in red pepper stew.

"Kimchi fermenting in clay pots," Ernie said. "That smell is like life."

"Like *our* life."

We passed an open-fronted restaurant with wriggling sea creatures splashing in an iridescent blue tank. Below that, a sign read NAKJI.

"You ready for some octopus in hot sauce?"

"I'll pass," Ernie replied.

We wandered around for a while, not bothering to ask for directions because we wanted to get a sense of the layout of the ville. ASCOM City is probably, in terms of people per square foot, the most jam-packed GI village in Korea, teeming with business girls, bars, and tailor shops. The villages at Tongduchon outside the 2nd Infantry Division and, of course, Itaewon in Seoul are larger in terms of geography, but none have a more buzzing, intimate atmosphere. We wandered down a narrow lane until we reached its end. Oddly, just a few yards from where the buildings stopped, the rice paddies started. ASCOM City was a gold mine to those seeking frivolity, but it was also plopped down in the middle of a vast agricultural area.

Ernie pointed south. "So out here are the fields, and up north are the railroad tracks, the MSR, and that ASCOM compound."

"A pretty small area," I said.

"Yeah," Ernie replied, "but it's got everything I could ever need."

We turned back to the darkness and looked for the Wild Lady Nightclub. The front door was only a beaded curtain. We pushed through and entered a well-appointed room with a long bar on the left, tables on the right, and a small wooden stage in the back. Only one girl sat on a stool behind the bar. She stared so intently at her celebrity magazine that she hardly noticed our approach. Finally, she looked up.

"You early," she said.

"Yeah," Ernie replied. "Early."

She was very young, with her hair still cropped in a Buster Brown haircut—the type middle-school girls are required to wear. Thick-rimmed glasses sat slightly askew atop her nose.

"*Meikju olmayo?*" Ernie asked. It was his favorite Korean phrase: How much is beer?

She told us.

"Beats the hell out of Texas Street," Ernie said, ordering two. When she served the beers and set down our change, I pulled a photo from my pocket and pushed it toward her. It was of Corporal Holdren, late of the 44th Engineer Battalion.

"You know him?" I asked.

It was the black-and-white copy of the photo attached to his personnel file, the same one that would've appeared on his military ID card. Interested, she studied it carefully, but within seconds her eyes lost focus. Furtively, she glanced at us and then back at the photo. Finally, she set it down and slid it back to me.

"*Moolah*," she said. I don't know.

There was a slight quiver in her voice; she was afraid.

"Don't worry," I told her in Korean. "We're just old friends of his."

She nodded skeptically.

"Have you seen him before?"

She shook her head until her straight black hair swished silently past her ears. Ernie, apparently, saw what I saw and decided to change the subject.

"When do the other girls come in?" he asked.

She didn't understand, so I translated. She said that some of them should be in soon, and she had to order their midafternoon meal from the Chinese restaurant nearby.

Chinese food is popular in Korea, and local Chinese restaurants primarily do business through takeout and delivery. They serve dumplings—fried, boiled, or baked—and *jajangmyon* noodles in black bean sauce, or various permutations of other types of noodles in vegetable or fish broth. Oddly, the Park Chung-hee dictatorship won't allow them to serve rice. The given reason is to slow overall consumption, so precious dollars aren't spent on importing foreign-produced rice. But some of the more skeptical diplomatic observers believe the real reason is that Park Chung-hee fears consortiums of Chinese businessmen cornering the rice futures market and conspiring to suck the wealth out of Korea, as he believes they've done in other countries.

As we sipped our beer, the young girl switched on the sound system, which banged out an American rock tune that was far too loud. She lowered the volume slightly, then pulled her stool over to the phone behind the bar and dialed, scooting as far away from us as the phone cord would allow. She bent forward and covered the side of her mouth with her hand, so the person on the other end could hear her over the music. I strained to hear her food order. In any case, the women at the Wild Lady Nightclub were doing pretty well financially if they could afford Chinese takeout. Most of the business girls in Korea had to settle for leftover rice, stale kimchi, and the thin gruel that the bars and nightclubs and brothels served to their employees. I watched her nod and reply in the affirmative. Whoever was on the other end of the line must have been repeating her order back to her. She frowned and said something, but her voice was drowned out by the sound system, which was now assaulting the three of us with something by a British rock band.

I still found the idea of Englishmen playing rock and roll rather odd, since the genre was clearly an amalgam of indigenous American country music and southern blues. But they'd done it successfully for the last decade or so, and I wondered when other countries would get in on the act. Korea had some excellent bands; they often played at the NCO and officers clubs on base, but as far as I knew, none of them had ever made it Stateside. Maybe one day.

As this random thought flitted through my head, Ernie said, "We're not getting anywhere here."

"Be patient," I said. "She's ordering chow. That means business girls can't be far behind."

"You think they'll know something about Holdren?"

"I'm sure they will," I said.

My assumption about the women at the Wild Lady Nightclub turned out to be about as wrong as the one about Englishmen and rock and roll. Three business girls arrived minutes later, and I showed them Holdren's photograph as Ernie horsed around with them. They said they had never seen Corporal Holdren, much less known of him having a girlfriend at the club.

Before their noodles arrived, Ernie and I finished our beers and left.

Outside, we wandered the back alleys, exploring ASCOM City with no particular destination in mind. We found ourselves in a small circular plaza surrounded by shops. A

Chinese food delivery boy carrying a suitcase-sized metal box almost knocked us over.

"*Mi-an,*" he said, bowing his head as he scooted past us. Sorry.

We turned to watch him go. As we did so, I sensed movement in the passageways that ran off from the central intersection like spokes from a wheel. Without warning, shadows blocked all the exits.

"Trouble," Ernie whispered to me.

Young men, some carrying short-handled hoes, others dangling bicycle chains from their fingers, stood blocking our pathway to each of the narrow lanes, all grim-faced. They ranged from their teens to mid-twenties, some with scars on their faces or oddly shaped reptilian tattoos on their forearms. As if on cue, they all moved forward, tightening the enclosure.

Ernie edged toward a shop with wooden bins full of secondhand plumbing supplies. He tossed me a two-foot-long lead pipe and then pulled a long-handled plunger from a pile of junk. Thus armed, we faced the men.

I thought of saying something to stall them, but before I could come up with the right words, a bicycle chain flew in a great arc toward my head, resembling a whirring buzz saw.

-9-

Ernie hopped forward and jabbed upward with the wooden plunger until it met the swirling metal and the chain wrapped three times around its handle. He didn't yank backward, as the nearest thug expected, but instead charged forward, sticking with his classic strategy for handling trouble when outnumbered. I'd known that he would, and by the time he charged, I was already at his left flank, flailing away with the short lead pipe. Two of the guys backed off, and then I pivoted and hit the one who'd thrown the bicycle chain in the back of his head. He went down, and I hoped I'd pulled my swing enough that I hadn't killed him.

The *thunk* of lead on skull had a sobering effect on the other men. The bicycle chain was still wrapped around the wooden plunger handle, so Ernie flung it back and charged at the two men on his right. One of them managed to catch his elbow, and I backed up to protect him, swinging and yelling and clanging my pipe against their clubs. Amidst all this shuffling, an escape route opened up. Ernie and I took it, sprinting down one of the alleys. It was so narrow that there was hardly space to swing a lead pipe, much less a bicycle chain, and the men behind us had to follow in single file; I jabbed periodically at the closest one to keep him from reaching us. After about fifteen yards, we reached the open rice paddies. We stood there for a moment, holding them off at the opening. Ernie asked, "Which way?"

To either side of us were the backs of residences belonging to the people who lived and worked in ASCOM City. The only break in the brick and mortar was a few high windows, probably leading to bathrooms. Either way we went, we'd have to sprint along a narrow pathway on the edge of the mud-filled rice paddies. We had only seconds to decide.

"Take your pick!" I yelled.

Ernie did. Instead of angling along the backs of the homes, he ran straight along one of the elevated berms into the rice paddy. I thought he was crazy. The thugs could easily follow us, and eventually we'd fall off one of the narrow walkways and end up wallowing in knee-deep mud, which would make fighting them that much more difficult. But Ernie had seen something I hadn't.

A group of women with conical hats held in place by silk bandanas, wearing long shirts and gloves, were trampling through a dry field, moving forward in a roughly straight line. In unison, they bent forward and hacked with short-handled sickles, then hoisted and dropped thick heads of *peichu*—Napa cabbage—into loop-handled straw baskets.

We ran straight toward them, the thugs close on our heels.

Once we reached the women, Ernie stopped where two perpendicular berms met. He grabbed my elbow, pulled me past him, and stepped forward to use the long-stemmed plunger like a bayonet, jabbing at the thugs to slow them down.

Surprised, the women stood up, some of them placing a hand on the smalls of their backs, leaning backward, and loosening their spines. Each had their sickle in hand.

As they watched us fight off the thugs, outnumbered at least four to one, the surprise on their faces turned to anger.

One of them shouted, *"Weigurei nonun?"* What's the matter with you?

Then they were all waving their wickedly curved tools, shouting in unison. The boldest amongst them approached the berm and swiped at a thug's ankle. He hopped back, shouting expletives and warning her off with his club. But the women kept shouting and waving their sickles in the air, and in the distance, from the straw-thatched farmhouses, people began to gather and point.

It wouldn't be long, I thought, until someone called the police.

And our pursuers must've realized it too. One of them shouted, *"Kaja!"* Let's go.

Others cursed, but in the end, they acquiesced and began

to back away along the berm. When they were a few yards off and sure that Ernie and I wouldn't follow, they turned and ran back toward the rat's warren of ASCOM City.

Ernie and I looked around at the vast countryside surrounding us, relieved. And glad to be staring into the smiling faces of the group of farming women.

After we thanked the ladies of the rice paddy and said we were okay, they asked us not to call the KNPs into this. The last thing they wanted was to be on the radar of a bunch of corrupt cops asking invasive questions. There wouldn't have been much to report to the KNPs, in any case. The thugs had taken all evidence of the attack with them.

"Who were those guys?" I asked the women in Korean.

"Chinese," they told me, "from Inchon."

There has been a Chinatown in the port city of Inchon since the late nineteenth century, when King Kojong, in an attempt to mitigate Japanese influence, overthrew Korea's long-standing isolationist policy and started to welcome trade with China. In 1949, thousands of Chinese refugees fled the Communist takeover by Mao Tse-tung and his Red Army. Many landed in Hong Kong, Taiwan, and other parts of the world, and a few thousand ended up in Inchon, just a half dozen miles from here. According to the women who'd helped us, when the US had set up the ASCOM compound shortly after the Korean War, a Chinese gang from Inchon had taken over the local rackets, and they'd been in charge ever since.

When I asked if the local KNPs had taken action, the women shook their heads. "They work for whoever has money," they said.

Ernie and I made our way back through ASCOM City, using the main drag so as not to be set upon again by the band of thugs. At least we weren't in danger of being shot at; Korea strictly enforces total gun control. Only the police and the military are allowed to carry weapons, and the penalty for trafficking in or using guns is so severe that even gangsters eschew them. Still, clubs and knives and tire irons can be as dangerous—and those no one is afraid to use.

Because of our experience in the rice paddy, Ernie and I were muddy and smelled awful. We crossed the railroad tracks and MSR to reenter the ASCOM military compound. At the Post Gymnasium, we showered, scraped some of the mud off our jeans and shoes, and wiped down the worst parts with moist paper towels. Finally, though still a little damp, we were ready to resume the case.

By now, the cannon had gone off for close of business. We sat at the ASCOM Snack Bar, sipping hot coffee and reviewing our options.

"We could file a formal report at the local KNP station," said Ernie.

I shook my head. "Like those women said—if the Chinese gang has been running the rackets here for years, then the local KNPs must be in on it."

"And the MPs?"

"They're completely in the dark. A Chinese gangster looks just like a Korean one to them, and if they can't even read *hangul*, how the hell would they be able to tell the difference between that and Chinese characters?"

I was the only American military law enforcement official in-country who'd bothered to study Korean. My night classes were sparsely attended, and even then, not by GIs, but by civilian workers who planned on staying here awhile. Everyone else, including high-ranking policy makers, relied on the Korean employees on base to translate for them. It often worked, but not always.

"We could roll out the big guns," Ernie said. "Call Mr. Kill."

As Chief Homicide Inspector of the Korean National Police, Mr. Kill had resources Ernie and I couldn't match.

"And tell him what?" I said. "That a bunch of Chinese gangsters tried to beat us up? We don't have any specific leads on the disappearances yet. Let's not ask for Kill's help until we know what we need. Something specific he can do for us. He's too valuable a resource for us to be calling on every time we hit a rough patch."

Ernie said nothing, which meant he agreed. He rubbed his collar. "I'm almost dry." He sniffed the air. "Still smell like fertilizer, though."

"Good," I replied. "Then we're ready."

"For what?"

"Let's go back to the Wild Lady Nightclub and have a talk with the girl who ordered Chinese food."

"And brought in the three business girls to delay us." Ernie set down his coffee cup. "You don't think she was just ordering extra egg roll?"

"No. As soon as we asked about Holdren, she got on the phone."

"You think she's one of the bosses?"

"No way. She looks twelve. And no crime boss would sit in a GI bar all day, reading some celebrity magazine."

"So she was just following orders?"

"Strict orders, considering how fast she moved," I said.

"Orders from who?"

"I'd sure like to know."

I chugged down the last of my cold coffee.

They played dumb at the Wild Lady Nightclub.

A new bartender was on duty, and he had no idea who the daytime bartender had been. When I told him about the short, middle school–style bob, the glasses, and the flat nose, he looked at me like I was nuts and said, *"Moolah."* I don't know.

Ernie wanted to drag him outside and beat the information out of him, but I said no. The place had almost twenty GI customers now, enjoying a drink while they waited for the band to start. There were also a half dozen business girls working the crowd, but the three Ernie and I had spoken with earlier weren't among them. As we sat at the bar nursing our beers, I listened carefully to the buzz of conversation. Between the business girls, the one waitress on duty, and the bartender, all communication was in Korean, and without any accent that I could discern.

"They don't *look* Chinese," Ernie said.

"What do Chinese people look like?" I asked.

"Not like Koreans."

"What's the difference?"

"Koreans have high cheekbones," he said.

I motioned toward the business girls. "You think all Koreans have high cheekbones?"

Ernie studied them. "No. I guess not."

"And by the way, some Chinese people *do* have high cheekbones. China is enormous; it has hundreds of different ethnic groups. There's no one way to classify how a Chinese person looks."

"They don't look like soul brothers," Ernie said, pleased with his line of reasoning.

I sighed.

"How about the way they talk?"

"That could give them away," I said, "but if they're from Korea, they'd sound just like any other Korean."

"Are they citizens?" Ernie asked.

"No. Park Chung-hee would never allow it."

"Why the hell not?"

"He doesn't trust foreigners. And he's seen the way Chinese communities operate in other countries. They stick together. They work hard, start businesses, accumulate wealth, and make sure their kids get the best education available."

"Sounds all-American to me."

"Yeah. But in his mind, they'll use their power to take over." This line of logic seemed irrational to us, but the history of Chinese aggression was a strong memory for many Koreans. Korea and China had warred on and off for hundreds of years, with Korea refusing to become a part of the Chinese empire.

Ernie had become bored with my dissertation. He peered at me curiously. "You're a real egghead, you know that, Sueño?"

I didn't bother to answer.

He finished his beer. "Fine. So anyway, how do we find that daytime bartender? Why don't you make a scene—start a fight or something? While everybody's distracted, I'll drag the new bartender out into the alley and beat some *freaking* information out of him."

I shook my head. "We have to be more patient."

"Why?"

"Because when we asked about Holdren, it was obvious we weren't from around here, and that bartender made her call. Whoever's in charge of those guys panicked. They figured they'd scare us off by beating us up."

"That didn't work."

"No. But we have to ask ourselves, what were they

protecting? Holdren was a regular here. Let's assume he went missing because of something—or someone—he ran into at the Wild Lady Nightclub."

"Like the gummy whore?" Ernie said.

"If Holdren is here all the time messing around with business girls, and all of a sudden he's seen with an older, upper-class Korean woman, someone would notice."

"So they were afraid that we'd talk to someone here who'd give us a lead to Holdren and the gummy whore."

"Right."

"But who?"

"I don't know. There are hundreds of GIs who come in here. And we can't be sure the ones we want to talk to—anyone who saw Holdren with the *gumiho*—will ever come in again."

"It could take forever to track him down."

"Right. And if someone who can provide us a lead is an employee or one of the business girls, they could already have fired her."

"Or moved her to another club," Ernie said. "I mean, if they've been operating the rackets here since the beginning of the Korean War, you can bet they've expanded their operation. A company has to grow or die."

"Where did you hear that?"

"*TIME* magazine," he said.

"I'm impressed."

"You oughta be." Ernie paused. "So now that they know

we're in the neighborhood, they're likely to shut down any source of information that will lead us to Holdren."

"Right."

"So we're spinning our wheels."

"Right again."

"I've been thinking about something," Ernie said.

"What?"

"We've been assuming that since Werkowski is dead, Shirkey and Holdren are at risk of being killed, too."

"Yeah."

"But what if they're just being locked up, being held for ransom or something?"

"The Army would've received a demand by now."

"Right. So maybe they're being held for some other reason."

"Like what?"

"I don't know. Something bad."

I thought of how frightened the woman at the Best Hotel near Camp Kyle had been when she'd mentioned the driver with the mangled face. And how Miss Kim had shivered upon hearing the term *gumiho*.

"So if they're alive . . ."

"Yeah," Ernie replied. "We don't have much time."

Ernie and I wandered from one flashing neon sign to another, drinking all the way, practically taunting the Chinese thugs to take another shot at us. I knew it was dumb, but I had no idea what else to do; they'd checkmated us. We weren't going to be able to find any information here in ASCOM City with the people who ran the place watching us. We just held onto a sliver of hope that we could find one or two of the thugs and give them a bad enough beating that they'd tell us something about who they worked for, or why they'd been sent after us.

It was unlikely, but we were down to that.

It was getting close to the midnight curfew, and we were walking down the well-lit main drag again when Ernie back-handed my chest. I stopped. His jaw had dropped open. Before I could ask what he was looking at, he took off sprinting. I ran after him.

We must've zigzagged through twenty dark alleys before emerging back on the MSR in front of the railroad tracks. About twenty yards to our right loomed the front gate of ASCOM compound, illuminated by floodlights.

"What?" I asked, huffing and puffing and leaning forward to rest my hands on my knees. "What did you see?"

"It must've been my imagination."

"What did you see?"

"You're not gonna believe this."

"Try me. What did you *see*?"

"Strange," he told me. "I saw Strange."

-10-

The next morning, back in Seoul, Ernie and I strode past two Honor Guard soldiers and into the 8th Army head-quarters building. The classified documents vault stood just past the foyer, wedged beneath the main stairway. Behind a barred window, Sergeant First Class Harvey—also known as Strange—sat at a small desk, thumbing through documents.

"What the hell were you doing in Bupyong last night?" Ernie said.

Strange nearly jumped out of his chair. He hurried toward the window and gripped the iron bars as if pleading to get out. His cigarette holder waggled nervously, and behind his nearly opaque sunglasses, I thought I saw his eyes dart back and forth.

"Not *here*," he whispered urgently.

Ernie grabbed for him through the bars, but Strange dodged backward. Officers in Class A uniforms and highly spit-shined low quarters padded silently down the carpeted hallway. One of them gazed at us curiously. I turned away.

Ernie realized that we wouldn't be able to break into the classified documents vault and drag Strange out. "Where should we meet you?" he asked.

"The Snatch Burr," Strange answered—the name he'd invented for the 8th Army Snack Bar.

"When?"

"I can't break out until noon."

Ernie pointed at him. "Don't mess with us, Strange."

"The name's Harvey."

"Whatever. Be there. At noon."

Strange swallowed. "I will."

Leaning up against the bars, Ernie jabbed his hand forward and managed to flick the tip of Strange's cigarette holder. It clattered off the edge of his desk and rolled to the floor.

When we returned to the CID Admin Office, Staff Sergeant Riley stood, hands on narrow hips, and gave us his usual warm greeting. "Where in the *hell* have you two been? And why haven't you delivered that *freaking* refrigerator?"

I explained our inability to dispatch a truck.

"Well, you better *shit* one. That broad Allsworthy came back and gave the Provost Marshal hell. He's getting sick and tired of it."

"So why don't you have Burrows and Slabem make the delivery?"

"I *told* you. They'd never find the place."

"They couldn't find their butts," Ernie told him, "if you gave them a color-coded topographical map."

"Don't be crude," Riley said, a stunning comment coming from him.

"So why don't *you* borrow a truck?" I said. "Make the delivery yourself."

"I have work to do."

"Paperwork," I said. I was angry. I knew it, but I kept going. "We have one GI dead, two missing. Nobody knows what happened to them, or whether they're alive or dead. For all we know, they're undergoing torture right now, as we speak, and all you rear-echelon pukes can think about is delivering a *goddamn* refrigerator."

Riley stuck out his bony cage of a chest.

"Who you calling a rear-echelon puke?"

"Is there somebody else standing behind that desk?"

"You better get your ass in gear, Sueño. The Colonel isn't going to tolerate that Katie whatever-her-name-is coming back in here and cussing him out again."

I clenched my fists. Then Miss Kim approached, and I unclenched them. She spoke in a soft voice. "Geogie," she said, "you received a phone message."

She handed me a pink slip of paper. She had written a phone number on it, one I recognized.

"Officer Oh," Miss Kim said, staring up at me, worried.

"Thank you," I said, stuffing the note in my pocket.

"Would you like some tea?" she asked.

"No, thank you," I replied, trying to muster a smile. "I have to steal a truck."

"Let me help you with that," Ernie said, patting me on the back. Together, we strode out of the office.

Instead of a truck, we stole a trailer. The two-wheeled kind that's usually covered in canvas and pulled behind a jeep. We didn't know whose it was and we didn't much care, but it sat in a line of vehicles in the parking lot behind the 52nd Supply Depot, and Ernie managed to unhook it quickly. I helped him rehook it onto the back of our jeep. We checked to make sure the brake lights worked, then drove off.

The refrigerator barely fit in the trailer. In fact, we had to tilt it at an angle and didn't have anything to tie it down with, but Ernie drove slowly through Seoul traffic. When we reached the Women's Power Coalition, we stopped and hoisted the refrigerator out, then banged on the front door.

It slid open, and the impressive physique of Miss Wang Ok-ja stood before us. She snorted and stood back, happy to let us carry it in. As Ernie reinstalled the transformer, I turned to her and thrust out some paperwork Riley had typed up.

"Sign," I said.

"Why?"

"To prove we returned it to you."

"You shouldn't have stolen it in the first place."

Her long hair hung past her shoulders, and her face was impassive. I let the silence grow, mainly to give myself more time to stare at her. Since Doctor Leah Prevault had been transferred to Hawaii, I'd only received a handful of letters. She was busy, she said, with a backlog of patients in the psychiatric ward that had built up over the years. Apparently, there were a lot of nuts in Honolulu. I was lonely and upset, and maybe desperate for someone to talk to who wasn't Ernie.

I considered asking Wang Ok-ja out, but in the end, I decided against it. The vision of Leah kept me on the straight and narrow. What I did think in that moment was that I'd contact Leah and demand that we set up a time and place to meet, somehow. After this case, I could take some leave and catch a military hop to Hawaii. Or she could come here. But things between us had to be resolved.

I realized that Wang Ok-ja was staring at me with curiosity. Once again, I offered her the receipt. She grabbed it from my hand, walked with it over to the kitchen counter, found a pen, and scribbled her signature. She thrust the receipt back at me.

Behind us, Ernie had apparently finished his work. The refrigerator's cooling unit began to hum contentedly.

When we returned to the 52nd Supply Depot, the jeep we'd stolen the trailer from was gone. We unhooked the trailer and left it in the same parking spot we'd found it in.

"He'll probably make an MP report," I said.

"Good," Ernie replied. "That'll give them something to do." We climbed back into our jeep, and he started the engine. "Think they'll solve the mystery of the purloined pull-cart?"

"Given time," I replied.

Ernie glanced at the trailer. "Maybe we should leave some more clues."

I groaned. He shifted into first and roared off.

"I saw you sizing up that dolly," Ernie said, "the one at the Women's Power Coalition. You gonna make a move on her?"

I shrugged.

"Don't wanna talk about it, huh?"

"Nothing to talk about."

"Still pining for Doc Prevault?"

When I didn't answer, he said, "Nice-looking, though. Worth chasing after."

"Now that they have the refrigerator back," I said, "I probably won't see her again."

"That's the problem with you, Sueño. You're too fatalistic."

"Fatalistic?" I said.

"Yeah. You settle for whatever the fates send your way."

"Don't you?"

"Me?" Ernie said, turning at the traffic light and heading back toward the main compound. "No, I don't settle for the hand fate deals. I make my own luck."

"Like when?"

"Like when I decided to put down heroin."

"After you came back from Vietnam?"

"Yeah," he said. "It ain't easy to turn your back on a sweet lady like that."

"And now?" I asked.

Ernie smiled. "And now I'm a drunk. Perfectly acceptable in polite society."

"I hadn't thought of it like that."

"So if I can do it," he said, winding down his lecture, "you can get into that lady's pants. Even if she is a Communist."

"She'd look good in red," I replied.

"Yeah," Ernie agreed. "Or wearing nothing but a Mao jacket."

Once we reached the snack bar, the first thing I did was enter the manager's office and borrow his phone. The 8th Army telephone exchange operator switched me to an outside line and dialed Officer Oh's number for me. It rang twice, and she picked up.

I identified myself, and she said, *"Jomkanman."* Just a moment.

As I waited, I stared out into the main floor of the snack bar. The lunch hour was just getting into full swing. GIs entered, along with civilian workers, most of whom were American. The Korean workers at 8th Army headquarters, of which there were hundreds, often brought their own small lunch consisting of a tin of cold rice and bean curd and vegetables, called a *toshirak*. Most of them didn't eat kimchi for lunch because they knew that Americans could smell it on their breath. I wasn't bothered by the smell; in fact, I found it pleasing, but many Americans complained bitterly about it. When these complaints came from people who'd been here for years, or even had a Korean spouse, I found it nuts. Ernie and I agreed that if you didn't like kimchi or the smell of garlic, you were definitely living on the wrong peninsula.

A voice came on the line. Chief Homicide Inspector Gil Kwon-up. Mr. Kill.

"Sueño?"

"Yes, sir," I replied.

"Where are you?"

I told him.

"You were in Bupyong last night," he said.

"How'd you know? The local KNPs spotted us?"

"Yes and no," he replied. "They spotted you, but they didn't report it to us. Not formally, at least."

"So how'd you know?"

"We have ways."

I took that to mean that he had eyes and ears—maybe an informant—in the Bupyong police station, and he didn't want that information spread around. I was flattered by the confidence. Ernie and I had worked with Mr. Kill and Officer Oh on a few cases now, and I believed we were developing a level of trust that was possibly unprecedented between US Army law enforcement and the Korean National Police.

He asked, "Were either of you hurt?"

"No, sir," I replied. Just a few bumps and bruises. And we'd washed away the mud from the rice paddies. Mostly.

"They tipped their hand," he said.

"By attacking us?"

"Yes. I believe it was a mistake. Possibly made by one of their low-level operatives when you walked into that bar. What was it called?"

"The Wild Lady Nightclub."

"Yes. What you're getting close to," he told me, "is very dangerous."

I still didn't know for sure what he was talking about. "What, sir? What are we getting close to?"

"The Chinese gangs. Don't underestimate them."

I wondered if that were true or if Mr. Kill was just displaying the very ingrained ethnic bias against the much larger Central Kingdom.

"Apparently," I said, "the Chinese run the rackets in ASCOM City."

"Yes. We've been trying to bring that under control for years. They've proven to be slippery."

And they had the KNPs in Bupyong on their payroll. But I knew better than to embarrass him with the assertion. Instead,

I asked, "So what do they have to do with the disappearance of the three GIs?"

"We need to talk," he said, "but not on the phone. We've found evidence."

"What evidence?"

"Not now. We need to move; we can't be sure how much time we have. I've formulated an operation, and it must begin tonight."

"Okay. Where should we meet you?"

He told me. I was surprised by his choice of meeting place, but this seemed urgent, and I didn't want to question his decisions. I promised we'd be there.

"And," he said wryly, "be sure to wear your running-the-ville outfits."

"Should we be armed?" I asked.

He hesitated before answering. "No. If they realize you're police officers, they'll kill you without hesitation, no matter how much firepower you bring."

He hung up the phone. I returned to the main dining room and sat opposite Ernie, thinking over what Kill had told me.

Strange was late.

He pushed through the big double door of the snack bar, glanced around the large room, and, after spotting us, took a surreptitious route to our table.

"He thinks he's Double Oh *freaking* Seven," Ernie said.

When Strange finally sat down, he appeared flustered.

"Couldn't break away," he said. He glanced around the room, and then, tightening his lips around his cigarette holder, he leaned toward us. "The gummy whore," he said.

"We know," Ernie replied. "You wrote it in sugar last time."

"Did you erase it?"

"Of course." Ernie folded his arms and leaned back. "We're up on our spycraft. Wouldn't want to leave anything for those Commie agents to pick up on."

"They're everywhere," Strange said.

"Okay, Strange," I said. "What the hell is this all about?"

"The name's Harvey."

"Yeah, sorry. Harvey."

He sat upright and straightened his khaki shirt. "Can't a guy get a cup of hot chocolate around here?"

That did it. Ernie leaned in, grabbed hold of Strange's shirt, and pulled him forward.

"Nobody has time for your bullshit, Strange. And no, I'm not going to buy you a cup of *freaking* hot chocolate. Now you better tell me what the hell you were doing in ASCOM City last night, or I'm going to drag you outside and beat about fifty pounds of lard off you. You got that?"

Strange's cigarette holder waggled, and his eyes seemed to squint behind the dark shades. "Got it," he said.

Ernie let him go.

Strange sat back and straightened his shirt. "Except I've been losing weight lately." We stared at him. He blanched and continued. "As I was about to say, and as I would've said earlier in a more civilized environment . . ." He glanced toward me for support, but didn't get any. "I went to Bupyong last night because I was hoping to make progress on a certain missing persons investigation that has apparently stalled."

"Cut the bullshit," Ernie said, his voice low and threatening.

Strange turned slightly away from him, angling toward me. "There've been reports," he said, "from the MPs up in the Second Infantry Division. They caught wind from the business girls about a gummy whore prowling the barrooms outside Camp Kyle."

"What's a gummy whore?" Ernie asked, feigning ignorance.

Strange shrugged. "Some sort of witch," he said, "or supernatural being. A nine-tailed fox from Korean lore. She preys on young men, forces them to have sex with her. Frantically. Using them, tossing them around, and—"

"Get to the point," Ernie said.

Strange straightened his collar. "When she's done with them, she tosses them aside like used-up rag dolls. Some people say she eats their liver and leaves the corpse to rot. She then goes back on the prowl and finds her next victim."

"Why didn't we get these reports?" I asked.

"The Second ID was embarrassed by them," Strange said. "Somebody slapped a Top Secret cover sheet on it, and since you guys didn't know about them, you didn't present a need-to-know request for the documents, and you didn't get them."

"They were buried intentionally," I said.

"Sure. Wouldn't you do the same thing? Talking about some horny old broad with magical powers and a hankering for internal organs isn't exactly beneficial to your military career."

And the welfare of their military career was what most soldiers put first.

"Okay," Ernie said. "I get how you found out about all this, but what were you doing in ASCOM City?"

Strange looked slightly offended. "Isn't it obvious?"

"No," Ernie snapped, losing patience. "It isn't."

"I was looking for the gummy whore."

"Oh, for Christ's sake. Don't you know there's no such thing as a gummy whore?"

"That's a matter of opinion."

"Suppose there was such a creature," Ernie said. "Once you found her, what did you plan to do with her?"

Strange's cigarette holder stood up.

"I was going to punish her." We waited. "Give it to her real good. You know, really plow a new row and . . ."

He started to raise his hands as if to explain further with gestures, and Ernie reached out and slapped his arm. "Don't explain," he said.

"And once this happened," I asked, "what exactly did you hope to accomplish?"

"I'd have had the best lay of my life, and she'd tell me where the missing GIs are."

I realized then that I pitied Strange. He was a senior NCO, a single man with nothing to spend his money on, nothing to do with his spare time except chase delusions of a woman who, if she did exist, was certainly no legendary creature. He wasn't authorized to check out a vehicle, so he must've spent at least thirty dollars on a cab to follow us to Bupyong.

"So you'd be covered in glory."

"I'd be covered in a lot of things."

"This document, who was it from again?"

"The Second Division MPs."

"And did they have any leads on the whereabouts of this 'gummy whore'?"

"No. But I knew you two had already gone up to Camp Kyle and had returned from Pusan. I figured Bupyong would be the next place you'd go, since that's where the last missing GI was from."

"And you wanted to help us out?"

"Yep. You'd need somebody who can hit the gummy whore hard, give her what she really needs. If you know what I mean."

Ernie stared at Strange for a long time, not quite believing what he'd just heard. "Sergeant First Class Harvey," he said, "you actually believe that this gummy whore exists?"

"Of course she does. She took those three GIs, didn't she?"

Ernie shook his head slowly. Then he pointed at Strange's nose. "If I find you in Bupyong, ASCOM City, or any other place we might go during this investigation, I will personally drag you into some dark alley and kick your butt until you're talking through your asshole. You got that, Sarge?"

Strange swallowed. "You need my help."

"No, we don't." Ernie stared him down.

"Yes, you do," Strange replied. "I didn't just read the 2nd ID MP reports. They match certain SOFA records." The Status of Forces Agreement, which covers all disputes, criminal and civil, between the American military and Korean citizens, amongst other things. Both ROK and US officials appoint members to the SOFA committee, which meets periodically to peruse SOFA complaints and adjudicate the less serious disputes and refer the bigger cases to either military court-martial or Korean civil court. "Those three GIs," Strange continued, "the ones who are missing, they all had SOFA charges brought against them." Which meant a Korean civilian had accused them of wrongdoing.

I'd known about Shirkey's attack on Soon-hui in Pusan, but the other two were new to me. I sat back, trying to hide my surprise. As calmly as I could, I said, "There was nothing about that in their personnel files."

"That's because all three charges were dropped," Strange replied.

"And you think that has something to do with their disappearance?"

"Of course it does. Somebody was pissed and sicced the gummy whore on them."

"Okay," Ernie said. "We'll check that out. But no more following us during this investigation. You got that?"

"Okay," Strange said. "No more gummy whore." He stood up. "But you owe me one cup of hot chocolate." And then he held up two fingers. "With *two* marshmallows."

Maintaining as much dignity as he could, Strange sauntered toward the exit.

-11-

"They're for official use only," Riley said. "You don't just go thumbing through the file of old SOFA cases. Not without *authorization*."

There was that word again.

"You can do it," Ernie said, grabbing Riley's copy of the *Pacific Stars & Stripes* and thumbing through it until he hit the sports page. "Nobody has contacts throughout this head-quarters like you do."

The flattery worked.

"Fine. I'll call Smitty," Riley said, "over at Personnel. Make sure it's true that if the SOFA charge is dropped, it doesn't show up in the soldier's permanent record."

"Makes sense," I said.

"Yeah, I guess it does."

"And find out what they were charged with," I continued. "As much detail as you can. Names, dates, everything."

Riley jotted down something in the notebook in front of him. "You don't ask for much, do you, Sueño?"

"Whatever you can get."

"After all," Ernie said, "we took that refrigerator back for you."

"Not for me. For the Colonel."

"There's a difference?"

Riley glared at him, deciding whether or not he should be offended.

"And our expense account," I said. "We've already run through our monthly fifty bucks each, what with the traveling and all."

"Fifty dollars is more than enough. You don't need to be wasting government money."

"We could drop by the Chief of Staff's office," I said. "See if he'll authorize more."

Riley made another note on the pad in front of him. "I'll run it by the Colonel."

"Good. We'll be off, then."

"Where you going?" Riley asked.

"To find a couple of missing GIs," Ernie replied.

"What about your reports?" Riley asked, turning to me. "You haven't turned in even one."

"I guess I'll have to consolidate them when we get back."

"No, not later. *Now.*" Riley pointed to the blotter in front of him. "Colonel Brace said he wanted a report turned in to this office, on this desk, every morning at zero eight hundred hours."

"Okay," I said. "You'll have one tomorrow at zero eight hundred hours."

I nodded toward Miss Kim, who stopped typing and waved toward me with her palm down, the Korean signal for "come here." I did. She reached into her handbag, pulled out a small book, and handed it to me. "For you," she said.

The title was written in *hangul* and translated to *Korean Folk Tales*. I thumbed through the contents page. There was a chapter on the *gumiho*. "Thank you," I said, sliding the book into my jacket pocket. "This will be helpful."

She nodded back at me, and I ran outside and jumped into the jeep.

"Where to?" asked Ernie.

"The banks of the Yellow Sea," I replied.

"What's out there?" he asked.

"China 'crost the Bay," I told him.

The United Seaman's Service is an international organization that provides home-away-from-home facilities for lonely merchant sailors. There was one here at the Port of Inchon, another at the Port of Pusan, and so I'd been told, many more scattered throughout the world. Their modest and generally quiet bar and restaurant operation was our designated meeting spot.

When we entered, Mr. Kill was waiting for us, sitting at a

corner table draped in a red-and-white checkered cloth. Ernie and I sat down.

"I see you're dressed for action," Mr. Kill said.

As he'd ordered, we were in our running-the-ville outfits, including the nylon jackets with embroidered fire-breathing dragons. He wore a businessman's coat and tie.

Ernie patted his breast pocket. "I feel naked," he said.

"You won't need a weapon," Kill said. "The Chinese triads here know better than to use violence against American servicemen. That would bring down the wrath of Park Chung-hee."

"I wish somebody would've told that to the boys in ASCOM City," Ernie said.

"I'm sure that was a mistake," Kill replied, smiling beatifically.

"Good," Ernie replied. "I'd hate to think it was intentional."

I leaned across the table. "You think this Chinese triad is involved with the disappearances of the three GIs?"

"Maybe," Mr. Kill told us. "Either involved, or they know something. Either way, they overreacted terribly to your sojourn yesterday into the . . ." He turned to me. "What is the place called again?"

"The Wild Lady Nightclub."

"Yes. The Wild Lady Nightclub. Something made them very nervous."

"Maybe it's that they killed one of our GIs," I said, "and

dumped his body into the Yellow Sea. Their 'nervousness' almost ended with us facedown in a cabbage patch with our heads bashed in."

"Yes. Not the way they usually do business."

"And what way is that?"

"Silver bullets."

"Payoffs?" I said.

He shrugged. "It works everywhere. But especially here in our poor country."

Mr. Kill was about to continue when a matronly Korean waitress approached. She brought us three menus and greeted Mr. Kill in Korean.

"Would you like to eat?" Mr. Kill asked us.

"You buying?" Ernie asked.

He nodded.

"Great," Ernie replied. He handed the menu back to the waitress. "I'll take the New York. Medium rare."

All three of us ordered steak. Which actually made us less conspicuous. Since the Cheap Charley—mostly Greek and Filipino merchant marines—seldom spent money at the United Seaman's Service Club, the only way the restaurant and bar operation stayed afloat was by selling "guest member-ships" to local Korean businessmen. These gentlemen loved nothing more than ordering steaks and imported scotch with-out having to pay the high customs duties they'd be charged at a Korean-run establishment. Besides, the quality of the food and drink was assured. The United Seaman's Service had an agreement with the US Army that allowed them to purchase their supplies from the military commissaries and PX.

Our salads were made of shredded cabbage. Iceberg lettuce was always in short supply at the commissary. I poured some dressing on mine and asked, "Where's Officer Oh?"

"On special assignment," Kill answered. Then he responded to our unspoken question. "You'll find out what that is tonight," he said.

When we finished our meal, we ordered coffee, and after the waitress left, Mr. Kill reached into his pocket and said, "Here's what we found."

He slapped his open palm onto the center of the table. His hand retreated, revealing a single dog tag threaded onto a small chain. Ernie and I both knew what it was. In basic training, every American soldier is issued a pair of dog tags, one of which is worn on a long chain that hangs around the neck. The other tag is attached to a shorter chain, which is in turn looped through the long chain. The idea is that if you're killed, the long chain and dog tag stay with your corpse. The short chain and second dog tag are taken by your commander, your buddy, or whoever is around to report your death. They turn the tag in up the chain of command. If everyone in your platoon is killed and there's no one left to turn in the small chains, then someday, hopefully, the Graves Registration unit will find you, uncover the dog tag, and officially report your death.

I picked up the evidence and examined it:

SHIRKEY, ALBERT M.

BLOOD TYPE: O POSITIVE

RELIGION: CATHOLIC

Shirkey was the missing soldier who'd worked at the cold storage unit at Hialeah Compound in Pusan. The GI who'd allegedly beaten the recently drowned Soon-hui, his ex-girlfriend at the Sea Dragon Club on Texas Street. And, according to Auntie Suh, had left with a "respectable woman" on the night of his disappearance.

"Where'd you find this?" I asked.

"Near Suwon, less than one kilometer from the Seoul-Pusan Highway. In a wooded area that many travelers use instead of the approved rest stops."

In the States, we're used to exits with fast food jungles and gas stations. But this is a new concept in Korea. When the government constructed the Seoul-Pusan Highway, they built rest stops with public restrooms and gas stations and noodle shops and souvenir shops spaced evenly along the way. For some reason, not everyone likes them. Perhaps the noodles are too expensive, the traveler is carrying contraband and wants to keep a low profile, or the car happens to have a kidnapped GI tied up in the trunk. As such, a few isolated spots near the highway have developed where people can do their business without government surveillance.

"You searched the area thoroughly?" I asked.

"Yes. We even used dogs. No corpse."

"That means he's alive," Ernie said.

"Yes. We hope so. They would've had no reason to take him out there if he were dead. They probably allowed him to urinate, and while he was doing so, he managed to toss this dog tag under a bush."

"And the local KNPs found it when they searched the area?"

"Yes."

The amount of effort the KNPs were putting into this search impressed me. They were more worried about the lives of these two remaining GIs than 8th Army was, no doubt because the deaths of three American soldiers could severely damage the Republic of Korea's relationship with the United States, especially with the culprit unidentified and at large. So far, the untimely death of Sergeant Werkowski had been kept out of the press, but there were AP, UPI, and Reuters stringers operating here in Korea. A single GI turning up dead was one thing. If all three GIs were killed, they'd definitely catch wind of the story.

I studied the dog tag and handed it back to Mr. Kill.

"The men who attacked you are part of the Sea Dragon Triad," Mr. Kill told us.

"Sea Dragon?" I asked. "We were just at a bar in Texas Street called that. Do they own it?"

"Yes," Mr. Kill said. "They operate down there, too. And across the Yellow Sea."

"In Communist China?" I asked, surprised. "How do they manage that?"

"The same way they manage it here," Mr. Kill said. "Payoffs. The Communist apparatchiks are hypocrites. All their professed dedication to the revolution and the thoughts of Chairman Mao is nonsense. They take bribes like anybody else."

This simple explanation reminded me of how well-educated Mr. Kill was, having attended the best schools in both of our countries. I knew what "hypocrite" meant; it came in real handy at 8th Army. But "apparatchik," I would have to look up. I glanced at Ernie. His face betrayed no confusion, though I suspected that was an act. GIs never admit there's anything they don't know.

"So these guys," Ernie asked, "the Sea Dragons. What's their main racket?"

"Smuggling," Mr. Kill told us. "Mostly Japanese electronics. Televisions, cameras, shortwave radios, stereo equipment. They ship it here to Korea, put it on a fishing boat or other small craft, and ferry the goods across the Yellow Sea to China. On this side they run nightclubs, bars, and high-end prostitution rings. I'm told that virtually every Chinese restaurant in the country pays them a stipend every month."

That was thousands of restaurants—a potential fortune. "For protection?"

"Yes, from the Korean gangs."

"Do they ever fight?"

"Occasionally. But the division of territory, as you might say, was set long ago."

"And ASCOM City belongs to the Chinese?"

"Yes. When the US army cleared a few acres of rice paddies and built the supply depot, the Sea Dragon Triad, which was nearby in Inchon, set up bars and brothels outside the main gate at virtually the same time."

"And they've managed to protect it from the Korean gangs?"

"Yes."

"Not just with muscle," Ernie said, "but also the cooperation of the local KNPs."

Mr. Kill sipped his coffee. "My country still has problems," he said.

Neither one of us wanted to press the issue. We just wanted to make sure we knew where we stood. Reliance on the local cops was not in the cards.

"Okay," I said, leaning forward. "What is it you want us to do?"

Mr. Kill had finished his coffee and ordered another. When the waitress finished pouring his, she offered more to Ernie and me, then flicked crumbs off the edge of the tablecloth and returned to the kitchen. Mr. Kill began to talk. He kept the plan as simple as possible. The only reason it had any embellishments at all was because the thugs of the Sea Dragon Triad kept a low profile. We had to draw them out. All without involving the local KNPs.

Our goal was to arrest one of the thugs of the Sea Dragon Triad. Straightforward enough when explained by Mr. Kill, but sure to be more difficult in execution.

"You, Sergeant Sueño," Mr. Kill said, pointing at me, "will play the most important role."

I sat alone in a Greek bar, a place called—appropriately enough—the Eros. I'd chosen it because it was the one place along the waterfront where I could have a couple of drinks without worrying about being spied upon by the Sea Dragon Triad. And I needed a drink or two.

The bar was about half full of drunken merchant marines—almost all Greek, with a smattering of Filipinos. The Greeks were notorious for settling their disputes with knives instead of fisticuffs. They all carried them, at least here in the port city of Inchon.

Korean business girls swirled about. A couple of them had already approached me, bleary-eyed—probably from sedatives—and greeted me by saying *ti kaneis*, the Greek phrase for hello. I replied with what I was told was the appropriate response, *kala*. After another exchange or two, the business girl would realize I wasn't Greek, and since most of the ladies here didn't speak much English, she'd move on. I also believed they walked away because if I wasn't Greek, I was imposing myself on what these sailors considered to be their exclusive territory, and trouble wouldn't be far behind. But I had no desire to get into a knife fight with a Greek sailor. I just needed a respite before the night's operation.

When the next business girl approached, I told her in Korean that I was sorry, but I had to leave. I rose from my seat and made my way through the smoke-filled room to the front door.

Outside, I breathed gratefully of the fresh night air. Heading north, my hands in my jacket pockets, I slouched beneath the flashing neon of the quiet Inchon waterfront.

Mr. Kill had laid out a map of Inchon and shown us the location of the Yellow Sea Teahouse, a known Sea Dragon hangout. No tea was sold in the Yellow Sea Teahouse. It was a "salon-bar," as Koreans called them—drinking establishments with small booths enclosed in curtains. Groups of businessmen could sit in relative privacy and be entertained by attractive young hostesses. The services the hostesses provided were more than just dropping ice cubes into glass tumblers, pouring scotch, and lighting cigarettes. They also smiled and giggled while their guests felt them up. One girl I'd interviewed on a previous case had actually cut a slit into either side of her blouse so her customers wouldn't fumble and rip the material.

"Less trouble this way," she'd told me.

What I already knew, and Mr. Kill did, too, was that generally, unless escorted by a pack of high-spending Korean businessmen, Americans aren't allowed into these places.

Not if they're alone, and certainly not if they're dressed like a Cheap Charley GI, which I was.

My job was to isolate a Sea Dragon gangster for arrest, which wouldn't be as easy as it sounded. According to Mr. Kill, the Sea Dragons mostly let their Korean underlings handle the day-to-day operations of their nightclubs, like tending bar or kicking out unruly customers. The Sea Dragons only showed themselves for cases their employees couldn't handle.

"They're cautious," he told us. "It's part of why they've been able to stay in business so long."

Just where the map said it would be, I found a tastefully understated neon sign that read YELLOW SEA TEAHOUSE. I took a deep breath, braced myself, and passed through the open door into a small, dimly lit foyer. Predictably, the young man at the entrance rose from his stool and started wagging his forefinger at me, motioning toward the waterfront bar district and saying, "You go. You go."

I grabbed his wrist and shoved him out of the way. "I'll go where I want," I said, and stepped into the Yellow Sea Teahouse.

The long hallway was lined with flimsy curtains. Behind them sat Korean and Chinese men, laughing and smoking with the young girls next to them, smiling as their paws wrestled their way toward their goal. One of the girls emerged from behind a curtain, glanced my way, widened her eyes in surprise, and hurried toward a short bar in the back that was suffused with reddish light. I headed toward it.

The plan was for me to make a scene—one serious enough that a member of the Sea Dragon Triad would be forced to step in and handle the situation. Ernie, of course, would have been perfect for this job. But it seemed Mr. Kill didn't believe in typecasting.

We only had one shot before my cover was blown, but he didn't want me taking unnecessary chances. And I didn't think I was in any serious danger, with Ernie following in the shadows and, according to Mr. Kill, a planted operative somewhere in the Yellow Sea Teahouse. That operative would remain undercover unless an emergency arose.

"What type of emergency?" Ernie asked.

"The type of emergency where your partner is about to be killed."

"Oh, *that* type," Ernie said. "No sweat. I'm sure he can handle it."

"Thanks for that," I said.

I sat at the back bar of the Yellow Sea Teahouse and ordered a double shot of bourbon. The bartender stared at me warily, but could tell that I wouldn't hesitate to reach across and grab him by the shirt collar if he didn't comply. Reluctantly, he reached for a glass and poured from a bottle filled with something the color of watered-down cola. I tasted it, grimaced, and threw it back at him. The glass shattered against the back bar.

"Bourbon!" I shouted. "Not this crap."

He stood back, offended—and still afraid—and before I could stop him, he took three quick steps and ducked through the low door at the end of the bar. Alone, I glanced around and saw no one. I hoisted myself up and sat on the bar, then swiveled my feet over and hopped down onto the planks. Kneeling, I perused the line of labeled spirits for a bottle that was watered down less than the others. Old Grand Dad—more commonly known by its Japanese nickname of "OG-*san*." I held onto it as I climbed back over the bar. I realized I'd forgotten to grab myself a glass, but instead of climbing back over to retrieve one, I simply twisted the cap off the bottle of straight Kentucky bourbon and began to slug down as much as I could. My nostrils burned, and I wiped my mouth and set the bottle down.

This was more fun than I'd had in a while. I could see the attraction of being a total miscreant. I began to feel a little more empathy for some of the GIs I'd handcuffed over the years. Maybe they weren't such bad guys, after all.

By now, some of the women down the hall had peeked out from behind the curtains. Even a couple of the Korean businessmen stuck their heads out to stare. I discovered another adrenaline rush: I was famous.

Ernie and Mr. Kill were concealed in the shadows outside. At least, they'd told me they would be. So when I heard a heavy back door creak open and the clatter of footsteps coming toward me, accompanied by urgent whispers, I was supremely confident of my own safety. I sipped on more of the increasingly tasty liquor provided by the venerable OG-*san*.

There were six of them.

None of them were armed, I noted with relief. Apparently, they thought manhandling a drunk wouldn't require such extreme methods. But my size did give them pause, and they furtively whispered to one another. I couldn't quite make out their words, but they definitely weren't speaking Korean. Would Ernie have realized that these were the Chinese gangsters we were looking for? Probably not, which explained why Mr. Kill had picked me.

The six men approached slowly.

The first one, grinning, launched a snap kick toward my groin. Apparently, he thought it would be a surprise. I sidestepped it and backhanded him in the head. He went down. Startled, the other five backed off, but only briefly. They reached into the folds of their clothing and came up with weapons. Clubs, brass knuckles, even a set of nunchucks.

I couldn't wait for them to regroup. I grabbed a barstool and jabbed it at them, then launched the bottle of OG-*san* at the lead thug. It twirled through the air and smashed him in the side of the head. The others came at me reactively. The barstool was kicked out of my grasp, but one of the fallen gangsters had left a gap just wide enough for me to squeeze through, which I did. Once I was past them, I headed for the back door. Of course, I didn't know the layout of the Yellow Sea Teahouse, so I went in the direction I thought might lead to an exit.

-12-

I ran down a long row of multicolored curtains, half-clothed business girls screaming and curling up to hide themselves and Korean businessmen puffing on flaming cigarettes and staring at me wide-eyed. Some were enraged, and drunk enough that they would've tried to beat the crap out of me if four other men weren't already barreling down the hall to do so.

I saw a white cement-block wall at the end of the row. My choice was right or left, and the thugs were so close that they'd be on me in a second, overpowering me with their numbers and their practiced attacks. As it turned out, I didn't have to decide, because an aluminum cart rolled out in front of me from the right. I dodged left, and the cart pulled back just enough for me to scrape past it.

Behind me, someone's yell was followed by a huge crash, and glassware and ice buckets went careening to the ground as the women nearby screamed. At the wall, I slowed and looked back. To my relief, behind the overturned cart was a jumble of thugs, sneakers, and wheels, all splayed out among the broken glass. A woman in a tight skirt and dark nylons was trying to help the thugs up, but kept slipping and making the situation worse—for them, not for me.

Something about her was familiar, but I had no time to think about it.

To my right, there was another wall, so I darted left, then turned right at a hallway with a double door at the end, a caged lightbulb glowing. I was hoping this led to a storage area, which might have a back exit or loading dock. Thankfully, I was right on both counts. I passed stacks of cardboard boxes sitting in the darkness, shoved open the door, and stepped out into the fresh salt air of the Port of Inchon. I hopped off the loading dock and hit gravel with a loud crunch before realizing the thugs weren't behind me.

Worried that they'd lost me completely, I stopped and looked back. The moment I did, four of them exploded out of the same double door and sprinted straight toward me—bruised, bloodied, and furious. I turned and ran downhill toward the waterfront, with a good twenty-yard lead on them.

I still had a half mile to go when I stumbled over a crouching stone *heitei*, a lionlike creature out of Korean mythology. I sprawled headlong down a cement walkway, my arm bleeding, and was so panicked that I used the downhill momentum of my slide to pull myself up and keep running. I glanced back; my lead had been halved. Ahead was a main street with potential witnesses to my murder, but where in the hell were Ernie and Mr. Kill?

By the time I reached the street, I was moving so fast that I was forced to veer left in a large swerving turn and was easily overtaken by one of my more nimble pursuers, who sliced across the arc to intercept me. He was only ten yards away, with nunchuks in his hand, and he was heading right at me. I had no choice but to stop and fight.

Frantically, I looked around for a makeshift weapon.

The only nearby object was a collapsed produce box of wood slat and wire. I reached down to grab it, then swung as hard as I could at the guy. Shocked by the blow, he raised his weapon, and I dropped the box, lunged, and popped him in the cheek with a straight left jab. He went limp, like one of the pieces of wilted cabbage stuck to the produce box. Dropping the chained sticks, he fell to the ground.

But the other thugs were still en route, about twenty yards back. Only two of them now. The other must've tripped over an obstacle in the darkness, as I had.

Headlights switched on behind me, an engine roared, and a blue-and-white KNP Hyundai sedan headed straight toward the thugs. They dodged in either direction, and I used the diversion to escape. I ran to the next intersection, turned the corner, and headed back uphill toward a massive Chinese arch—wooden stanchions painted bright red and tiled with green and gold on top, with a silver mosaic of a phoenix frolicking above the clouds. The sedan sailed along parallel to me, and as we passed beneath the archway, it slowed. Through the open window, I spotted Mr. Kill in the driver's seat. The back door popped open, and without hesitation, I leapt in.

Ernie sat in the passenger seat in front of me. "You hurt?" he asked.

"Not much. What about the triad? We have to arrest one of them."

"We already have one in custody," Mr. Kill said.

He made a left uphill from the arch and looped around back to where I'd stumbled over the ceremonial *heitei*. The same woman I'd seen pushing the aluminum cart inside the Yellow Sea Teahouse knelt next to a man who lay facedown on the pavement, his wrists handcuffed securely behind him.

Mr. Kill slammed on the brakes. Then he and Ernie hopped out, and in seconds they were dragging the man toward the car. They tossed him on top of me in the back seat. The woman in the tight skirt and nylons climbed in after him, and I scooted over to the far side of the car and pushed the hand-cuffed man upright into the middle seat.

I noticed through the rear window that two of the Chinese thugs had returned and were now running toward us, both of them waving short but lethal-looking bats. They must've real-ized we had one of their men.

Mr. Kill started the engine, made a quick turn at the corner, and sped back onto a paved road. In minutes, we'd driven away from the bar district and were on a nearly empty street that ran along the waterfront. Shadowy metal hulls loomed above us.

I glanced at the nearly comatose man sitting next to me. He was drooling from open lips, eyelids fluttering. He couldn't have been more than nineteen years old. The woman in the back seat opposite me peered around the man and said to me, *"Anyonghaseiyo?"* Are you at peace?

It was only when I heard her voice that I finally realized who she was. Dressed up in an elaborate hairdo—probably a wig—heavy makeup, a silk blouse, a tight skirt, and nylons was an unrecognizable Officer Oh, Mr. Kill's assistant. In my haste to escape the Yellow Sea Teahouse, I'd completely forgotten that Mr. Kill had mentioned an undercover agent.

"Nei," I replied. *"Anyonghaseiyo?"* Yes. Are you also at peace? She nodded.

Once I was assured that everyone was at peace, I leaned back and let out a sigh. Then I shoved open the door, leaned out, and barfed up about a pint and a half of Kentucky straight bourbon whiskey.

"Gross," Ernie said when we climbed out of the car at KNP headquarters in Seoul. "Some of that splattered back inside. You gonna leave it in there or what?"

"You have something I can clean it with?"

"A soldier is always prepared."

"Now you sound like Riley."

"You don't have to insult me," Ernie said.

He walked briskly inside to the men's room and returned with a huge handful of paper towels, some dry and others soaked in water. After fetching a few more, we wiped down the back seat of the sedan well enough that all it needed was a good airing.

"What a setback for Korean-American relations," Ernie told me.

I considered giving him the finger, but glanced at the nearby KNP guards and figured I'd been obnoxious enough for one night.

In a small seating area in the basement, Ernie and I made ourselves as comfortable as we could on two wooden benches. Exhausted, I dozed off for a while, but was jarred awake by a scream. I sat up, disoriented, looking around for its source.

"Go back to sleep," Ernie said.

"What was that?"

"Mr. Bam," Ernie replied. The lead KNP interrogator. "Doing what he does best."

"Think this is really necessary?"

Ernie shrugged, closed his eyes, and fell back asleep.

I started to doze off again, trying my best to ignore the screams that followed.

At dawn, after receiving the results of the interrogation, Ernie and I caught a cab back to Yongsan Compound. In the barracks latrine, I showered, shaved, brushed my teeth thoroughly, and gargled with mouthwash. Back in my room, I donned fresh clothes. Feeling somewhat human again, I walked downhill to the CID office. The place was dark, empty; even Riley hadn't arrived yet. I unlocked the door, flicked on the lights, and sat down at my favorite Olivetti typewriter. Carefully layering a clean white piece of paper atop both green and pink carbon-covered sheets, I rolled them into the carriage. After thinking a moment, I began to type.

I started the report by detailing our trip to Hialeah Compound. There was Shirkey's ex-girlfriend Soon-hui, who'd claimed she lost her baby. I also mentioned the fried fish vendor, Auntie Suh, and her description of the woman who was likely the last person to see Specialist Shirkey before his disappearance. I didn't mention the dog tag the KNPs had found near Suwon. No sense getting anyone excited up at the head shed. That was the type of information that could convince an officer trying to make a name for himself to send a search battalion to trample the area, generating a lot of noise that would just alert other higher-ups. Eventually, everybody and his brother would be ordering us this way and that—a lot of movement with little result. Best to keep quiet. I also declined to mention Soon-hui's death. It didn't fall under 8th Army's jurisdiction. Besides, that was more of a private matter, one I would avenge on my own.

I sat back and reviewed what I'd written.

As it stood now, the honchos at 8th Army were afraid to get involved any further than they had to into these disappearances. No one with ambition wanted their fingerprints on a case that had already resulted in disaster—namely, Werkowski's death. That left us free to investigate unimpeded. Or at least, as unimpeded as one can be in the Army.

But I also knew that as soon as someone caught wind of any progress we were making, both the Provost Marshal and the Chief of Staff, plus anybody else who could reasonably nose their way in, would line up to start telling us what to do. Best to head them off now, make them avoid the case like the plague. And I knew just how to do that.

In my report, I added an extra line break, typed in Roman numeral two, and dedicated an entire section to the *gumiho*.

I cited testimony from eyewitnesses in the ville outside Camp Kyle about an older woman seducing Sergeant Werkowski and possibly driving him off in her chauffeured sedan. Then I laid out the legend of the *gumiho*, the nine-tailed, thousand-year-old fox that had been transformed into a woman. Anyone at the head shed who read this would write us off as crazy. In fact, 8th Army honchos would find this so embarrassing, they might pull us off the case. Which was why I'd asked Mr. Kill to submit a formal request to the ROK Ministry of National Defense for me and Ernie specifically to be assigned to work with the KNPs for the duration of the investigation. Based on experience, I knew

8th Army wouldn't reject such a request, not when it came from such a high level in the Korean government. And not when a denial would be reviewed personally by the US Ambassador to the ROK.

From 8th Army's point of view, what were two crackpot low-level GIs, more or less? To avoid diplomatic brouhaha, they'd certainly let us go. And more importantly, by not raising an objection one way or the other, fewer people would know that the initial CID report was largely centered on rumors of a mythical creature.

When I'd finished with Camp Kyle, I started on ASCOM City, but by then Riley had shown up.

"'Bout *time!*" he shouted, seeing me at the typewriter. "I'll burn copies of these and get them sent in. You done yet?"

"Almost," I said.

Next to me, hidden from Riley, sat the pink carbon copy of the pages I'd completed. I always kept an extra set for my files—an accordion folder in the back of my wall locker in the barracks.

Riley busied himself with the big silver coffee urn in the back of the room. We had forty-five minutes until the zero-eight-hundred start of the business day. As the urn started to perk, Riley wiped down the counter and shuffled a few things around, and on the way back to his desk, he glanced at me. "What the hell happened to you?" he asked.

I shrugged.

"Some dolly out in the ville get fed up and hit you with a *mongdungi*?"

A *mongdungi* was a cudgel used to beat dirt out of laundry. And occasionally for other purposes, like disciplining recalcitrant husbands. I was impressed Riley knew the word and wondered if I'd been underestimating him.

"Actually," I said, still typing, "I was doing my job."

"Great," Riley replied, plopping down in his seat. "I'll put you in for a Purple Heart."

The coffee stopped perking, leaving the room silent just as I finished my report. I wanted to give it another once-over, maybe make some changes, but Riley wouldn't hear of it.

"If I don't get this in right now," he told me, "Colonel Brace'll ream me another asshole."

"You have such an eloquent way of phrasing things," I said.

We both made our way for the coffee urn. I pulled a mug and offered it to Riley, then made one for myself.

Riley squinted at me for a moment. "What the hell's wrong with you, Sueño?"

"What do you mean?"

"You're too *freaking* polite."

"Spanish manners."

Riley didn't reply, but gave me a hard stare. Finally, he said, "You don't belong here, Sueño."

"What do you mean?"

"I mean you don't belong in the army. You should be

doing something else. Like something at a university, maybe. Or something artistic."

"Thanks."

Riley grimaced. "Don't think that's a compliment."

"What is it, then?"

"It's me telling you not to fuck it up for the rest of us. Colonel Brace is a good man. He doesn't need you embarrassing him all the time." Before I could respond, he went on. "And you'd be better off doing what the bosses told you to do for once. Just shut up and finish the job."

I could've defended myself. I could've told him about Soon-hui and the way she'd been treated, the cruel fate she'd been subject to. I could've told him about the Women's Power Coalition being jerked around just because two officers' wives couldn't get along. I could've told him about how Ernie and I had to fight and connive our way through every damned investigation just to make sure we'd be allowed to do what was needed to carry out actual justice. Instead, I said nothing. It was all too long, too complicated. And I knew that Staff Sergeant Riley would never care enough to understand. He followed the lifer's motto: just do what the Army tells you to and shut up.

On the other hand, I couldn't let him get away with insulting me, not even with something as oblique as this. Not in this man's army. I set my coffee mug down and stretched myself to my full height, angrily looming over him.

He paused, realizing he'd gone too far. "Okay," he said. "Sorry, Sueño. But you act different from everyone else." When I didn't answer, he elaborated. "You're too proper. You give a shit about things like spelling and grammar. And you're nice to Miss Kim, even though you're not trying to get in her pants. You just seem like you're in the wrong place," he continued. "Like you don't belong here."

"Try to kick me out," I challenged.

Riley looked down at his coffee. "Sorry," he said again.

But I understood what he was getting at. Sometimes I felt it, too. I didn't belong in the Army. I was different. For most soldiers, the rank they manage to achieve is their only measure of self-worth. But sometimes to me, the more rank you've achieved, the more you've compromised your ethical standards, the more you've done whatever the brass told you to do, regardless of how stupid or how harmful, and the more of your soul has been auctioned off to the demons of war.

"I'll read the report," Riley said. Then he turned and walked back to his desk.

Another thing I'd left out of my report was the result of Mr. Bam's interrogation. It turned out the Chinese thug we'd captured in Inchon was a recent recruit of the Sea Dragon Triad. He'd been smuggled into Korea illegally aboard a Hong Kong fishing vessel less than two months ago as part of a large influx of young toughs, recruited mostly from Fujian Province in southern China. The Sea Dragon Triad was expanding its manpower.

The question was, why? What did the Sea Dragon Triad have planned that would require more human capital?

Mr. Bam had hammered away on that point—quite literally—but the young Fujianese gangster repeated over and over that he didn't know anything.

"He probably doesn't have that information," Mr. Kill told me and Ernie just before dawn. "He's also never heard of any person who matches the description of the woman we're calling the *gumiho*, though when our Chinese translator said the word in his Fujian dialect, he seemed quite shocked. According to him, Chairman Mao looks down on such folklore, but he admitted that before his parents died, they believed in such things."

"So he does, too," I said.

"Of course. The Communists have wiped out many institutions, but amongst the uneducated peasantry in China, old superstitions still run deep."

Ernie found this irrelevant to the case. "Okay, so he doesn't know anything. What's our next step? He's never heard of the gummy whore and knows nothing about the missing GIs. So this was all a waste of time?"

"No," Mr. Kill said. "Not a waste of time. The Sea Dragon Triad is bringing in more muscle, which means they have a bigger plan—a new enterprise, or something they're protecting.

I suspect you two have already stumbled onto part of that, which is why they went after you in ASCOM City."

"Do you have any idea what it is?"

"They could be expanding their smuggling operation. The more product they sneak into China, the more money they make."

"What would that have to do with missing GIs?"

"They could have witnessed something they weren't supposed to," Mr. Kill said.

"Unlikely," I said. "None of them were doing the type of work that would bring them into contact with any sort of smuggling operation."

"Or maybe the triad needs insurance," Mr. Kill said. "Hostages. Maybe they need something they can barter if things go wrong."

I sat up straighter on the bench, staring at him. Kill knew he'd caught my attention. "And what could be more valuable to Communist China," I asked, "than bona fide members of the most powerful military in the world?"

"Perhaps," Mr. Kill said, "but they'd risk US retaliation." He shook his head. "We still don't know."

"Shirkey's ex-girlfriend in Pusan," I said, "worked in a bar controlled by the Sea Dragon Triad."

"Soon-hui?" Ernie asked.

"Right. And she turned up dead. In ASCOM City, Corporal Holdren, another of the missing GIs, was apparently seeing a woman who worked at the Wild Lady Nightclub, also controlled by the Sea Dragon Triad."

"And when we snooped around there," Ernie said, "they attacked us."

"It's tenuous," I said, "but there seems to be some link between this *gumiho*, the missing GIs, and the Sea Dragon Triad."

"Right," Mr. Kill said. "So what we need to do is track down the *gumiho*."

"How do we draw her out?" Ernie asked.

"We need bait." Mr. Kill gazed back and forth between us. "She seems most interested in Americans."

We both looked at Ernie.

"Oh, no," Ernie responded. "A rich woman with means and education? Not my department. That's you, Sueño."

Ernie was right. Mr. Kill and I both remained silent.

"The real question is," Ernie said, "how do we find her?"

We looked at Mr. Kill, who shrugged. "She operates in your GI villes, as you call them. That's your area of expertise, not mine. Which is the justification I used in the formal request for you both to temporarily join our investigative team."

"I think I know how we might be able to find her," I said.

"How?" asked Ernie.

"It's a long shot. I'll tell you when we get back to the compound."

Ernie and I rose from the bench.

"Thanks for the fine accommodations," Ernie told Mr. Kill.

"Anytime," he answered.

-13-

Later that morning, Riley received the SOFA complaint records he'd requested from Smitty. I was going over them when Katie Allsworthy stormed into the office. Her tiny frame hovered over my desk.

"You!" she said, pointing a manicured forefinger at me. "*You* told Mrs. Frankenton that you took the refrigerator back to the Women's Power Coalition."

The idea that I'd have the occasion to communicate with someone as high up in 8th Army as Mrs. Frankenton, President of the Officers' Wives Club and wife of the Chief of Staff, was so ridiculous that I didn't bother to answer. Instead, I sat dumbfounded with my hands over the SOFA report.

"And the other bozo who went out there with you. What's his name?"

Again, I didn't answer.

Mrs. Allsworthy continued, "That witch Frankenton had our power shut off. *Apparently*, she mentioned the refrigerator to one of the officers in the ROK Army Liaison committee, who mentioned it to an official in the Ministry of Energy, who mentioned it to the lowlifes who actually control the switch. And they turned off our section on the grid. Because of you." She was pointing at me again. "So you're going to fix it. Do you understand me? I want the electricity at the Women's Power Coalition back on *today*, before close of business, and I'm holding you personally responsible. What's your name? Sween-o? My husband will have you up on charges so fast— insubordination to the wife of a superior officer. Malingering. Spreading rumors detrimental to good order and discipline. You name it, you'll be charged with it. Do you understand me, soldier?"

Colonel Brace had to be hearing this from his office down the hall. But no sound came from that direction. Staff Sergeant Riley, however, felt some responsibility to protect one of his troops.

"Ma'am," he said, stepping out from behind his desk. "Maybe if we talked this over . . ."

Without even looking at him, Katie Allsworthy said, "You keep out of this. I want an affirmative from this man, and I want it *now*."

Miss Kim was practically cowering behind her *hangul* typewriter. She was the sole earner for herself and her mother, and the thought of being caught up in anything that would cost her this admin job terrified her. There was no social safety net in South Korea, unless you counted standing in the street and begging.

Ernie had quietly placed himself five paces behind Mrs. Allsworthy. I could almost read his mind. If she pulled a weapon or made a move to strike me, he'd be on her. But her attack wasn't physical. She was quickly losing precious resources for the WPC, so in her desperation to protect the women there and their cause, she'd chosen to resort to threats. I wondered whether she might actually take these accusations to her husband or someone even higher up in the 8th Army hierarchy.

Katie Allsworthy was still waiting for her answer. My irritation with the situation had slowly graduated into fury; I'd wanted neither of the assignments with the refrigerator, and electricity at the Women's Power Coalition was no more my responsibility than the man in the moon's. But then I remembered something I'd seen in the summary of Status of Forces complaints I'd been studying.

"When was your electricity turned off?" I asked.

"Nine o'clock this morning."

"Did somebody come out to unhook it, or was it disconnected remotely?"

"I don't know. There were workmen there."

So somebody had gone out to manually shut off their power. I figured as much. Remote switches weren't common in Korea.

"Okay, so I'll have to talk to one of your associates. Who was there?"

"Wang Ok-ja—you've met her. She tried to fight them off."

"All right," I said. "Tell her to stand by. I'll be there in a few minutes."

Mollified, Katie Allsworthy stepped away, briskly slid on her overcoat, cinched its belt tightly around her waist, and marched out of the room.

In the silence that followed, Ernie was the first to speak. "I would've decked her."

Riley whiffed roundhouse punches through the air.

Frowning, Miss Kim hurried outside to the ladies' room.

Colonel Brace's office remained silent as a tomb.

I sat back down. Ernie placed both hands on the edge of my desk. "Why'd you promise to get their electricity back?" When I didn't answer, he said, "Oh, I know. You want to see that *yoboseiyo* out there. What's her name? Sandy Koufax—the one with the fastball."

"It's not that," I said.

"Don't lie to me, Sueño."

"Okay, maybe that's part of it."

"And the rest?"

"I think they've got something for us out there."

"Like what?"

"Information that can help us track down Strange's new obsession."

"The gummy whore?"

"Just so," I replied.

Ernie walked over to the Moyer Recreation Center and caught the military bus that ran once per hour over to the Army Support Command in Bupyong. He promised me he'd stay away from the Wild Lady Nightclub and take a cab from ASCOM to the United Seaman's Service Club in Inchon to retrieve our jeep.

Riley came through for us with another fifty bucks in petty cash allotment, so Ernie had stopped at 8th Army Finance on his way to the bus station to pick up some money.

A few months back, Ernie and I had busted a guy named Potocki for a black market violation. When we found out his wife was sick, we let him off with a warning and didn't file official charges. He was grateful and knew that he owed us one. As it turned out, he was an electrician for the 19th support group, maintenance, and repair facility. As Katie Allsworthy had chewed me out, I'd decided he would be getting a call. He answered on the first ring, and promised to meet me with his repair truck, just asking where and when.

Within an hour, Sergeant First Class Potocki and I were in front of the Women's Power Coalition. He walked around the building, studying the wiring, then jumped into the truck's hydraulic lift bucket and raised himself above the level of the roof. Within minutes, he was fiddling with the cable and rehooking it to the utility pole.

Wang Ok-ja came outside. She wore a long woolen dress and a black scarf with embroidered peacocks. "Katie says you'll fix this," she said. "You have to."

I didn't argue with her, just smiled and nodded.

"Who ordered it turned off?" she asked.

I shrugged and said, "Someone who's afraid of Mrs. Frankenton."

"Are *you* afraid of Mrs. Frankenton?"

"No."

"Why not?"

"Because her husband needs me right now."

"For what?"

"For a case I'm working on." I looked her over. She was a sharp one. "You can help me on that case."

"Me? How?"

"Some women were hurt," I told her, "by GIs. I need to look at the details on the SOFA charges."

She pulled the long ends of the scarf closer around her neck. "I don't know."

"Katie will approve it," I said. "It's to help the women."

She glanced up at Potocki, who'd unhooked a few wires but appeared to be far from finished.

"I'll call her," she said.

"Please."

She turned and hurried back into the office.

When Sergeant Potocki eventually climbed back down, he

said, "They have juice now. And the good news is"—he pulled off his thick gloves—"I bypassed the meter. They won't have to pay for it, and no one will know unless the utility techs stop by to inspect."

"When will that be?" I asked.

"Maybe never."

I thanked Potocki, offering him a handshake.

"You don't need a ride back?" he asked.

"No. I'm going to stay awhile."

Officially, I was at the Women's Power Coalition on a disappearance and murder case.

What I was looking for was access to the records of women who'd filed claims with the Status of Forces Agreement Committee in recent years, specifically for domestic abuse involving US servicemen. In the SOFA data Riley had provided, I'd discovered that the WPC represented a number of these young women. No wonder 8th Army had come to view them as more than an annoyance. They had been marked as a legitimate threat.

The problem was that the data Riley had made available to me, all of it marked FOR OFFICIAL USE ONLY, had few particulars except the names and dates of each case. The accusations were left vague, like "assault" or "harassment" or the old standby "mutual confrontation." As if a hundred-pound Korean woman would be eager to fight a two-hundred-pound American GI.

I needed to know the details of the accusations these women had made. Their stories, their understanding of what had taken place. And I knew there was a good chance the Women's Power Coalition had these in their records.

I told Wang Ok-ja that I'd met Soon-hui on Texas Street in Pusan and become aware that she'd been beaten so badly by her GI boyfriend that she'd suffered a miscarriage. I explained that I was an investigator on a missing persons case, and I had reason to believe that several of the missing men had recently been up on SOFA charges. I asked for more information on Soon-hui's incident and the others, with the promise that when I confronted the GIs involved, I'd be in a better position to bring them to justice. I neglected to mention Werkowski, whose actions had already caught up with him.

We sat at the wooden table in the center of the WPC common room. Miss Wang pursed her lips, studying me warily. "Why do you want to help these women?"

I switched to Korean, telling her how I felt. It didn't matter to me whether the victim was Korean or American; justice shouldn't serve one over the other.

"What will happen to the GI?" she asked me.

"He'll be punished," I said. How harshly, I couldn't guess. Often, it was just a slap on the wrist: restriction to compound, pulling of an overnight pass. "And everyone will know what he did," I added. Even if fellow GIs weren't informed officially of the results of the SOFA investigation, gossip spread fast in the Army.

She remained silent, but nodded. Hoping to lighten the subject, I complimented her on her English. She told me she had spent time as a foreign exchange student in the States. She'd even helped to create a course on Korean literature at the University of Washington. She'd wanted to include more on Korea's female writers, but in the end only the *sijo* poetry written by ancient *kisaeng* had been incorporated. Suddenly, she seemed to remember why I was there and said, "Okay, the files."

She brought me to the next room, where I was greeted by a row of wooden file cabinets arranged in order by the *hangul* alphabet. I pulled out my notebook and went to work.

After a few minutes' search, I hit pay dirt. A lot of it.

First was the file on Corporal Kenneth P. Holdren, the missing GI from the 44th Engineer Battalion in ASCOM. When Holdren's Korean girlfriend had first become pregnant, he was furious. He'd walked out on her. Wouldn't help her at all.

A few weeks later, she'd appeared at the Women's Power Coalition branch office in Bupyong, outside of ASCOM City. They'd explained her options for abortion as well as adoption. But she didn't have enough money to cover the hospital bills for either. The Women's Power Coaliton helped her fill out a Status of Forces Agreement request for compensation. Not for the child—per standard policy, the US never compensates anyone for having a GI's baby. But the request outlined the abuse that Holdren had heaped on her before he left. The specifics were difficult to read. Apparently Corporal Holdren, a dump truck driver, had a thing for beer bottles. Just for fun, he'd held his girlfriend down and forced them into her rectum and vagina. Sometimes the caps were off; sometimes they weren't. Sometimes they were full of beer, and sometimes he'd filled them with something else.

Holdren testified that it was all a lie, and since there was no evidence against him, the SOFA claim had been dismissed.

Meanwhile, his ex-girlfriend's pregnancy advanced. When she was seven months along, she visited the compound out of desperation. She convinced a GI at the front gate to escort her on base to the Enlisted Club and waited for Holdren there. She begged him for money. When he tried to ignore her, she began to cry and grabbed his arm, screaming for him to help her. The master-at-arms, reluctant to drag her outside in her condition, ordered Holdren to get her out, which he did. He grabbed her by the hair and pulled her out of the club and off compound through the pedestrian exit. According to her, he then let go of her, and his demeanor changed completely; he was as nice as he'd been at the start of their relationship. They walked together toward the room that a sympathetic landlady in the village had allowed her to use temporarily; pending the money she would receive when her GI boyfriend moved back in with her.

They never arrived. In a dark alley, Holdren beat her senseless, smashing her head against brick and leaving her for dead. Only she wasn't dead. An hour or two later, she regained consciousness.

I read on, stomach churning, seeing this report as yet another example of how damaging our presence here in the ROK could be.

She then returned to the Wild Lady Nightclub, waddled up onstage, and, with the rock band still playing behind her, used a butcher knife to cut her own throat. She bled out before her body arrived at the hospital in Bupyong. No heroic efforts had been taken to save her child, since there was no head of family to sign for her or make an advance payment.

A month later, Corporal Holdren disappeared.

I tried to push the sordid details from my mind and analyze this new information through a broader lens. There was more than one similarity between these cases.

Corporal Holdren had met his ex-girlfriend in the same place she'd committed suicide—the Wild Lady Nightclub, whose young bartender had sicced several members of the Sea Dragon Triad on us. Likewise, Specialist Shirkey in Pusan had been involved with Soon-hui, a business girl on Texas Street, in another nightclub controlled by the Sea Dragon Triad.

Could Werkowski's disappearance from Camp Kyle—and eventual murder—have also involved the triad? But the Chinese gangs stuck close to port cities, since their main source of income was international smuggling, and Camp Kyle was outside Uijongbu, which was far enough inland that Korean gangs ruled the roost.

So how could Werkowski's case possibly connect to the Sea Dragon Triad?

Two of the three missing American GIs had abused their pregnant Korean girlfriends. Holdren's and Shirkey's cases both involved territory controlled by the triad. The *gumiho* had been spotted with both Shirkey and Werkowski. The only place we weren't sure whether or not the *gumiho* had been was ASCOM City, since we'd been chased out before we had the chance to interview any possible witnesses.

I had a question for the young Sea Dragon member in KNP custody.

The next morning, Ernie and I drove to KNP headquarters in downtown Seoul. Officer Oh greeted us in the lobby and walked us downstairs to the interrogation rooms, where Mr. Kill was waiting. "You have a question for our young Fujianese mobster?"

"Yes," I said. "Camp Kyle. Does the Sea Dragon Triad have any investments in that area?"

"Interesting," Kill said. "Camp Kyle, on the northern edge of Uijongbu?"

"Yes," I replied.

"Let's ask," he said.

He told us to wait. We sat down on the hard wooden

benches we'd slept on and tried to ignore the screams once again. A half hour later, Kill returned.

"He doesn't know," he said. "Bam's sure he's not holding anything back. And his lack of knowledge actually makes sense; if the Sea Dragons were expanding their operation to Uijongbu, they wouldn't entrust that information to a low-level thug fresh from overseas."

"Is there any other way for us to find out?" I asked. "In the other two cities where our GIs went missing, they were involved with business girls at Sea Dragon operations."

He nodded. "I'll send a man up to Uijongbu to see if anything suspicious has been going on there in recent months."

"Good. And their new operation," I said. "The one they're bringing more men in for. Any progress as of yet?"

"Not yet. I have people working on it, but the Sea Dragon Triad is very secretive."

Ernie had been quiet up till now, but rose suddenly from the bench and began to pace. "Why not check Itaewon?" he said.

We both looked at him. "What do you mean?"

"Think about it. If you're a gang with pride and you've been tussling with the Korean gangs over money and territory, you're going to want to spit in their face and dare them to do something about it." He continued to pace. "As it stands now, you have a run-down nightclub or two down on Texas Street in Pusan and a titty bar you call a teahouse in Inchon, plus the Wild Lady Nightclub in ASCOM City. All those places are fine, but they're out on the fringes. So where's the center of the action? Where's the next place you're going to want to expand?"

"Seoul," I said.

"Right. The capital, where all the glamour is. So you can show the world how much money you're making, how smart you are and, more importantly, how tough you are. And the best bar district in Seoul is . . . ?"

He waited for us.

"Myong-dong," I answered.

"Yep. But that's smack in the middle of downtown Seoul, and it's for Koreans. Not an international crowd. So maybe the Sea Dragons aren't quite ready for Myong-dong yet. What would be the preliminary step? The second largest bar district in the city?"

"Itaewon," I said.

"Right. Every foreigner in the country eventually gravitates there. And Itaewon is also likely because thousands of American GIs hang out there. Not to mention that all these disappearances have happened in GI villages."

"And Itaewon is the biggest GI village of all," I replied.

Ernie nodded.

"Maybe you're right," I said. "But where does that leave us? There have to be a hundred bars and nightclubs jammed into Itaewon."

"So we narrow our choices," Ernie said. "If the Sea Dragon Triad is bringing in muscle as part of a big push, they must be starting something new. So what's new in Itaewon? What's everybody talking about?"

I thought about it. "I don't know," I admitted.

"Christ, Sueño. You've been working too hard. There's a new trendy nightclub out there that has people standing in line to get in."

"Standing in *line*?"

I'd never heard of such a thing. On New Year's Eve, maybe, but usually the bars in Itaewon were begging for business.

"An American guy runs it. Or at least, he's the face at the door. Don Yancey. You've seen him around compound. Mr. Fancy Pants. Slicked-back hairdo. Always wearing nice clothes. Imported from home, not from the PX or shops around here."

"The guy Strange hates."

"Right. He holds court every day at the 8th Army Snack Bar. Late in the day, around close of business. A couple of hours before he opens his place, the Harbor Lights Club."

"That one," I said. "I've heard of it. Out on the MSR, just on the edge of Itaewon."

"Hot and cold running women," Ernie said. "And most of them aren't even business girls. Guys tell me that there's so much free action at the Harbor Lights Club that it's cutting into Itaewon's bottom line. The local business girls are thinking of organizing a *demo*." A protest demonstration.

"But this guy, Don Yancey," I said, "he can't actually *own* the Harbor Lights, can he?" The ROK government requires that any long-term business lease be cosigned by a Korean.

"I guess not," Ernie replied.

We both turned to Mr. Kill.

"I'll get the information on the business title." He called for Officer Oh.

She trotted lightly down the stairs.

"*Nei,*" she said, bowing with hands clasped in front of her skirt. Mr. Kill told her what he wanted, and she bowed again and marched back upstairs.

"It could take awhile," he told us. "Some of these land deeds are convoluted."

There it was again—his displaying a vocabulary that was beyond the ken of most of the Americans we worked with.

"Once we find this information," Kill asked us, "what will the next step be?"

Often, I felt as if Mr. Kill steered our conversations like a professor conducting a seminar. It didn't bother me; I was happy to learn from someone who essentially held a PhD in criminal investigation.

Ernie, however, seemed to have lost patience with coopera-tive analysis. "You're the head honcho," he said curtly.

Mr. Kill smiled.

"I have an idea," I said.

"Don't you always," Ernie replied.

"Well, like you said, I don't get out much. About time I met this new king of Itaewon. I think I'll pay Don Yancey a visit and check out the action at the Harbor Lights Club."

"I'll go with you," Ernie said.

"No. I think I have to go this one alone."

-14-

When we returned to the CID office, I convinced Riley to take me to 8th Army Personnel for a meeting with Smitty. Once we arrived, we were ushered into a small office cluttered with stacks of paperwork and three-ring binders full of 8th Army supplements to US Army regulations. Fronting his desk, Smitty had a mother-of-pearl nameplate that identified him as the NCO in Charge, Personnel Operations. He was a big man with a bushy mustache, probably in his late thirties, and clearly already balding. He wore his khaki uniform proudly, and his Master Sergeant stripes shone yellow off his sleeve.

"What can I do for you two gentlemen?" He leaned back in his chair, lacing his thick fingers across his belly.

I told him.

He laughed out loud. "By God, that's a first."

"Hey," Riley said, motioning with his hand. "Keep it down, Smitty. This one's on the QT."

"QT?"

"You know. Hush-hush."

"Oh, getting all British on me, huh? Okay, I'll keep a stiff upper lip." Smitty guffawed at his own joke. Eyes filled with mirth, he looked at us again. "You have to admit it's a rich one. Sergeant Sueño here wants to bring himself up on SOFA charges?"

"ASAP," Riley said. "Here, I've written up a scenario." He tossed a sheet of paper across Smitty's desk, and Smitty snapped it up like a barracuda capturing its prey. He read as fast as his flitting eyes allowed.

I turned to Riley. "You didn't tell me you wrote something up."

"When you called me from downtown and told me how urgent it was, I figured I'd get a jump on it."

"Good Lord," Smitty said, looking at me agape with something like newfound respect. "You did all this? To a helpless woman?"

"I didn't do anything," I said. "The idea is to make people *think* I did something. That some abused Korean business girl has brought me up on SOFA charges."

"Who the hell do you think is going to read this? Nobody but a bunch of old farts on the SOFA Committee."

"Maybe," I said.

Smitty was nothing if not shrewd. His eyes narrowed as he set the sheet of paper down. "You think someone's leaking information," he said.

"We *know* someone's leaking information," Riley told him.

We didn't really, but it was our working hypothesis. The *gumiho* seemed to have somehow gotten wind of the crimes committed by Specialist Shirkey and Corporal Holdren, which we suspected had led to their abduction.

"Does this have anything to do with those three GIs who disappeared?" Smitty asked.

I held my hands up. "Hold on there, Sergeant Smith. You're moving too fast. This whole thing has to be kept under wraps, or it has no chance of working."

"Hey, I get it. You think I'm a newbie?" He stared at the paper again. "I'll take this over to Frances. She runs the admin shop over there at SOFA. I'll tell her to slip it in when nobody's looking."

"Can she backdate it?" Riley asked.

"Yeah, probably. No more than a week, though. Otherwise it'll look suspicious. She'll just claim that the charges were so upsetting that she couldn't bring herself to type out the paperwork right away."

I looked at Riley. He grinned sheepishly. "They're that bad?" I asked.

"Man," Smitty said. "If I ever see you in a dark alley, I'm running the other way. Bogus charges or no."

"Thanks," I said. "I think."

We were now fairly sure that the Sea Dragon Triad had a hand in the disappearance of the three GIs, but had yet to figure out exactly how that tied in with a legendary one-thousand-year-old fox-turned-woman. It did seem that where the Sea Dragons went, the *gumiho* followed, with the possible exception of Camp Kyle.

Then I received a call from Officer Oh, who explained that just a few months ago, a new fish processing plant had been built on the outskirts of Uijongbu. The ownership title had been purposely obscured, but it was rumored that the Sea Dragon Triad had funded the plant's construction. She also discovered that the Harbor Lights Club's building belonged to an investment consortium, but the lease to the club itself had been signed by a woman named Roh Hyun-ah.

"Who's she?" I asked.

"A wealthy woman," Officer Oh told me. A pause as she riffled through her notes. "Married to a foreigner. His name is Donald P. Yancey."

Ernie and I approached Don Yancey at the snack bar. He sat with his legs crossed and a cup of tea in front of him, and one of his disciples had just gotten up and walked off. It was late, an hour after the five P.M. cannon, and the snack bar was almost empty. Yancey, we figured, would finish his tea and head out to his club in Itaewon. He didn't seem surprised when we sat down.

"Howdy, gentlemen. I'm Don." He reached out and shook our hands. His fingers were soft, pudgy, and spangled with three or four rings.

Ernie took the lead. "We know who you are. We need your help."

Yancey gazed at us pleasantly, with his perfectly coifed hair, light blue eyes, and air of relaxed friendliness. "How can I be of service?" he asked.

"Your new club, the Harbor Lights," Ernie said. "We understand you're doing well out there?"

"Praise be to God."

"You're religious?"

"Only when it comes to business," Yancey said, smiling.

Ernie flashed his CID badge. "My partner and I are looking for a couple of guys. They have money, and we've been told they love to hang out at Harbor Lights."

"Oh?"

"They're not dangerous," Ernie said, "as far as we know. But they are slippery. So we'd like your cooperation."

"Always happy to help law enforcement," said Yancey.

"It won't take much," Ernie told him. "My partner here will spend some time in your club by himself, staying out of the way and watching for these guys."

Yancey nodded.

"When he takes them down—if they show up, that is—we expect there to be no disruption to your operations."

"I see," Yancey said.

"He'll start tonight," Ernie told him.

"All right, then," Yancey said, checking his watch. "I have

to be on my way." He stood and said, "Oh, if you're not a member, my security guard won't let you in."

"How much does membership cost?" Ernie asked.

"Oh, there's no cost. I give it out free to friends. Here." Yancey reached into his jacket pocket and pulled out what appeared to be a calling card. He scribbled something on the back and handed it to Ernie. "A key to the kingdom," he said.

"Thanks," Ernie said, handing the card over to me.

Yancey shook our hands again and left. As we watched him push through the door, Ernie said, "That was easy."

"He'll want something in return someday," I warned.

"Yeah. But he didn't ask for anything. Or even hint that he'd want something in the future. I think he's nervous."

"I think so, too."

Back at the barracks, I sat alone on my bunk. Listlessly, I picked up the book Miss Kim had given me and opened to the chapter on the *gumiho*. About every third sentence, I had to stop to look up a word in my Korean-English dictionary. When I was done, I rubbed my face, trying to put what I'd just read out of my mind. It wasn't easy.

I glanced at the framed photograph in my wall locker of me and Leah Prevault in front of Changgyong-won, the royal palace in downtown Seoul. We were both smiling as a ferocious stone *heitei* snarled behind us. I knew Doctor

Prevault was busy in the psychiatric ward at Tripler, which was a huge military hospital, but it still bothered me that she hadn't found more time to write. Her last letter had been friendly, joking even, but impersonal. I'd answered it right away, and though I hadn't yet received a response, I was already considering sending another.

I showered, shaved, and changed into the best pair of slacks I owned. Ernie kept saying I was moping around too much. According to him, I hadn't been the same since Leah had left. He probably liked the idea of my solo mission at the Harbor Lights Club because hanging around some fancy nightclub would give me the chance to find someone new.

"She's gone," he'd told me. "No one ever comes back. We're young. Time to live a little."

I slipped into a starched shirt with long sleeves. Before leaving the barracks, I slapped on some aftershave.

I walked up stone steps. A GI I recognized from the weight room at the Collier Field House on Yongsan Compound South Post sat on a stool outside the main club entrance, wearing blue jeans and a too-tight sweatshirt. Emblazoned across his chest was the flaming logo of the Harbor Lights Club.

"You're moonlighting," I said.

"Yeah." Dead-eyed, he asked, "You a member?"

I showed him the calling card Yancey had signed. He

studied it suspiciously. Finally, he reached for the phone. "I'll call him."

I snatched the card back from him. "Don't bother," I said. "I'll talk to him inside."

I breezed past the bouncer, forcing him to decide whether to strong-arm me. He stayed on his stool. But he did lift the phone and dial.

After passing through a short hallway, I entered the Harbor Lights Club proper. It was a huge space, considerably larger than most of the nightclubs in Itaewon, and bustling with people. There was a long L-shaped bar on the right bathed in the blue glow of elevated round bulbs. It was packed with single men. To the immediate left was a stage about ten yards wide, and in front of that a round parquet-covered dance floor with a mirrored ball hanging so low a basketball player would've had to duck his head. The band must have been on break, because a too-loud song about rocking some sort of boat was being piped in through an overhead sound system. Cocktail tables were spread across the room, covered in white cloth and spangled with candles glowing red in netted glass holders. Along the far wall, shrouded in shadow, stood a row of high-backed, padded leather booths. Ghostly figures haunted the darkness.

Despite being in my best shirt and slacks, not to mention a highly spit-shined pair of Army-issue low quarters, I felt like a bumpkin fresh from the cabbage patch. Everyone else here was decked out in the latest fashion, especially the women. Most of the female clientele was Korean, but I spotted several Caucasian and a few African American faces. Some men sat with their girlfriends or wives at tables, while the single men stood together at the bar or chatted up business girls. Everyone seemed anxious to dance except the guys at the bar. I would normally have joined them, but on this mission I had to at least make the attempt to socialize.

Way in the back, I found a small, round cocktail table with a single chair. The joint was so busy it took ten minutes for a waitress to reach me. By then the band had started up, and I had to shout to be heard. I ordered a Heineken, since no one here was drinking domestic OB. When I paid, I was shocked to learn they were charging 1,500 *won*. Three bucks a bottle. Outrageous. It was more than we'd paid on Texas Street, and easily three times as much as I'd pay for a beer at any of the old, run-down nightclubs in Itaewon. But this place was so trendy. Which was what people paid for, right? To see and be seen in the most fashionable of places.

Disgusted, I slowly sipped my beer.

A half hour later, Don Yancey pulled up a chair and sat down across from me, all smiles. He offered his hand and I gave it a firm shake.

"Everything going as planned?" he asked.

I nodded.

"I didn't catch your name," he said.

"Sueño," I said.

"Oh," he replied, confused for a moment.

"Just call me George," I added.

He was back to his stock smile. "These guys you're looking for. Maybe you could describe them to me? I can keep an eye out."

"Better if you don't," I said. "They could be dangerous."

He frowned, the expression out of place on his visage. "Your friend told me there wasn't going to be trouble."

"There isn't, as long as I spot them before they spot me."

"I don't want any violence here in the Harbor Lights Club."

"That why you have a bouncer?"

"Randy's a good man."

"One guy," I told him. "Muscle-bound. Wouldn't be much use in a fight." I nodded toward the back, over by the men's room, where a plastic sheeting hung down. "You expanding already?"

Yancey beamed proudly. "Yes. We're partnering with the WVOW. You heard of them?"

I had, on my last big case. "The Wounded Veterans of Overseas Wars?"

"That's them. The Seoul city government approved an expansion of their charter, so we'll be able to open a WVOW operation here at Harbor Lights."

"A casino," I said.

"Yes. Isn't it great?"

"Wonderful," I agreed. *So you can rip off more GIs*, I thought, still smiling. "That's a hell of a managerial responsibility, what with all the cheats out there."

"I've got a great manager lined up. A casino boss from way back. Twenty years of experience," he bragged, raising his eyebrows at me expectantly.

I played along. "Let me guess," I said. "Your new manager's from the Sheraton Walker Hill." The big casino on the eastern edge of Seoul.

"Nope," Yancey said. "The Olympos Hotel and Casino. You ever heard of it?"

The Olympos Hotel and Casino sat on the edge of the Yellow Sea, just a few yards from the main train station in Inchon. Right in the heart of Sea Dragon country.

I did my best to hide any reaction. "Oh, yeah. Class operation."

"I'll say."

Yancey snapped his fingers as a waitress passed by. "Miss Lee," he said, "Heineken *hana*," and he pointed at the almost empty beer in front of me. *Hana* meaning one.

I thanked him.

"Don't mention it," he said, getting up and shaking my hand again. "You need anything, just give me a holler."

"Thanks, Don," I said. "There is one thing."

He sat back down.

"It's about a—a misunderstanding I had," I stammered, forcing the words out.

"With a girl?" he asked.

"Yeah. A Korean girl, here in Itaewon." He leaned forward and listened patiently, like a priest in confessional. Information and wheeling and dealing were Don Yancey's stock-in-trade.

"She filed a SOFA charge," I went on.

Yancey nodded knowingly.

"It's phony," I said, "just a ploy to make money, but it's official now, and the SOFA Committee will be taking it up soon."

I stopped and stared at my beer.

"So you're asking if I know anyone on the SOFA Committee?" he said.

"Do you?" I said, looking up hopefully.

"No. But Don Yancey always knows somebody who knows somebody." He stared at me hard, knowing that a CID agent in 8th Army had plenty of power to make life easy or make it difficult. "I'll see what I can do."

"I appreciate it," I told him.

When he left, I glugged down the last of my Heineken. The waitress arrived with a fresh bottle and retrieved the fallen soldier. I watched her sashay back toward the bar, wondering where Don Yancey found all these beauties to staff his nightclub—maybe a modeling agency. He had connections, that was for sure. I sat back, feeling the bubbling suds wash their way through my stomach. I gave myself permission to enjoy the night now that step one of my job had been completed. This could all be a dead end. But, with any luck, we'd dropped enough crumbs in the forest for someone to follow the trail.

"You were right," I said, plopping myself down in the seat next to Ernie's.

It was a routine morning in the CID office: Riley shuffling through a stack of disposition forms and Ernie reading the paper as a fresh pot of coffee brewed on the back counter.

"Of course I was," Ernie said. Then he looked up. "About what?"

"About the Sea Dragon Triad making a move on Itaewon."

He pointed to his cranium. "It's all up here," he whispered loudly.

"Ain't nothing there but mush," Riley retorted.

"Beats bull crap," Ernie replied.

After Don Yancey had left me, I'd spent the rest of the night sipping one green bottle of imported Heineken after the other. How many I'd actually consumed, I wasn't sure, at least until the next morning in the barracks when I counted my money. Including the one Yancey had bought for me, I'd had eight bottles. Not nearly enough to give me a hangover. Which was why I was up early this morning, having called Inspector Kill's office before he'd even arrived.

"I left a message with Officer Oh," I told Ernie.

"She never sleeps, does she?" Ernie asked.

"Guess not. I asked her to check out the new WVOW charter at the Seoul City Hall. All the other American veteran groups—like the VFW and the AmVets—operate little casinos elsewhere in Kyongki Province." Still in the region, but outside of Seoul.

"Not in the city itself," Ernie said.

"Right. It's not allowed."

"Which means that Yancey has connections," Ernie said.

"He works for them," I replied. "He's always smiling and shaking hands and doing favors." I thought of his sympathetic stare last night as I unloaded my woes about the made-up SOFA case. "I also asked Officer Oh about the casino boss from the Olympos Yancey claims is going to be running his new gambling spot."

"The Olympos?" Ernie asked.

I nodded.

"That's in Sea Dragon territory."

"And it all comes together," Riley said flippantly.

Ernie turned slowly toward him. "Why don't you just take care of your paperwork, and we'll take care of the investigations."

"Up yours," Riley said, but he still grabbed a folder out of his inbox and snapped it open.

Ernie and I walked over to the coffee urn. "So Officer Oh called back?"

"Yeah. Just talked to her."

"What'd she say?"

"She says it's long been known that the Sea Dragon Triad unofficially controls the Olympos Casino. They even fly in high rollers from Hong Kong."

"They must lure 'em with girls," Ernie said. "Or whatever else they want."

I nodded and sighed. "We've been compiling all this info, but in terms of concrete evidence, we're not really closer to finding the missing GIs than when we started."

"Yeah, it's frustrating," Ernie said. "Did Officer Oh have anything that could help us connect the Sea Dragon Triad to the disappearance of the three GIs?"

"Not yet. But she said something that has me worried— *mot kidaryo*."

"What does that mean?" Ernie asked.

"That we can't wait."

"Did you ask her why?"

"I didn't think to before she said goodbye and hung up," I said.

"So you think Kill's going to make a move?"

"It's possible," I replied.

"But what good will that do?" Ernie asked. "If the remaining two GIs are still alive, Kill could endanger them and drive whoever's holding them even deeper into hiding."

"Yeah. But this case isn't his only priority. The Korean

government might be pressuring him to crack down on the gang activity."

"If those GIs are killed, it'll be a PR nightmare for the ROK," Ernie said.

"The Koreans will blame it on the Chinese Communists."

"The Chicoms," Ernie said slowly, his eyes widening as he saw the sense in it. "And there will be three American martyrs the ROK can use to lobby for more US aid in countering not only the foreign gang problem, but the influence of the Communist Chinese government."

"They might be looking at it that way. It's a gamble, but from their point of view, it could both alleviate the problem and convince the US congress to open up its purse strings."

Ernie thought it over. "That's a helluva gamble. So what do we do?"

"We can't stop the KNPs. It's their country, after all. So we'll have to join them. And try to make sure our missing GIs aren't collateral damage of Cold War politics."

"So it's up to us." Ernie glugged down the last of his coffee. "If we were smart, we'd run all this by the Provost Marshal. Get his blessing."

"Going through Colonel Brace or the Chief of Staff will take too long. They'll dither over the decision and might still decide to do nothing."

"Right," Ernie replied. "If we want to get something done, the last thing we want to do is ask for permission."

I grabbed my coat.

"Where in the hell are you two going?" Riley asked.

"Out," I told him.

"This'll piss the Colonel off."

"It's better to be pissed off," Ernie said, "than pissed on."

"Thank you, Confucius," Riley replied.

-15-

Our first stop was the Military Police arms room.

"Forty-five, huh?" Palinki said. "Good choice. Easy to carry in a shoulder holster. Plenty of firepower. Off a lot of bad guys."

He handed me the weapon; it was perfectly clean, well oiled, and generally in excellent shape.

"Thanks for taking care of this, Palinki," I said.

"No sweat, bro. After reading comic books," he said, pointing to a two-foot-high stack in the corner, "nothing else to do. I clean weapons. Pass the time."

Palinki was a huge man, over six feet tall and maybe two hundred forty pounds, most of it muscle. He had been one of the best MPs on patrol in Seoul until he'd made the mistake of taking his police work too seriously. He'd severely beaten three GIs who'd attempted to rape a high school girl on her way home. They were hurt so badly that at first, the medics at the 121st Evac thought one of them was going to die. The GI pulled through but was permanently confined to a wheelchair, for which he receives a monthly check from the VA. Fuck up and move up, as they say. The other two were in serious condition for over a month but eventually recovered, at which point they were court-martialed and dismissed from service with bad conduct discharges. As far as the rank-and-file MPs were concerned, Palinki was a hero.

But when one of the would-be rapists returned to the States, he hired a lawyer who claimed that his client's rights had been violated. Palinki had stopped the three men from committing a horrific crime, but instead of handcuffing them and taking them into custody—a cozy holding cell on compound—via proper procedure, he'd trapped them in a dark alley and challenged them to an open-handed fight. None of them wanted anything to do with the big Samoan, but they'd had no choice, and he'd systematically taken the three men apart. An investigation found Palinki guilty of unprofessional conduct. A letter of reprimand had gone into his personnel file and ever since, he'd been stuck in the arms room.

He handed me a full magazine, which looked tiny in his hand. "You need more ammo?" he asked.

"If I can't get the job done with seven rounds," I said, "it's not getting done at all."

He grinned. "Right on, bro. The spirit of the gunfighter." He turned to Ernie. "How about you? More ammo?"

"Yeah," Ernie replied. "Give me a box. Two of 'em."

Palinki handed over two fist-sized cardboard containers.

Ernie stuffed one in his left jacket pocket and the other in his right. When I glanced over at him, he grinned back like a greedy kid who'd just been discovered pilfering the last chocolate chip cookie.

Palinki said, "Big operation, huh?"

"Could be," I replied.

"MPs got a new commander," he told us. "Maybe he'll take a look at my record. Let me back on the street." He paused, embarrassed.

Ernie figured it out. "You want us to ask for you?" he said.

"Can you? If the CID needs help, asks for Palinki by name, maybe the commander will say yes. Worth a shot."

"Yeah. It is worth a shot." Ernie looked over at me.

"I'll run it by Riley," I said. "We gotta go."

I thanked Palinki again as Ernie and I climbed back up the stone steps.

The Korean National Police operation that Officer Oh had tipped me off to turned out to be massive—paramilitary, really. The Korean National Police are controlled by the central government of the Republic of Korea, or more specifically, by President Park Chung-hee himself. For this mission, as Officer Oh explained, the KNPs had been charged with eliminating possible Communist Chinese influences that were infiltrating the ROK via the Sea Dragon Triad. After all, the Chicoms had invaded South Korea during the Korean War, and despite the relative economic boost the Sea Dragon smuggling operations had brought about in certain areas, the government still considered the People's Republic its mortal enemy.

"Park Chung-hee order," Oh said. "Chief Inspector Gil Kwon-up, he do."

It appeared so.

Ernie and I stayed close to Mr. Kill. Our job was ostensibly to arrest any Americans caught in the sweep, but in reality, we would be looking for any leads to the whereabouts of the two remaining GIs.

The ROK's objective of this operation was, of course, to clean house.

For years, the Inchon KNPs had accepted bribes to protect the overseas gangs. Who knew how many KNP children from Inchon had had their college tuition paid with money derived from the suffering of young girls who'd been forced into prostitution? Or how many homes had been purchased in the surrounding hills with the ill-gotten gains of international smuggling? These answers would likely never come to light, but Mr. Kill was hell-bent on making sure such graft would come to an end.

Starting with the Sea Dragons.

The building right behind the Yellow Sea Teahouse was a barracks of sorts: a three-story concrete slab, the top floor jam-packed with girls who were farmed out at night to various Sea Dragon nightclub and bar operations. The first and second floors had roomier accommodations for the muscle who enforced Sea Dragon Triad operations. These men traveled to Chinese establishments throughout the Inchon and Seoul corridor, an expanse of a couple of hundred square miles, to collect protection for the Sea Dragons. This extended not only to restaurants, but mom-and-pop takeout dumpling houses, grocery stores specializing in Chinese foodstuffs, and most lucratively, herbalists that depended on international imports for their remedies. Unusual items like ground-up tiger bone, red peony root, Chinese foxglove, dried seahorse, and ultra-expensive powdered rhinoceros horn—for wealthy old gentlemen with hopes of recovering the stamina of their youth—fetched quite a price.

Mr. Kill's mission started in the midafternoon with a sweep of low-level thugs and prostitutes. With information from Mr. Bam's field interrogations, the task force then moved a step up the ladder to a few mid-level Sea Dragon managers who lived in luxury apartments in the city center. Doors were kicked in, women and children dragged outside. Even grandparents, many of whom had been smuggled over from China, ended up in the street. The interrogations grew yet more intense, with a small coterie of specialists with Chinese language skills and fancy tape recorders working the Sea Dragon bosses. That was where things bogged down. These gangsters either didn't know anything about the higher-ups or, more likely, were too afraid to talk. And no amount of mercilessly administered "persuasion" would loosen their tongues.

A merchant ship flying the Liberian flag was boarded, this time by the Korean coast guard. They found evidence of passengers who'd departed the ship, none processed properly by Korean immigration. A thorough search also produced numerous Chinese medicinals, all slated to be exchanged for high-end Japanese electronics.

From the start of the Cold War, Red China has been embargoed economically by most of the free world, following the notion that this would prevent Chairman Mao and his allies from stockpiling foreign exchange by exercising free trade in international goods. The Sea Dragon Triad's actions, with the cooperation of the corrupt Inchon police, were considered a violation of that embargo.

The Liberian ship's Dutch captain was placed under arrest and dragged down to the Inchon Police Station, where Chief Homicide Inspector Gil Kwon-up had set up temporary headquarters. Ernie and I hung around outside his office; Ernie spent most of his time ogling the attractive female police officers, all of whom seemed to have been handpicked by the male commanding officer of the Inchon KNPs.

"Nice setup," Ernie said, languishing on a vinyl-covered couch and sipping a can of chilled guava juice he'd found in the breakroom refrigerator.

"Yeah," I agreed. "Free money from China, good-looking

hires to make you coffee and light your cigarettes, hobnobbing with the rich and famous."

"Is Kill gonna bust the old fart?"

"I think that's where this is headed. Officer Oh told me the Inchon chief of police is holed up in his villa on the outskirts of town."

Ernie sat up. "A shootout?"

"Probably not," I said. "Once Park Chung-hee announces a warrant for this guy's arrest, he'll know he's toast."

"Why?" Ernie asked. "He didn't pay off enough people?"

"There's no one left to pay around here, now that Park Chung-hee is cutting the triads down to size. The penalties for being caught resisting now could amount to treason, or who knows what else."

"But President Pak isn't getting rid of the triads entirely, is he?"

"He'll leave them be, but on a much smaller scale. Just enough to provide some of the medicines and other Chinese products Korean society demands."

"Like letting steam from a valve."

"Exactly," I said.

"Okay, fine," Ernie said. "And what about our two boys?"

"Bam's been asking about them," I said. "But Officer Oh says no one knows anything."

In a long, looping arc, Ernie's empty can of guava juice sailed into the metal wastebasket, landing with a loud *clang*.

"Didn't even hit net," he said.

Officer Oh entered the room, motioning for us to come with her. Ernie and I hopped to our feet and followed her down a carpeted hallway lined with glowing celadon vases on stainless steel stands. At the end of the hallway, we entered an office furnished with seascape artwork hanging above plush, leather-upholstered chairs. Mr. Kill sat behind a polished teak desk, shaking his head. "The Sea Dragon leadership," he said, "they're a tough nut to crack."

"Not getting any information?"

"We're getting plenty of information. About their operations, and which KNPs have been turning a blind eye for money. In fact, we have so many names and accusations that it will take us awhile to sort them all out and formulate a coherent set of charges. But on the two missing GIs," he continued, "and the dead one, nothing."

"What about the gummy whore?" Ernie asked. "And the driver with the scars, did you ask about that?"

"Yes. Mr. Bam didn't forget. He and his staff interrogated these men from top to bottom. Not a single one claims knowledge of the *gumiho* or any of the three abducted Americans."

"Does he believe them?" I asked.

"His tactics are . . . effective. I believe most of them aren't lying. Most of the low-level thugs are recent recruits with little loyalty to the organization—they wouldn't be privy to certain information. But the gang bosses, the ones whose penthouses we raided, would know something."

"And he can't get it out of them?"

"He hasn't been able to yet," Inspector Kill said. "And if they're not giving in to his methods, it's because the consequences of betrayal are far worse."

Mr. Bam employed an almost medieval level of brutality; I couldn't imagine what could be so much worse.

"They must be pretty damn scared," Ernie said.

"They are. And they're well trained. Their faces go completely blank at any mention of the *gumiho*. They just shut down."

"But Bam will keep trying?" Ernie said.

"Of course. Just don't expect much. Not only are the few who know anything too afraid to talk, but we believe that the information we need has been highly compartmentalized." When we stared at him, puzzled, he said, "It's a technique similar to those used in espionage. Each spy ring is broken down into cells of three or four people. What one cell knows isn't shared with any other cell. So if someone is captured and interrogated by the enemy, it won't necessarily compromise the entire operation."

"So the gummy whore is still out there," Ernie said, "haunting GI villages and Sea Dragon operations."

Mr. Kill nodded.

"It's been over two weeks since Holdren went missing," I said. "Seems like it's almost time she struck again."

"Possibly," Mr. Kill answered. "But where?"

"That's the question," I said.

"Won't this raid disrupt her schedule?" Ernie asked.

"It might," I said. "But we're not sure what exactly determines her modus operandi."

"No, we're not," Mr. Kill said. "In fact, the correlation of these disappearances with the uptick in Sea Dragon activities might be nothing more than coincidence. It's unlikely, but not impossible that there's no connection."

"So what do we do?" Ernie asked.

"We keep looking," I said. "Hope for a break."

"The only break we're going to get," Ernie said, "is when she strikes again."

To my dismay, Mr. Kill didn't disagree.

The raid had taken most of the afternoon. On the drive from Inchon to Seoul, the red sun was already setting behind us.

"He's just using us," Ernie said.

"Who?"

"Mr. Kill."

"How's that?"

"He's probably wanted to get rid of the crooked cops in Inchon all along."

I thought about it. Since I'd known him, Mr. Kill had always been embarrassed about the corruption in the KNPs and the broader South Korean government. All he could do to counter it was keep himself and his own subordinates clean.

Ernie continued. "He needed the pressure of the missing Americans, one dead, to force Park Chung-hee to move off the dime. Someone high up must've been sharing in Sea Dragon profits. Maybe even the president himself."

"You don't know that."

"You're right," Ernie said. "I don't. But Kill has what he wants, which is the Inchon chief of police out on his butt. Meanwhile, we don't have squat."

As we approached Seoul, Ernie said, "You going back to the Harbor Lights tonight?"

"Doubt it. I'm not sure it would do any good." Then I remembered something. "Can you drop me at the Women's Power Coalition?"

Ernie smirked at me, ignoring traffic for a moment. "You devil, you," he said.

I pointed. "Get your eyes back on the road!"

He did. And barely in time to swerve around a three-wheeled truck loaded with cabbage.

"Which one is it?" he asked. Enjoying the game, he ventured a guess. "That big Korean broad. The one with a right arm like a World Series pitcher."

I didn't answer.

"I should've figured you'd hook up with a Commie," Ernie said.

"She's not a Commie."

Pleased with himself for getting it right on the first guess,

Ernie grinned from ear to ear all the way until he dropped me off at the front door of the Women's Power Coalition. There was no point in trying to disabuse him of the notion that I had a romance going with Wang Ok-ja. He wouldn't have believed me, anyway.

There didn't appear to be anybody at the WPC office. I slid the door open, slipped off my shoes, and stepped inside. In the far corner, the transformer blinked and the refrigerator hummed. Loose documents were scattered on the main table, where a sheet of fresh paper had been rolled into a portable Smith-Corona typewriter.

"*Yoboseiyo?*" I ventured. Hello?

No one answered.

A sound came from the back room. Angry words. I grabbed the handle and opened the door.

"*You!*" she shouted.

Katie Allsworthy sat on a straight-backed chair across from a sobbing Wang Ok-ja, both of them studying a document on the table. Katie stood to face me.

"You son of a *biscuit*," Katie raged. "You come in here to the Women's Power Coalition, acting concerned, claiming you want to help abused women, and the whole time, it's nothing but a *scam!*" She threw the document at me. "*Here!*" she yelled. "Your secret is out. We know what you are. A rapist and a murderer."

I reached down and smoothed out the document, which was stamped CONFIDENTIAL. It was a copy of the report that Riley and I had sent in to the SOFA Committee through Smitty, which I hadn't had the chance to read earlier. Like all classified documents, it was assigned a serial number that included a Julian date and said *Copy 6 of 7*. I quickly scanned it. It detailed the horrific rape of a young Itaewon business girl, and said I'd badly beaten her with a bat and thrown her into the Han River after finding out she was pregnant. Riley had really done overkill on this one.

"Who gave you this?" I asked.

"What does that matter? We know. And we found out just in time to stop you from doing more damage."

I wanted to explain to her that nothing in this report was true. But I couldn't. Word needed to get out, either through the WPC or from leaks elsewhere in the SOFA Committee. I held onto the slim hope that the *gumiho* would catch wind of it, just as she'd found out about the other GIs. I owed it to the dead soldier Werkowski, and to Shirkey and Holdren, who were still missing, to find the killer. Even if it meant sacrificing my reputation and the respect of Katie Allsworthy and Wang Ok-ja, I had to follow this plan through to the bitter end.

"Did you pay someone for this?" I asked, holding up the paper.

"*Pay?* With what?" Katie Allsworthy swept her arm across

the small office. "You think we have enough money to *pay* for anything?"

"If you don't represent this woman, then you're not authorized to have this," I said. "So you must've stolen it."

Eyes narrowed and fists clenched, she took a step toward me. "You have the gall to accuse us of that? After what you did to an innocent young woman?" Her voice went low. "We don't *have* to steal things. We have people who help us—people who believe in what we're doing. "

Wang Ok-ja reached out and touched her forearm. This seemed to calm Katie down. She stared up at me, brushed her hair back, and held out her palm. "Give it back."

I hesitated, glanced at the serial number one more time, and then handed the document back to her. Katie stepped back.

Both women stared at me as if I were something that had just oozed up out of the muck of the city sewer. Feeling like about two cents, I turned on my heels and walked out of the Women's Power Coalition.

-16-

I couldn't find Ernie. Riley had gotten off work at seventeen hundred hours, and instead of staying late in the office as he often did, he'd returned to the barracks. Once there, he'd purchased a can of cola out of the lobby vending machine and repaired to his room, whereupon he proceeded to start on the bottle of Old Overwart he kept hidden in his wall locker.

By the time I went to talk to him, the rye whiskey had already made him stupid. He threw a few punches in the air and told me that he was going to kick some ass, and I shoved him down on his bunk and told him to sleep it off. Mumbling incoherently, he closed his eyes.

What I wanted to do was tell Ernie, or at least Riley, that we now had a way to find out who'd passed the information on my bogus charge to the Women's Power Coalition. That meant there was at least one crack in the bubble of confidentiality of the committee. Whether this leak was the same one the *gumiho* was getting her information from, I had no idea, but at least we could interview the guilty party and find out. But that would have to wait until tomorrow, until we could locate the breach and confront the perpetrator with what we knew.

I went to the latrine to shower and shave, then returned to my room. Donning a fresh shirt and the same slacks I'd worn last night, I checked myself in the mirror. I felt like shit after my second fight with Katie Allsworthy, but I wasn't looking too bad. As I slipped on my highly polished low quarters and combed my hair, I wondered if my shy solo act at the Harbor Lights Club would ever attract female interest. Probably not.

I felt like I was spinning my wheels, but I couldn't think of any other way to move this investigation forward—until we tracked down the leak tomorrow—so I slipped on my jacket and made sure I had my wallet, my money, my keys, and my CID badge. Then I looked at the shoulder holster with my .45 automatic. I was supposed to either carry it with me or return it to the MP station and turn it back in to whoever was on arms room duty. Both seemed like way too much trouble, so I did something I shouldn't have. I stashed the pistol in the back of my wall locker.

When it comes to weaponry, the Army is fanatical about safety and accountability. We're not allowed to leave loaded weapons around willy-nilly. The weapon, and associated ammunition, had to be properly checked out and then properly secured or on one's person at all times. I felt guilty about taking this shortcut, but if I was going to pump people for information at the Harbor Lights Club, a pistol strapped to my chest was probably not the most appropriate conversation piece.

I snapped my wall locker shut and stepped out into the hallway. Then I remembered that I'd told Ernie I wouldn't be going to the Harbor Lights Club, but that was before I'd found out about the SOFA Committee leaking like a sieve. Now, what had appeared to be a stalled investigation was moving forward again. I was excited; I wanted to keep the momentum going, and getting out to the Harbor Lights Club before anyone else found out about the leak provided at least the outside chance that more information would fall into my lap.

Still, it's not good practice to leave your investigative partner unable to find you. So I wrote a note to Ernie that mentioned not only Harbor Lights, but also the leaked confidential document and its serial number, along with the fact that the document was copy number six of seven. After perusing the classified documents issue log, we'd know who the recipient had been. Returning to Riley's room, I stuck the note into his scuffed low quarters, figuring the houseboy would find it early tomorrow morning and give it to him once he was sober enough to read it.

Outside the barracks, the air was fresh and bracing.

Twenty minutes later, unencumbered by lethal weaponry, I was climbing the broad cement steps of the Harbor Lights Club.

■   ■   ■

I drank too much. It hurt me to shell out so much money for Heineken, a European beer I didn't even like, at 1,500 *won* a pop. So I switched to bourbon. Price-wise, that certainly didn't help. They charged 2,000 *won* per shot. But the pour was generous, and wasn't watered down. Don Yancey lived up to his reputation for running a class joint. After a couple of shots, I wandered toward the back of the nightclub where the expansion would be taking place. I pushed past dusty plastic sheeting and entered a room floored in powdered concrete. Oddly shaped chunks of lumber lay about, and cans of paint and cleaning solvent were piled in a corner. I'd been in there for less than a minute when staccato steps approached me from behind. I turned around.

A young Korean woman in an expensive-looking red dress and a long pearl necklace stood a few feet from me, arms folded across her chest. She was tall and slender; she could have been a fashion model. In keeping with her sharp beauty, her eyeliner swept upward past the corners of her eyes, like a jet taking off into the sky. Her cheekbones were carved like shelves on the side of Mount Rushmore.

"What in the hell are you doing here?" she asked.

"Oh, sorry," I said, gesturing to the room. "I wanted to see the progress on your new casino. Don told me about it."

She was unimpressed by my name-dropping. Her frown remained fixed. I studied the dark hair falling to one side of her face, her manicured nails, and the flashy rings constraining the flesh near her knuckles. It occurred to me that she was younger than I'd originally thought, which the makeup and jewelry were intended to hide.

"You're the CID agent," she said.

No point in denying it. I grinned and opened my palms wide. "You caught me. How'd you know?"

"Don told me." When I stared at her quizzically, she said, "I'm his wife."

She didn't seem thrilled by the fact. An awkward silence followed. I was willing to bet she was anticipating my unspoken question: *Isn't he a little old for you?*

With a sour expression, she turned and strode toward the far wall. Abruptly, she stopped and pointed. "See this shit?" she said. Lumber had been hammered into the outline of a half-finished bar. "Piss-poor workmanship," she said. "Before I went to the States, Koreans knew how to do a good job. Now?" She scoffed. "All they want is to get paid. Smile and bow and take your money. Korea's gone to hell."

We both stood there, contemplating the Hermit Kingdom's long slide into perdition. The silence grew.

"How long were you in the States?" I said in a weak attempt to make conversation.

"I immigrated with my parents when I was in the tenth grade." She laughed. "Didn't speak a word of English." She turned to face me. "You can imagine how awkward I felt in an

American high school. The only *chink*," she said bitterly. "But I survived, and as soon as my diploma was under my arm, I headed straight to New York. Drove my parents crazy, of course; they wanted me to be a freaking accountant. After landing a few modeling jobs, I grew restless and came back to Korea on my own. Then I met Don." She opened her arms to her kingdom. "And now I'm going to run this."

"The casino?" I asked.

She nodded, re-folding her arms across her chest.

"So you have experience," I said.

"Six months," she said.

Don had told me twenty years. Just a slight variance. "In Vegas?" I asked, still playing dumb.

"No," she replied vaguely. "Here. As a marketing director."

"For the Olympos, right?"

She narrowed her eyes at me. "How'd you know?"

I shrugged. "Don mentioned it."

"Him and his big mouth."

"Was it supposed to be a secret?"

"No. It's just that he can't keep anything anyone tells him to himself."

I gestured back at the very busy floor of the Harbor Lights Club. "Seems to work for him," I said.

"Sure," she replied. "Don Yancey, everybody's friend."

I wanted to ask her more about her relationship with her husband, but it seemed impertinent. And I didn't want her assuming I was interested in her. Most men would be—she was one of those gorgeous young gals who walked into a room and took everyone's breath away. Exactly the type of woman Don Yancey would go after. But not me. As Ernie always said, I was too introverted to want a woman who sucked up all the air. And I was still hung up on what Wang Ok-ja must think of me—not to mention my confusion over Leah Prevault and the sudden distance between us.

She seemed to sense my withdrawal and changed the subject. "Are you a gambler?" she asked.

"Only when I have the edge."

"The edge?" she asked.

"A mathematical advantage."

"Hard to find in a casino."

"Very."

Someone shoved through plastic sheeting. "Pooki," said Don Yancey. "There you are." *Pooki*'s eyes didn't exactly light up. "I see you two have met."

"I wanted to take a look at the construction," I said.

"You find your fugitives yet?" Don asked.

"Not yet. I better get back and keep watch."

"If you need anything," he said, smiling, "give me a holler."

"Will do." I turned to Don's wife and said, "Nice to meet you."

Her arms were still crossed. "My name's Agnes, by the way, not Pooki."

Don Yancey slid his arm behind her waist. "Pooki's what I like to call her."

I nodded to Don and hurried back to the noise and tobacco smoke of the main ballroom.

As I sat at my table, nursing another shot of bourbon, I went back over my conversation with Agnes and Don. As usual, I'd been awkward, which was why I usually avoided social situations. I preferred confronting people in the capacity of criminal investigator; I knew what I was in for when I approached someone and introduced myself as a CID agent. But in non-Army social settings, I had no idea what I was after. I was certainly no Don Yancey.

Yancey must've first spotted Agnes while out gambling at the Olympos. His presence at a high-end joint like that meant there was a good possibility he had a connection to the Sea Dragon Triad. I wondered if today's raids by Mr. Kill and the KNP would put the kibosh on WVOW sponsorship of Don's and Agnes's new casino. Maybe dry up funding, force the triad to abandon the project. I wasn't sure of how much the Sea Dragon's money and influence had been diminished, but we'd see soon enough.

I thought of Agnes. How deeply was she involved with the Sea Dragons, if at all? Had she encountered them in New York, or had she approached them and applied for a job at the Olympos? Certainly they'd seen her potential. A stunning

Korean woman who spoke fluent English—an ideal hire for an international, high-rolling operation like the triad's. Of course, that didn't mean she'd joined their ranks as a criminal.

The waitress brought me a double shot of bourbon. Noting my surprise, she said, "From Don."

I thanked her, and she left. After I tossed back half of it, my worries began to fade. In fact, I was getting closer to my goal of not having to think altogether. I wanted to stop picturing the corpse of Sergeant Werkowski, staring up at me from between tangled strands of concertina wire, and the sad, small body of Soon-hui laying on a cold metal slab before she'd ever had the chance to become something other than a disdained business girl. I wanted to stop worrying about what might be happening to the two missing GIs and the abuse they had inflicted upon their Korean *yobo*s. I wanted to stop asking myself why Leah Prevault had stopped writing, and I wanted to stop seeing the hatred in the eyes of Katie Allsworthy and Wang Ok-ja.

After I finished the double bourbon, the same waitress brought me another. Setting it down, she asked, "You want Heineken?" When I didn't answer, she said, "Don say okay."

Apparently, Don Yancey wanted me on his side. I told the waitress I'd take the Heineken. As I sipped on it, I remembered the folktale I'd read in the book Miss Kim had given me. The one in which the nine-tailed fox, in the form of a beautiful woman, rolled up her right sleeve, slathered her forearm in sesame oil, and stuck her hand down the throat of her comatose lover. Reaching, reaching, reaching, until her fingers found what she wanted. She plucked out his liver, letting the rest of him fall to the ground, and as the folklorist put it, "devoured it with relish."

After finishing the Heineken and my third double bourbon of the night, I worked up the courage to ask a woman to dance.

More drinks came from the same waitress, who almost seemed to be following me around. I vaguely remember dancing. Wildly. Doing something called the frug. A girl dragged me out on the dance floor, and when she was done with me, another woman took over. There was a long row of laughing faces. I must have put on quite a show.

As I staggered down the steps of the Harbor Lights Club and out onto the sidewalk, I was still too drunk to regret anything. I was just pleasantly aware of my newfound popularity and assumed vaguely that, by tomorrow morning, I would probably find the memory less pleasant. For some reason, this made me laugh.

A Korean couple eyed me nervously as they walked past, and the young man steered the woman he was with toward the far side of the pathway. *"Yoboseiyo!"* I practically shouted the greeting at them.

A big bus rolled past. The small crowd waiting for the next one stared at me, unmoving and wide-eyed.

"To hell with you," I said. Or at least, I think I did. Then I staggered down one of the back alleys, climbed a long flight of stone steps, and reached the front of a Korean movie theater with a huge, mural-like painted sign above it advertising the most recent epic. The huge faces of Korean actors and actresses stared down at me. One belonged to a man in the traditional robes of an ancient warrior. The other was of a young woman who was wearing a silk *chima-jeogori* and a jade tiara atop her head. As I passed, I pressed my fingers to my lips and threw her a kiss.

Suddenly, I was walking downhill toward the central Itaewon bar district. Neon signs flashed on brightly and then off again, as if rolling over in their beds and settling down for the night. Women cooed at me from doorways. I didn't want to hear their offers. I didn't want to see the sadness in their eyes or feel their desperation. I veered into another dark alley, this one running behind the bar district whose illumination still shone above the two- and three-story buildings.

I reached another abandoned road, one that ran atop the main drag of Itaewon, and turned right, heading for where it intersected with the hill that overlooked the busiest part of the neighborhood. Up there, I knew there would be kimchi cabs waiting, ready to zoom down as soon as they spotted a likely customer emerging from one of the bars. They took turns. And if there was a long wait, they'd climb out of their cabs, light up a Turtleboat cigarette, and exchange gossip and insults with their fellow cab drivers. Bleary-eyed, I could see the intersection. There were maybe a half dozen cabs waiting there. But they were disappearing fast. The midnight curfew was approaching, and people were fleeing Itaewon like first-class travelers abandoning the Titanic.

I leaned forward and tried to hurry, not wanting to be stranded out here. But I wasn't making much progress. My eyes were focused on a lit-up menu written in *hangul*, shining from the front window of a chophouse to my left: *bibimpap, mulmandu, dubu jigei*. It moved closer to me, then away, then closer again. I forced my brain to deduce why: I was staggering. Moving faster sideways than forward.

This made me chuckle. And as I laughed, a dark sedan slowly rolled up and stopped about ten yards in front of me, blocking the way. I paused, still swaying involuntarily back and forth, studying it warily. The front door popped open, and the driver, whose brimmed cap obscured his face, emerged. He wore a black vest over a white shirt, rushing around to the rear of the car and pulling open the door. He stood at attention as if waiting for the Queen of England. The thought made me laugh again, though I had no idea whether that was out loud or just in my head.

When he reached out a white-gloved hand, slender fingers grabbed it, and a woman climbed out. She took a regal step forward, sporting a black skirt and red waistcoat over a frilly white blouse. Her face was pretty and perfectly heart-shaped, though not particularly young. Cascades of black hair were piled intricately atop her head. What impressed me most was her bearing. She smiled at me as if we'd known each other for years. With an open palm, she gestured for me to climb into the back seat.

I thought about it, noting that she certainly didn't have nine tails. I attempted to study the face of the driver, but it was dark and his head was tilted downward, as if to intentionally hide his expression. I couldn't make out his features, but he was a husky fellow. Small and self-contained, like the sawed-off trunk of a mighty oak. His mistress continued to smile, as if reading my thoughts, but instead of rushing me, she waited patiently as I made my decision.

Even in my drunken state, I knew a trap when I saw one. And that if I stepped into that sedan, I might never get back out. Not in one piece, anyway. But I also believed that I was being offered a chance to find out who had murdered Sergeant Werkowski and, more importantly, whether or not Corporal Holdren and Specialist Shirkey were still alive.

I thought about what I had to lose. As Staff Sergeant Riley had so obligingly pointed out, I had never fit into the Army, anyway. Though I'd committed my life to the service, I would always be an odd duck. Leah Prevault, meanwhile, had all but forgotten about me. The only thing that set me apart from my fellow soldiers was my work—my ability to solve cases. And here I was, being offered the chance to find out why three

American GIs had been taken. An opportunity potentially unlike any other I'd ever be offered.

Unsteadily, I stepped forward. When I was very close, I nodded to her, and the nod somehow turned into a bow. When I straightened up, she smiled and motioned again with her hand.

Time to step through the looking glass.

With a deep breath, I ducked through the door and into the back seat of the sedan.

Silently, she took the seat beside me, smelling sweetly but subtly of roses. The driver shut the door, ran around the vehicle, and resumed his position behind the steering wheel. He started the engine, backed up, and drove carefully down the main drag of Itaewon, avoiding drunks and swerving around half-naked business girls.

We turned left at the Main Supply Route, heading for the outskirts of the city. Within minutes, we'd crossed the Third Han River Bridge, turned right, and followed the moonlight on the water stretching west toward the Yellow Sea. With her cool palm, the *gumiho* patted the back of my hand, reassuring me that I'd done the right thing. She smiled again, and I sighed and leaned back in the soft leather seat.

"*Chak-hei,*" she said. Well done.

And then, as if a great weight had just fallen from my shoulders, I slept.

-17-

Sunlight filtered through a curtain of hanging bamboo slats. The translucent wood swayed in the cool breeze. I sat up. Beneath me lay an inch-thick sleeping mat, swaddled in linen. Rumpled in a heap next to me was a silk comforter, embroidered with a Siberian crane rising from the reeds, angled wings flapping.

My stomach heaved. I opened my mouth, and a loud burp emerged. Bile bubbled angrily halfway up my throat, then subsided. My head throbbed, but gently, as if being squeezed by giant hands covered in cotton gloves. The sharpest pain, I knew from experience, would come later.

My lower abdomen felt distended—a goatskin brimming with wine. Cautiously, I crawled toward the porcelain chamber pot and lifted the top. After relieving myself, I replaced the lid.

I looked around; there was no sign of another person having slept here. No strands of long black hair, no sweet smell of perfume. Apparently, I'd been dumped here alone. I searched for my clothes. They weren't hanging from nails pounded into the wall, as they would be in a cheap *yoguan*—a Korean inn. Instead, there were varnished hand-carved pegs screwed into similarly varnished stanchions. But none of them held my clothes. Even more worrisome was my missing wallet and 8th Army CID badge.

Still in only my underpants and T-shirt, I began to search the room. The antique wooden furniture had drawers and cabinets full of linens and extra bedding. One drawer held the loose pantaloons and silk vest of *hanbok*, traditional clothing for a Korean gentleman. I shuffled along the immaculate floor toward the oil-paper-covered door and slid it open. No one outside—just a long, polished wooden hallway.

"*Yoboseiyo?*" I called, not wanting to holler yet.

Silence. A long, deep silence. For a moment, I felt as if I'd been transported back in time to the Middle Ages, when fewer people roamed the earth and a man's voice could carry off into eternity. Impatiently, I shrugged off such thoughts and slid the door shut.

I stood and tried on the *hanbok*. To my surprise, it was large enough to fit just about perfectly. I tied the belts and fastened the buttons. Thus outfitted, I took a deep breath, stepped toward the door, opened it, and walked out.

The wooden planks squeaked beneath my feet.

It was a giant traditional Korean house, the type lived in

during the Chosun Dynasty by either royalty or by the *yang-ban*—the educated elite. Of course, to sustain themselves, the *yangban* generally had more than just education. They owned the land that everyone else was forced to work on.

The house appeared to be square-shaped. In the center past the mosquito screens, I spotted a garden, and I thought I heard water running. Maybe a fountain sat amidst the greenery. Back here, where I was wandering, there were at least two dozen small rooms, each with paneling that could probably be shifted to combine spaces. I thought of the old drawings I'd seen of Korean musicians sitting at one end of a long rectangular hall, rows of low tables lined up before them. People in brightly dyed silk robes sat on cushions, clapping with the music, eating, drinking, and generally having a wonderful time. At least, as wonderful a time one could have before the age of electricity.

A deep ping reverberated down the hallway. A single note on a stringed instrument, perhaps a zither. A higher note followed, then a few more in rapid succession, flowing into a rising scale that stopped on a prolonged vibrato. I hurried toward the music; at least I wasn't alone in this huge mansion.

My feet flapped on wood as I hurtled down the narrow hallway. Suddenly, a figure blocked my path. Startled, I came to an abrupt halt, realizing as I did so that he had a foot-long steel knife in his right hand.

The *gumiho*'s driver.

I could see his pockmarked face clearly now. One eye was swollen almost completely shut. On the left side of his mouth, the lips were mangled, as if burned until they'd turned to crisps, and on his face were dozens of small craters that looked as if they'd been made by tiny asteroids. It was probably all from one horrific accident that had ruined his face forever. I suspected it may not have been such a great face to begin with; his head was small and square, his nose flat, and his ears pulled back as if stapled to his skull. He wore a traditional silk cap over his hair, as well as a silk blouse and pantaloons. His long, thin knife gleamed even in the dim light, appearing sharp enough to cut cleanly through ice.

The welcome of last night had disappeared. Spite shone out of his dark eyes; he looked like he wanted to cut out my spleen and feed it to me for breakfast. I wasn't sure how I'd engendered such hatred, but if he was about to shove that knife into me, I didn't want his last memory of me to be one of a helpless fool. I held completely still, thinking frantically about whether anything I'd seen so far could be used as a weapon. Nothing but sliding doors and smoothly varnished floors.

He let his breath out slowly, softly hissing like a viper in its death throes.

Down the hallway, the music stopped. Just as quickly as he'd appeared, the driver stepped back into the doorway he'd emerged from and disappeared.

Hesitantly, I took a step forward. When he didn't return,

I proceeded down the hallway toward where I thought the music had come from. I could barely resist the urge to look back.

At the end of the hall, double sliding doors to the left opened into the largest room I'd seen in the house thus far. The rafters were high, and on a raised dais against the far wall was the *gumiho*. She sat on a flat cushion, legs folded beneath a huge, flowing blue silk skirt.

She was beautiful, with flowers and jeweled pins punctuating her waves of lush black hair. Behind her was a painting of snarling dragons that swam through a foamy sea, as other creatures did their best to scurry out of the way. Across her skirt lay a flat, stringed bass zither I knew to be called a *komungo*.

She pointed toward the square cushion below the dais and said, *"Anjuseiyo,"* the polite but familiar way of offering a seat. I crossed my ankles and lowered myself to the cushion as elegantly as I could, falling the last few inches. She pretended not to notice.

She clapped her hands, and in seconds a young maid in a plain white vest and purple-hued cotton skirt came in with a short four-legged table and set it in front of me. She then placed a porcelain pot of hot tea carefully atop it. Using both hands, she poured the steaming concoction into a handleless cup. I thanked her, but she gave no acknowledgement that she'd heard me and backed out of the room as soon as she was done. I lifted the cup with two hands and gestured toward the *gumiho*. She nodded in response and said, *"Duhseiyo."* Please partake.

I did. The tea slid down into my roiling stomach, warming its lining. Soon, the caffeine would take effect and my recovery would start. In my short life, I'd been through so many hangovers that I knew exactly how each part of my anatomy would make its way back to health. In the Army, almost everybody drank—booze was cheap and provided abundantly in the enlisted clubs, officers clubs, snack bars, bowling alleys, Class VI liquor stores, and even vending machines in the barracks, which were always well stocked and could be counted on to pop out endless cans of cold Falstaff. Functional alcoholism was about the only thing I could think of on which Ernie and I were fully aligned with 8th Army.

The *gumiho* set her zither aside and peered at me. "Sueño," she said. "What does it mean?" She must've gotten my name off of my ID card or my badge.

"Dream," I replied. "Or sleep."

"Kum-ul kuhyo," she said in Korean. Which meant "to dream."

"Yes."

"That's a good name," she replied. Her English was clear and precisely pronounced; I concluded that money must have bought her a top-notch education. "Mine is Moon Guang-song."

I was surprised she'd revealed her first name; it was something Koreans rarely did, especially upon first meeting. I wondered if this boded poorly for me. I didn't have any backup, no one knew where I was, and I wasn't armed.

A long silence followed. Apparently, it was my turn to talk. I had to find out how Sergeant Werkowski had been murdered, and hopefully locate two still-living GIs, while somehow preserving my own safety. I decided to lay everything on the table, if only to forestall the inevitable moment of truth.

"At Camp Kyle," I said, "north of Uijongbu. Do you know what the barmaids there call you?"

"No. What?"

"Gumiho."

She smiled. "They called me that?"

"Yes."

Suddenly, she was laughing, patting her silk-clad knee. "Oh, that's good."

"Yes. And in Pusan, they thought you were old-fashioned. Too high-class to be seen with an American GI."

She stopped laughing and stared vacantly at me. For the first time, I looked directly into her eyes. They were a deep, lustrous brown, and just slightly crossed. It gave her an air of concentration. And it was slightly unsettling, as if you couldn't be certain which part of your soul she was peering into. I pressed on.

"There was a young American soldier near Camp Kyle,"

I told her, "named Werkowski. You took him in your sedan, probably the same one we were in last night, which was driven by the man in the hallway—the blacksmith."

She tilted her head. "Blacksmith?"

"Daejang jang-i," I said.

She shook her head. "His burns are from the war. A white powder."

During the Korean War, there was one likely culprit. "White phosphorous?" I asked.

She nodded.

Some groups considered white phosphorous a chemical weapon, and therefore a breach of international treaties. The US used it anyway—liberally. In Basic Training, they'd taught us all about the powder. It burns the skin upon contact, and left to its own devices, will sizzle a hole right down to the bone. And it sticks to the flesh. The only way to get rid of it, we'd been told, was to use our bayonets to carve it from our bodies.

I heard a slight movement from behind one of the walls; was her guard here, listening to us discuss his past? I moved back to the subject of the missing GIs.

"A week later, you traveled to Pusan and met another GI named Shirkey. He tried to force you into the Cheil Yoguan, but you resisted. The two of you argued loudly. The proprietor locked you out, and you took him with you."

I pictured the KNPs finding Shirkey's dog tag near the

Pusan-to-Seoul Highway, a hundred miles north of where he had gone missing and thirty miles east of where we sat.

The *gumiho* sat in silence, her fingers idly strumming the strings of her zither.

"And the third soldier missing. Corporal Holdren, from ASCOM City. Did you take him, too?"

She sighed a long, drawn-out breath. "Why would I do any of these things?"

"That's what I'd like you to tell me."

"And why should I?"

I took a guess. "You want someone to know. Especially Eighth Army. And America."

She frowned. "Why should I care what America thinks? I've built myself a place of refuge, completely removed from the modern world. You have no idea what it costs to try to preserve traditional art and music." Her fingers rested across the strings of the *komungo*, but didn't pluck them. "I know about your interest in our language, our culture." When I didn't answer, she sat back up and said, "But you're just another soldier."

"Yes, I am," I replied. "And I want to know why you did it. Why would you kill Werkowski?"

She clutched the strings of the *komungo* so tightly, I thought they might snap. "You *dare* to ask me that?" For a moment, I thought she might hurl the zither at me. Instead, she carefully set it aside and turned back to me, muttering, "*Sangnom sikki!"*—a rather unladylike insult about being born of a base lout.

Then she rose from the dais in one graceful move and floated toward me in her silk gown like an enormous blue flower. I rose to meet her, and when she reached me, her right hand swung upward in a broad arc and slapped me across the face.

Surprised, I staggered backward, hit the small table, and overturned it. Porcelain shattered and tea splashed, flooding across the immaculately polished wood-slat floor. The bodyguard burst through the door, knife still in hand. The *gumiho* nodded to him before sliding open one of the side doors to exit, and he launched himself toward me. I reached for the edge of the low table, and at the last second swung it in front of me like a wooden shield.

The knife slammed into the varnish, the table shuddered, and to my surprise, its sharp tip sliced through the thick top as if it were a sheet of plywood. Cold steel slid toward me. Still clutching the table legs with both hands, I twisted it to slow the knife's progress. Just before reaching my neck, the blade stopped, its handle hitting the wood.

I used all my weight to wrench the table to my left, then leapt forward and planted a kick between the guard's legs. He buckled over in pain, and I shoved him backward. As he struggled to regain his balance, I sprinted past him through the open sliding door into the hallway.

At top speed, I covered the length of the house, spotting a

short passageway that led toward the kitchen. Two women, hair covered by white bandanas, stared at me in fear. I pushed past them, involuntarily feeling hunger as I nearly knocked over pots and pans and a steaming bowl of bean curd soup. I emerged onto a long lawn that sloped toward a rise about fifty yards away.

I ran uphill, bare feet slapping atop a flagstone walkway and then giving way to cool grass that stabbed at my soles. Off to my left, past a line of birch trees and up near the top of the rise, sat a squat stone building. To my right, a tall stone fence.

In a few seconds, I reached the top of the ridge and stopped. A dead end. Worse than that, a cliff. A hundred feet below, roiling surf pounded against jagged rocks. I turned and looked back. Climbing uphill steadily was the stout driver, still holding his knife, which looked no worse for wear after its encounter with the table. Behind him, skirt held in front of her, tottered the *gumiho*.

Movement caught my attention on another rise about two hundred yards away, on the far side of the house. A man knelt in a firing position, aiming a rifle directly at me. Keeping my hands to my side and visible, I glanced around in a slow arc, spotting an armed guard every hundred yards or so around the perimeter of the small valley that cradled the *gumiho*'s estate.

So much for my fantasy of escape.

My pursuers plodded uphill steadily. I was trapped, they knew it. I supposed they didn't expect me to leap off the cliff and onto the rocks below, or they didn't care much if I did.

I studied my surroundings more thoroughly. On my right now was the stout stone building, looking as if it could withstand any typhoon the Yellow Sea might hurl its way. Off to my far left, maybe ten miles away and partially obscured by mist, stood the Inchon skyline. From here, the giant mechanical cranes at the Port of Inchon looked small, like bent chopsticks, and the hulls of merchant ships resembled torn sheets of dried seaweed.

My heart pounding, I stared out at the magnificent vista, breathing in salt air for a moment. If escape was impossible, I could at least study my surroundings and commit every detail to memory, in case any of it turned out to be of use. I turned back toward the *gumiho*'s palatial home. It sat on a level plane carved into a gentle slope. About a mile beyond the edge of the estate were farms: fields of cabbage and Korean radishes, and beyond that, rice paddies. At the farthest edge of one of the muddy fields, a small boy rode the back of an ox.

The *gumiho* and her bodyguard were almost on me now. I searched my surroundings for something I could use as a weapon—maybe a tree branch, or a large rock. But neither would be much good against that wicked knife. Black-and-white magpies flitted between the trees.

If only I could fly.

The bodyguard stopped just below the top of the ridge. Motioning for him to hold, the *gumiho* stepped past him, her skirt and loose silk sleeves billowing in the wind.

I considered making a mad dash for the *gumiho*, grabbing

her by the neck, and threatening to toss her off the edge of the cliff if her bodyguard didn't back off. As if reading my thoughts, he took two steps closer to her.

So much for that. But I'd fight. Even if all I had was dirt, I'd toss it into the bodyguard's mangled face and run as far as I could before he gutted me with his blade. As these grim images ran through my head, the growling of a combustion engine in the distance began to compete with the roaring of the waves behind us.

The *gumiho* looked back, smiled and said, "They're here." A van had pulled up to the edge of her estate. After traversing a bumpy dirt access road, it rolled to a halt, the back door slid open, and a crew tumbled out, bearing oddly shaped cases.

"Who?" I asked.

Turning back to me, she replied, "The musicians," as though her answer were obvious.

She began to walk off, ordering her bodyguard to bring me along.

His knife now sheathed, he bowed, and followed behind me closely as we headed back to her palatial home.

"What the hell happened to Sueño?" Riley asked.

Miss Kim stopped typing, her forehead creasing in worry.

Ernie pulled himself a cup of coffee from the silver urn and plopped down in the straight-backed chair in front of Riley's desk. "He's probably with a girl," Ernie said.

"I don't give a damn if he has a date with Raquel Welch,"

Riley replied. "He's required to report here at zero eight hundred hours, standing tall and ready for duty!"

"Bite me," Ernie said, grabbing Riley's copy of the *Pacific Stars & Stripes* and peeling it open to the Major League Baseball stats.

Miss Kim never involved herself in the incessant arguments between Staff Sergeant Riley and Agent Ernie Bascom. But this time, she did. "He's not with woman," she said.

Both men looked at her, astonished. "How do you know that?"

"Because he still think of his girlfriend, Doctor Leah."

Ernie and Riley were now balking. In their minds, if a GI could get laid, he wouldn't care if he'd just had a royal wedding presided over by the Pope.

Riley said, "So you think he should be here?"

"Yes," she replied.

Something fell out of Riley's newspaper. Ernie picked it up. "What's this?"

"I found that this morning. Somebody must've stuffed it in my low quarters."

"Your houseboy?"

"No, he's the one who found it, when he was shining them. Somebody else must've left it there."

It was a lined slip of paper, corners tightly tucked into the center, as was habitually done in Korea with private notes.

"Have you read it?"

"I meant to," Riley replied. "My head hurt a little too much at the time."

"So you were gonna wait until you had your coffee and your Alka-Seltzer?"

"Doesn't everybody?"

Ernie unfolded the note.

"Hey," Riley said. "That's my personal correspondence."

"Not anymore," Ernie replied. "It's from Sueño." He scanned it quickly. When he was finished, Ernie used the newspaper to backhand Riley across the chops. "You dumb shit."

Riley batted the paper away and said, "Just tell me what it says."

"It says here that Sueño decided to go to the Harbor Lights, after all. Apparently, the ploy with that phony SOFA complaint worked like a charm." Ernie continued to read. "There's a serial number here for a classified document."

Ernie read it off and Riley copied it down. Without being asked, Riley called Smitty over at personnel. Five minutes later, Smitty called back. Riley thanked him and hung up.

"What'd he say?" Ernie asked.

"The classified document was originally issued to a Professor Fulton from Yonsei University. According to Smitty, he's on the SOFA Committee."

"He must be the guy leaking information," Ernie said.

"Why'd Sueño write all this down in a note?" Riley asked.

"I'm not sure."

"He's worried," Miss Kim said. They both looked at her

again. She swallowed and said, "He's worried that maybe something bad happen at the Harbor Light Club. So he write down where he go."

"Sueño? Worried?" Riley asked.

"That's all he ever does," Ernie said. "He's a worrywart. I'm always telling him it's a waste of time."

"Why?"

"It just *is*," Ernie explained.

Miss Kim became exasperated. Glaring at both of them, she stood up and stomped her foot. "You go *find*," she said.

Not only had neither Riley nor Ernie ever heard Miss Kim give her opinion on an investigation, they'd never once heard her raise her voice. She grabbed a tissue out of the box in front of her, held it to her nose, and stepped around her desk. They both listened as she clattered in her high-heeled shoes down to the ladies' room.

"Maybe she's right," Riley said.

"There's always a first time," Ernie replied.

"Not the first time," Riley told him. "She was right about dumping you."

"She didn't *dump* me," Ernie said.

"Then what do you call it?"

"She figured me out."

"That'll do it," Riley told him. "Every damn time."

-18-

The small orchestra set up in the central garden near a miniature waterfall flowing into a blue-water goldfish pond. A few of the musicians were young, others wizened. The men wore loose white cotton pantaloons and silk vests, and the women multicolored flowing skirts and long-armed blouses. The *gumiho* was clearly meant to be the focal point of the group. She played fluidly on her long-stringed zither as the others joined in with a wooden clapper, a gourd-shaped fiddle, a bamboo flute, and a double-headed drum. Though my head was still pounding from the hangover, I eventually began to find the music enjoyable. I pretended to sip the short glass of *soju* the maid had served, knowing my life could depend on remaining sober.

Taking a break, the *gumiho* joined me at the small table, her expression surprisingly pleasant despite our earlier misunderstanding. The musicians played around with a new tune, laughing and bantering amongst themselves. They ignored me completely, as if I didn't exist. The *gumiho*, however, stared expectantly at me.

I offered her a full glass of *soju*. She raised her eyebrows in astonishment, but to my surprise, she accepted. I wished I could jolt back my shot, but remembered the pale corpse of Werkowski, floating in the Yellow Sea.

Sipping her drink, she began to tell me her story.

A GI had gotten her pregnant.

The relationship had begun quite innocently. In preparation for university, she'd signed up for conversational English classes. Virtually all higher-level academic textbooks are in English, so after a certain point in most disciplines, knowing the language is crucial. The 8th Army Civil Affairs Office recruits GIs to teach colloquial English throughout the country. These classes are in high demand, though the number of GIs willing to take the time off from drinking and whoring is fairly low.

"His name was Barry," she told me. "Barry Krassler. After class, we went to coffee shops and talked."

"And you ended up in a *yoguan* with him."

She flinched. "Barry left me, went back to States, didn't write a single letter. My maid and I hid the pregnancy from my father. He was so busy, he didn't even notice. Until the night the doctor came to our house and the baby was born. My father was furious, screaming at me about causing him shame by bringing the child of an American into our family. He beat the doctor, threatening him with death if he ever said anything. He almost killed the maid; she barely escaped. Then he came after me. I only remember the first few blows before I went unconscious and he took the baby."

She paused now. The musicians were packing up. I put a hand atop hers. "What was the baby's name?"

"He never had a proper name like my father would have given him if he'd accepted him into the family. So I gave him the name I wanted him to have."

"What was it?"

"Bok-su."

"Moon Bok-su?"

"Yes."

Before the musicians left, they all bowed to the *gumiho*. She dismissed them and turned to me. "Let's go outside."

I acquiesced.

We crossed the same expanse of grass we'd crossed earlier in the day, but this time, the bodyguard remained under the awning of the main building, glowering after us. Apparently, now that I'd been taught that escape wasn't in the cards, I could be trusted to a small degree.

I asked her about the stone building. "What is that?"

"What do you think it is?"

"A tomb," I replied.

She nodded, and we continued to walk toward the cliff. At the edge, we stared out at the red sun setting into the Yellow Sea and the thick wall of fog rolling in slowly toward us.

The *gumiho* started to murmur something. I couldn't hear the first part, and leaned in to try to make out the words. Her voice, filtered by the swirling wind, lilted: "I was a child and she was a child, in this kingdom by the sea . . ."

I recognized the words, but from where? The breeze picked up, and I stumbled over a rock, once again unable to understand what she was saying. I stepped forward more carefully after that, watching for crags, and as I moved closer to her, the wind blew in my direction.

Her voice had lowered to a whisper as she finished. "In the sepulchre there by the sea—in her tomb by the sounding sea."

We stood just a few steps from the stone edifice, and she had gone quiet. In the distance, the wind howled. Even an uneducated simpleton like me recognized what she'd recited. A poem.

Edgar Allan Poe's "Anabelle Lee."

We stared out at the sweeping blue waves.

"My father," she said, "took the baby and walked down that pathway." She pointed. "He walked down the edge of the cliff to the Yellow Sea." She was crying now. "He walked into the waves and lowered my son into the water."

The tears stopped. She looked at me. "I died, too, that night."

"And later, when your father died, you decided to carry out your revenge."

"Not revenge. Justice. GIs who murder their own children will be forced to honor my child, to lie next to him like the man who loved Anabelle Lee."

"In a tomb by the side of the sea."

"Yes, by the side of the Yellow Sea."

Until that moment, I had been internally poring through the list of Korean vocabulary words I'd spent so many months memorizing. Finally, I dredged up *bok-su* and realized what it meant: revenge.

That night, the maid served a lavish dinner of bean curd in hot pepper stew, diced turnip kimchi, chopped squid tentacles, and mint leaves in soy sauce. As we ate, the *gumiho* opened up about her past. She'd been born into wealth. Her great-grandfather had been a Chinese merchant who'd accompanied an expeditionary force sent to Korea in 1883. Their mission was to enforce the Ching Dynasty's claim of extraterritoriality rights in Korea. Because China, Japan, and even Russia were vying for influence in Korea at the time, this didn't last long. When the Chinese were expelled, many of the soldiers and almost all of the merchants remained in Korea, and a Chinatown of sorts was set up in the heart of the port city of Inchon. At its peak in the early twentieth century, the Chinese population reached 65,000. But that number had greatly dwindled over the years, and only a fraction now remained. During the Korean War, Moon Guang-song's father made a fortune selling legally imported and black market foodstuffs to the hundreds of thousands of refugees streaming down from the Communist north. When the ceasefire was signed, her father, along with a small group of well-connected Chinese allies, formed the Sea Dragon Triad.

After divulging this half of her family history, she paused, waiting for me to ask about the Sea Dragons. But instead, I decided to focus on her personal life. "And your mother?"

Surprised, she mumbled, "How odd. You're the first one to ask about her."

I simply nodded, and she took a deep breath and continued.

"My mother was Korean," she told me. "She was marvelous at the *komungo*. Listening to her play are my happiest memories. She died when I was still young, but not before giving her instrument to me. She's the reason I've refurbished this estate and hired musicians—I've built a repository of classical Korean culture in her honor."

Suddenly, her face darkened.

Alarmed, I asked, "Is something wrong?"

She looked at me sharply and said, "I believe my father murdered her."

"Why?"

"Korean leaders have abused the Chinese," she told me. "Levying taxes exclusively on Chinese merchants, denying them the right to buy or sell rice in bulk out of fear they'd corner the market. Sending spies to make sure they don't betray their Koreans counterparts. Some of my father's men have even disappeared without a trace."

"And he blamed your mother for this?" I guessed.

"Yes," she replied bitterly. "As if *she* had any control over the police or government officials."

"And after your mother passed away," I asked, "it was just you and your father?"

She nodded. "I looked after him for almost two decades, watching without a word as he brought one concubine after another into our home."

"And when your father died, you inherited leadership of the Sea Dragon Triad."

"Not without opposition," she said.

"But you won."

"Yes," she said. "And we're expanding. But our men are not as disciplined or loyal as they should be; I have higher hopes for the new recruits."

"What about your bodyguard?" I asked. "Did you inherit him from your father, too?"

"No. A refugee family left him with us when I was an infant. My father had him trained extensively in martial arts, and assigned him to watch over me from about ten years old."

"I see." I paused, then decided to risk it. "What's his name?"

"Gui-mul," she told me.

"Gui-mul?"

"Yes."

I knew what it meant: monster.

■　■　■

A skulk of foxes nipped at my face. I awoke with a start, sweating onto my warm sleeping mat. For five minutes I lay perfectly still, listening. The only sound was the feint drip of a faucet in the kitchen. The main advantage I had over the previous three hostages was that I knew what to expect, and it wasn't good. I rose and slipped into my pantaloons and vest, then slid back the oil-papered door and padded as quietly as I could down the hallway. Slouched outside of one of the doors was *gumiho*'s guard, Gui-mul, snoring softly. His knife lay across his lap, and a set of keys hung on a large ring at his belt.

-19-

Later that morning, I was re-awakened by a severe wind rattling the windows and the walls. The maid knocked on my door and brought in a low table with my breakfast. Rice gruel and *muu malengi*, dried turnip. After she'd left the room, I sat cross-legged at the table and shoveled the hot gruel into my mouth. I chewed on the dried turnip a bit, grinding my teeth into its tough hide, but was rewarded only with bitter juice. In the end, I couldn't stomach more than a small sliver.

Outside, a car engine started. I stood and rushed over to the high window. The *gumiho*'s sedan was driving off; I thought I spotted her in the back seat. I sat down and finished my meal. After the maid took the table away, I got dressed and paced around the building, ending up out back, closest to the ocean. I spotted just two or three guards uphill and noted their positions. A thick mass of clouds was rolling in. I went back into the house and waited for lunch, slowly formulating a plan.

Later that afternoon, I snuck back outside, keeping

carefully out of the line of sight of the guards. Despite the wind gaining in strength and starting to blow cold rain into my face, I started up the path toward the stone sepulcher near the cliff's edge. As droplets became fistfuls of water, I saw the first of the guards in an Army-issue poncho run for cover, his M-1 bouncing behind his shoulder. As the others followed, I recalled Moon Guang-song's lament about the fading competence of the members of the Sea Dragon Triad.

I stumbled in the relative darkness up the incline, careful to stick to the shadows of the birch trees.. When I reached the fork in the pathway, the thunderstorm was full-blown; I hurried toward the sepulcher. I stood for a moment in front of the tall stone doorway, recognizing the Sea Dragon insignia engraved into it—a furious, terrifying image of a scaled reptile, rampant in the waves, devouring ships and men alike. The carving was so lifelike that it seemed to move as the rain pelted against it. I grabbed the iron ring on the left edge of the door and pulled. Complaining loudly, the door screeched back to expose a large, dark entrance.

The smell hit me all at once. Elements of it were familiar—feces, urine, and the body odor of someone who hadn't bathed in weeks. But decaying flesh? That, I couldn't detect. I held out hope that I hadn't risked my life for nothing. Still, I inched forward, hesitant to head straight into the pitch black.

It took a moment for my eyes to adjust to what little light was coming in from outside. The floor of the sepulcher was dirt, the walls made of stone. On the far side of the sepulcher sat a small box atop a rectangular stone platform. On a second platform closer to me lay a long, dark mass. I had to move closer to make out thin protrusions, which I soon realized were arms and legs.

"So you've found it."

I swiveled.

The *gumiho* stood soaked at the door to the sepulcher, a tranquil smile on her face and Gui-mul behind her. He carried a glass lantern that softly illuminated the room.

The shape groaned. In the light, I saw that it was a man, shackled by the wrists and ankles to the platform. I stepped forward and peered at him, lightly tapping his sunken cheek. Blue eyes popped open. He opened his mouth and croaked, emitting a strong stench. I turned away, but I knew who he was. Specialist Shirkey from Hialeah Compound in Pusan—the last GI taken.

I examined the clamps around his wrists and ankles. Not padlocked, but apparently hammered to fit securely. I straightened up and backed away, keeping my eyes warily on Gui-mul. "What about the other one?"

Moon Guang-song shrugged. "He's gone now."

"Gone where?"

She nodded toward the Yellow Sea.

So Corporal Holdren was a corpse floating in the Yellow Sea, just as Werkowski had been. I glanced back at Shirkey, prostrate on the stone platform. "Please, let him go," I told the *gumiho*. "This isn't right."

"*Not right?*" she said, eyes blazing. "How dare *you* tell *me* what's not right?"

Gui-mul shifted his stance, keeping his distance from me, holding the lamp out with his left hand and with his right hand gripping the hilt of his sword.

"Please," I said, "cut him loose."

"Never *hachi!*" she screamed. Never happen. GI slang that she must've picked up from the business girls in the GI villages she'd been visiting.

"What do you want?" I asked. "Money?"

"Money?" She was incredulous. "You think I'd take *money* for what GIs have done to me?"

I paused. This wasn't just about the loss of her child. Boksu's murder was the final straw, but she had been forced to cater to her mother's killer for decades, sinking into madness as she was exposed to her father's derision. And now she had the means at her disposal—money, hired muscle, a strong, skilled guard who was faithful to her, a vehicle, a massive seaside estate in which to hide—to execute her desired revenge. But her father was no longer here to accept his punishment, so American GIs had taken his place. A GI had once betrayed her, so his fellow GIs would pay the price. She'd been selective, relying on her apparent access to SOFA complaints to determine which GIs were deserving of torture and murder.

Whether she'd bought access through the SOFA committee or a different conduit, I couldn't say. But, based on how much she knew about me, I guessed the Sea Dragon Triad had spies placed very centrally within 8th Army.

Spies serving a vigilante, gone completely off the rails.

"Okay," I said. "Not money. So what do you want?"

She was silent for a moment.

"You know about the crimes that GIs commit," she said. "You see the women they hurt. All you need to do is tell me. Tell me and the Sea Dragons; we'll take care of it. Soon, GIs will stop hurting women."

When I hesitated, she continued.

"I'll pay you well," she said. "And I'll let you go—I know you didn't do the things in that report. You're not the same as your fellow soldiers."

The phony report Riley and I had run through Smitty. She'd already seen it, but her inside knowledge was so sophisticated, she'd known it was bogus. She must've gathered intelligence on me, realizing how dissatisfied I was with the madness of 8th Imperial Army. She'd figured she might be able to exploit my disaffection. She'd assumed that within military law enforcement, I was the weakest link in the chain, the most likely to betray the command.

I pretended to consider her proposal in order to buy time. What Riley had said about me not fitting into the military involuntarily replayed itself in my mind.

By now, Gui-mul had shifted his position to completely block the sepulcher's entrance. Looking around this ugly, cold place, I saw no weapons with which to defend myself. Bare hands against a skillfully employed sword in a small, sealed-off space. Little chance of escape. I had to keep her talking.

"What was this tomb built for?"

"My father's burial," she said.

"Is he still here?" I asked.

"No. I pulled his body out and tossed it into the Yellow Sea, where it belongs," she said.

"And in here," I said, motioning toward the tiny box on the bier. "This is your son?"

She stepped toward the casket and gently laid her hand on it. "Yes. Bok-su," she said, tears starting to stream down her face.

Her pregnancy and abandonment, the murder of her child—it was a horrible story, and I did sympathize with her, having been separated from my own son due to circumstances beyond my control. But then I looked over at Shirkey, emaciated and chained to unforgiving stone. I remembered Werkowski's corpse, floating in the concertina wire. And the spot on the back of his skull, rubbed raw from laying on the same stone platform, his head scraping against it. The wound to his chest through his heart, rising to exit from his back that perfectly fit the dimensions of Gui-mul's curved sword.

If I was going to escape from the *gumiho* and, more importantly, be the cop I had sworn to be, I had to save her last surviving victim. Despite what these GIs might've done, she didn't have the right to take the law into her own hands.

Moon Guang-song and I stared down at the tiny casket. My only true weapon was surprise. I reached out as if to touch the small casket. Before she could protest, I'd lifted the tiny coffin from its pedestal and hurled it at Gui-mul. The top of the coffin swung open, and a tightly wrapped bundle fell out.

The startled bodyguard stumbled backward out of the entrance in horror, eventually tripping and falling, the lantern slipping from his grasp and shattering, its flame extinguished by the rain.

Moon Guang-song screamed, rushing to pick up the casket and its contents. I burst outside and headed straight for Gui-mul, who was still struggling to regain his footing. Night had fallen, and the overcast sky was thick with angry gray clouds that had rolled in from the Yellow Sea, wind and rain whipping themselves into a frenzy. With any luck, the guards on the surrounding hills wouldn't be able to spot us.

I put the guard in a chokehold and grabbed his knife before he could retaliate. He struggled against me for nearly a full minute before going unconscious.

When I looked back up, the *gumiho* was gone, along with her child's corpse. The coffin I'd thrown at Gui-mul earlier lay in pieces on the ground. Shirkey was still chained to his stone platform, unmoving except for shallow breathing.

Putting the *gumiho* out of my mind, I unhooked the key

ring from Gui-mul's belt and began testing rusty keys on Shir-key's shackles. He groaned, seeming to regain consciousness.

"Where are Werkowski and Holdren?" I asked, despite knowing Werkowski was dead. I hoped he might be able to give me new information. And I hoped against hope that the *gumiho* had been lying to me about Holdren, and that I could somehow return him to Camp Kyle.

"Who?" he asked.

"The two GIs taken before you," I told him. "They were here, too. Probably not at the same time."

With a great wrenching of iron, one of the cuffs snapped open, freeing his right wrist. I moved on to his left.

"Who?" he repeated.

I explained again. Finally, he responded, "They were taken away."

"Where?" I asked.

Feebly, he shook his head. "Don't know."

"Was it just one man or two?"

He thought about it for a moment. "Two," he said.

"Were they locked in here with you?" I said.

"Yes," he said. "First one, then the other."

So the *gumiho* had let them die of hunger and thirst next to her lost child until she found their replacements. I wondered if, given time, I would have been the next in chains, or if I would've been spared, given that I hadn't committed the same crimes as the others. It was unsettling that the *gumiho* knew me better than 8th Army did—how much more I aspired to than military rank, and where the fissures in my loyalty were, and what she had to do to pry them open. I tried not to think about what would happen if those cracks widened, or whether Moon Guang-song might one day be able to exploit them completely.

I had opened the first ankle chain and only had one more leg to free. Before I started on it, I listened carefully. A great whooshing sound entered the chamber. I panicked for a moment, thinking the *gumiho* had come back with a weapon, or her guard had awoken. But then I realized it was rain, blowing in from the Yellow Sea.

I went back to unlocking the last shackle.

Agent Ernie Bascom searched the barracks, the 8th Army Snack Bar, the Post Library, and everywhere else he thought Agent George Sueño might be found. Finally, he gave up and drove to downtown Seoul to show Mr. Kill George's note. After brief deliberation, they decided that they'd pay a visit to Yonsei University.

The two of them walked through the leafy campus, led by Officer Oh, whose job was to stop students and ask for directions. Ernie, meanwhile, smiled and waved to each passing gaggle of female coeds, who tittered and walked on arm-in-arm. They located Professor Fulton in his office in the Humanities Building, speaking quietly with a couple of colleagues while going through papers at his desk. Fulton was a tall, thin man with a wispy brown goatee that made him look like a young Lenin. He didn't seem surprised by Ernie's appearance, though he looked a bit puzzled at the KNP's presence.

Officer Oh went over and whispered something to Professor Fulton. He glanced at Ernie and Mr. Kill, and the group stepped outside into the hallway.

Unafraid, he faced Mr. Kill and Ernie. "I'm told this is important."

"It is," Ernie said, inviting Mr. Kill to take over the questioning.

At first, Fulton claimed ignorance of the leak. But under Kill's withering interrogation, he revealed that a law firm in Inchon had offered him an "honorarium" for information on SOFA accusations.

"For their clients," Fulton said. "The ones who aren't properly represented. They track them down and offer pro bono assistance in their claims against Eighth Army. It's a worthy cause."

"What do you mean, not 'properly represented'?" Ernie asked.

Professor Fulton spread his fingers. "This firm has a specialized knowledge of the Eighth Army claims process."

"So they have inside connections," Ernie said.

Fulton shrugged. "I wouldn't know about that."

"Easy work for you," Ernie said.

"It's honest work," Fulton replied. "These victims deserve competent representation."

"And you deserve an honorarium."

"I donate all of it to the Women's Power Coalition. Someone has to strike back when you consider all the sexist mayhem the American military is perpetrating on the women of Korea."

"I'm sure you don't keep a penny," Ernie said.

Fulton raised himself up and replied, "I don't, in fact."

Mr. Kill pulled Ernie away.

Out of earshot, he said, "Three things. The Sea Dragons are based in Inchon. Sergeant Werkowski's body was discovered off the nearby coast. And a law firm there is the one buying information on SOFA charges."

"We need to go there," Ernie said, "and talk to the Sea Dragons. The ones who are still around, anyway."

"Yes. And if whoever is behind this has taken Agent Sueño, we don't have much time."

"He could end up like Werkowski," Ernie said.

"Yes."

Ernie checked his watch. "I can be out there in an hour. Two, with backup."

"We'll meet at the Inchon KNP headquarters."

Before they parted, Mr. Kill said, "Bring as many men as you can. But don't make this official yet."

"Why not?"

"I'm afraid the culprits might be given advance warning."

Ernie understood. There were plenty of bureaucrats within 8th Army and the Korean National Police who were willing to sell information. Until he and Mr. Kill had pinpointed exactly who this *gumiho* was and who was facilitating her crime spree, it was best to hold close what little information they had.

Mr. Kill gave a quick command to Officer Oh, who nodded vigorously. The pair of them stepped toward Professor Fulton, who by now was back at his desk arranging his papers. When Officer Oh placed him under arrest, he didn't resist, apparently expecting the handcuffs before they were snapped on.

Speechless, the other professors in the office waved goodbye to Fulton as he was hustled away by the all-business Officer Oh.

Once he was back at 8th Army CID, Ernie checked in with Staff Sergeant Riley.

"I've called everybody I know," Riley told him. "Still no sign of Sueño."

Getting permission to drive out to Inchon with a real MP patrol would take too long, and the request might even be denied. So Ernie took matters into his own hands. He asked Palinki to turn the keys of the arms room over to his second-in-command and make the trip with him and Staff Sergeant Riley.

"Back on the street?" Palinki asked. "Busting heads, enforcing the law? You *got* it, brudda!"

The big man set down the M60 machine gun he'd been working on, cleaned off his fingers with solvent, and was armed and ready in five minutes.

-20-

The last chain holding Shirkey to the stone platform groaned and fell open. I lifted his back so he was sitting up for the first time in days.

"Can you walk?" I asked.

He put his feet on the ground and tilted himself forward. He was about to crumble, but I caught him and held him upright. Together we'd started hobbling toward the door when I realized this would take too long.

"Here," I said, crouching. "Get onto my back."

I used a fireman's carry. Shirkey wasn't a big man and had lost weight in the last few days. It was easy enough to lift him off the platform. After a half mile or so of slogging through mud, I knew he would feel a hell of a lot heavier, but we had to get out of here.

Balancing his weight across my shoulders, I pushed open the stone door of the tomb.

Outside, the driver was still out cold. A massive deluge was coming down. There was little difference between the sky and the sea below. I waded uphill away from the cliff until I reached the rise overlooking the main house. At the bottom of the slope shone a few lights. If she hadn't fled already, the *gumiho* would be down there. I needed to get ahold of the keys to the sedan—the only car I'd seen on the compound thus far—so Shirkey and I could get out of here.

Halfway down the ridge, headlights glistened through the rain. A convoy of vehicles was winding up the long driveway to the estate. I knelt behind a large rock, allowing Shirkey to slide off my shoulders and sit in the wet grass beside me.

"Who's that?" I asked.

His eyes were closed.

"In those cars," I said.

"Her boys," he whispered. "They came out there once to see us. Smoking and laughing."

So she'd called backup. I wondered if there was any way to escape without a confrontation, which meant on foot without a vehicle. Up north, toward the road, there was nothing but farmland until Inchon. And down south, more farmland. We could hide, but they could easily fan out and find us in the morning.

"Come on," I said, lifting Shirkey back onto my shoulders. I kept far to the right of the big house, and we made our way into a small orchard of pear trees. After a half mile or so, I set him down again, this time into a thicket of untended brush. When I stood up, he said, "Where are you going?"

"To steal a car," I said.

"When will you be back?"

"Can't say for sure."

I found a half-rotted pear, tore off and threw away the most rotten chunk, and let the rain wash off some of the dirt.

"Here," I said.

"I can't eat nothing."

"You have to," I told him. "Take one small bite, chew it thoroughly, and then when you're ready, do another."

He reached out and took the pear. "If you don't come back," he said, "I'll understand."

"Don't worry," I told him. "I'm coming back."

I walked off, staying within the shadows. As I approached the main house, I blessed the rain for the decreased visibility. Lightning flashed, and I saw two of the Sea Dragons smoking in the closest of the five sedans lined up out front. I suspected they were supposed to be outside of the car, pacing the perimeter of the property on lookout for us, but they didn't seem to be operating under much discipline. I figured that the *gumiho*'s growing obsession with revenge had probably left her little time for disciplining her father's arrogant gangsters.

Lack of discipline in an enemy was always a good thing.

I crawled through the mud until I was behind the car. I grabbed a large rock, crouched down, and waited, rain pelting the back of my head.

They finished their cigarettes and climbed out of the car.

Without surveying their surroundings, they sprinted through the downpour toward the overhanging roof in front of the main building. When the driver ran past, I reached out, grabbed him around the throat, and struck him with the rock. He fell like a sack of wet millet, out cold. I dragged him behind the sedan until he was safely hidden and grabbed the keys from his pocket.

The one who'd been in the passenger seat, once safe under the overhang, turned around and looked back, surprised that his partner wasn't there. He called out.

"Ni gan shemma?" he said. I couldn't speak Chinese, but guessed he was asking after what his partner was doing.

When he took a few steps closer, I moved out of hiding and leapt at him with my full weight. He fell backward, and I landed squarely on him, jamming my elbow into his ribs. A great *whoosh* of air erupted from his lungs, and I used the same rock as before to knock him out cold. Worried that I might've gone too far, I double-checked that they were still breathing—all clear. I dragged both unconscious bodies behind a nearby bush and ran back to where I'd left Shirkey.

The untouched pear lay in the mud next to him. I picked him up and half-carried, half-dragged him to the car. Neither of the unconscious Sea Dragons had moved, and I prayed that any damage I might've done wouldn't be permanent. I forced the thought from my mind as I shoved Shirkey into the back seat of the car. Then I squeezed into the front, scrambling for the lever that would allow me to slide the seat back—at six foot four, I wasn't designed for these foreign compacts. I never could find the lever, with every damn car made differently. But this was no time for a letter of complaint to the Hyundai customer service department.

Hands wet with rain and Shirkey's filth, I fumbled with the key until it slipped into the ignition. I started the car and reversed it past the rest of the line, then threw it back into drive. As I accelerated up the gravel driveway, my knees were up so high I felt like they might touch my cheeks.

Someone must've heard me start the engine, because they ambled from the house onto the front porch. The blurred form pointed and shouted. They might not have known exactly what was going on yet, but they realized something was wrong. No one was supposed to leave the property, I guessed, without permission.

I stepped on the gas so hard that my tires spun on the wet rocks, and I had to ease off the accelerator before we rolled uphill toward the road that led to the main two-lane highway. I had almost reached pavement when a dark figure lurched out of the wall of trees on the far side. I swerved to avoid it, but whatever it was deliberately stepped forward to remain in my path. I accidentally clipped the figure with my left bumper, and only as we drove off did our rear lights illuminate the form.

Gui-mul was bent forward slightly at the waist, straining to remain upright, and in one clenched fist was an M-1 rifle.

Lightning flashed as he aimed it straight at me.

I jammed my foot onto the gas, but despite horrible conditions, the bullet nearly reached its mark, hitting the rear window first and then whizzing past mere inches from my head through the driver's seat window. Its impact shook the little Hyundai like one of the big brass bells the Buddhist monks rang in downtown Seoul. Glass splintered inward, covering both me and Shirkey. I closed my eyes and leaned away from the window, my foot still on the gas.

Though he was now much smaller in my review mirror, I saw Gui-mul fall in the middle of the road, rifle still in hand.

Shirkey, despite being covered in glass and rain, struggled to sit up. "Are you all right?"

"Yes," I shouted. At least, I was pretty sure I was—I was shaken by the gunshot, but conscious and, as far as I knew, uninjured.

Finally, we reached the main road. There were no cars in sight in either direction, so I headed north toward Inchon. I'd spotted flashes of light in the rearview mirror as we'd fled the compound—probably the other sedans, soon to be on our tail. The little car lurched forward as I stepped on the gas. I was still having trouble controlling the steering wheel with my knees jammed up alongside it. But I did my best.

In the back seat, Shirkey lay down and groaned.

By the time we reached the outskirts of Inchon, the Sea Dragons had almost caught up with us, their cars swerving around corners and obstacles like a pack of angry hounds. I guessed it was about nine P.M., meaning reasonable traffic, but not so much that I had to slow down. I maneuvered around slower cars, which meant all of them, and took advantage of the fact that Inchon still employed policemen instead of traffic lights at traffic circles. The ones who were still out, in their raincoats and white gloves, blew their whistles as I whizzed past, but I couldn't afford to stay within the speed limit. The question was, where could I go? Certainly not the Inchon Main Police Station. Mr. Kill had long since abandoned his temporary headquarters there. I had no desire to hand myself and Shirkey over to a gaggle of corrupt cops who'd not only been on Sea Dragon payroll, but who'd just been embarrassed by the Chief Homicide Inspector of the KNP at my behest.

Though it was the biggest tourist spot in town, which would otherwise have been convenient, I had to stay far away from the Olympos Hotel and Casino, property of the Sea Dragon Triad. For that matter, I wasn't sure which local bars they might have their hand in, seeing as Inchon was their home base.

There was only one place in town I was fairly sure they didn't own, and where the clientele might have the moxie to help me. The Eros Club.

I roared up to the Eros, just missing two merchant marines smoking out front but raising a large enough tsunami to thoroughly soak their pants. They were furious, and when I leapt out of the car, both men approached, shouting in Greek. I ignored them and yanked Shirkey from the back seat. Just as we reached the entrance, another half dozen cars pulled up, causing a tidal wave to break over the entire front of the Eros Club. This gave the two men something else to be angry about. I pushed through one of the swinging front doors to the club.

A sailor was dancing by himself onstage, bouncing around to stringed-instrument Greek music. Inadvertently, I'd stumbled into two or three tables and several chairs before the wet Greek sailors from outside stormed in. The ones whose drinks I'd knocked over were raising hell and reaching into their back pockets for what I presumed would be switchblades.

Following close on the heels of the two men I'd originally angered, a group of Sea Dragon men burst into the Eros. They shoved their way through the crowd, pointing and hollering, and I kept moving until I managed to duck behind the bar, Shirkey still clinging to me like a koala. I crouched and hid as best I could. From my liquor-lined trench, I grabbed several empty beer bottles and lobbed them into the crowd.

A cringe-inducing screech erupted from the sound system, and immediately everyone was shouting and shoving one another. The Sea Dragons were befuddled by the sea of angry Caucasian faces around them, wondering what they'd stumbled into. I remained hidden behind the bar, unsure of my next step until three or four police sirens screamed up to the front door. This should've brought relief, but considering the local KNP corruption, this cavalry might turn out to be more dangerous than the ongoing brawl.

One of the Chinese gangsters peered over the edge of the bar, face dripping with perspiration. When he saw us, his mouth opened, but before he could shout, a bar stool swung in a great arc toward his head. He barely ducked in time.

"Come on," I said to Shirkey. "We have to get out of here."

He stared at me and asked, "How?"

I searched the back wall of the bar. There was a small door, meant to be crawled through. I shoved it open and stuck my head inside. Sure enough, it led to a liquor storage space.

"Come on," I said.

Shirkey edged toward me. I went through the door, then reached back and pulled him in, shutting the little door behind us. There was no lock.

Wooden crates of OB Beer and plastic ones of Heineken lined the walls. I squinted in the glow of the dim yellow bulb, spotting what I thought might be the back exit. Behind us, something crashed, and someone cursed in Chinese. A hand reached through the door we'd come through. Motioning for Shirkey to remain quiet, I quickly stepped back to the side of the door and grabbed a full bottle of Jinro *soju* off the shelf. As the man crawled into the storage room, I smashed the bottle onto the back of his head. He fell into a lump. I pushed him back through the door and barricaded the passageway with a few crates before piling two more in the center of the room and climbing up to unscrew the dirty overhead bulb. In the darkness, I returned to Shirkey, squatted down, and pulled him across my shoulders. He complied, limp as a rag doll, and I shouldered open the back exit of the warehouse, accidentally hitting his head against a support beam.

"Damn," he whispered.

Outside, we stood in a dark alley, the air tinged with the salty reek of the sea. To my left, at the end of a gradual slope half a mile away, lights blinked from the masts of ocean vessels. A heavy bank of fog was rolling in quickly, enveloping the ships and turning one light after another into dim pinpoints. To my right, the darkness stretched off toward a catacomb of alleys. I heard crates being shoved out of the way behind us, then a big crash and yelling.

I headed away from the Eros toward the fog. The moment I rounded a nearby corner, the back door of the storage room burst open with a bang. Five or so pairs of footsteps pounded onto cobblestone, and the men's cursing reverberated down the street. I plowed forward, adjusting Shirkey's weight on my shoulders and hoping the Sea Dragons would decide this chase wasn't worth the effort. They didn't. As I rounded one corner after the next, the footsteps trailing me remained the same distance away.

I sped downhill, turning down new lanes as often as I could. I had no plan, and was starting to fatigue under Shirkey's weight. I hoped some sort of salvation would materialize.

Around another corner, a double string of lights swayed in the coastal breeze down below, stretching out toward the dark Yellow Sea. People walked along a wooden pier, milling about like small schools of fish and stopping at canvas-covered stalls. The fog bank crept ever nearer, ready to envelop all of it.

Between me and this idyllic scene was a busy four-lane road. Motorbikes and kimchi cabs swooshed past, none of the taxis with rooftop bulbs up for hire. They had no reason to be out here if they hadn't already caught a fare. Besides, who would stop for a sweaty foreigner with a half-dead man draped over his shoulders? I carefully made my way across the street toward the fish market. Perhaps being surrounded by a mob of people would make murder less of a viable option for the Sea Dragon Triad—only one way to find out.

"What was *that*?" Palinki turned around in the back of the jeep.

"What was *what*?" Riley asked from the passenger seat. Ernie drove. The three men wore fatigues and MP helmets, though the one Riley had on wasn't actually authorized.

"In the fog," Palinki said. "It looked like somebody carrying a dead body."

"A dead body? Of what? A fish?"

"Nah," he replied. "A person."

"No time for that now," Ernie said. "The emergency call came in from that Greek club. It's about two long blocks up that way. The caller mentioned a group of Chinese gangsters—I'm worried they caught Sueño in there."

"Let me out," Palinki said.

"What?"

"You two check out the Greek sailors. I'm gonna take a look over here, bro. Find out what that guy was carrying."

"But there's a *riot* up there. Don't you want part of that?"

"Maybe later. First, I check this out."

"We shouldn't split up," Riley said. "Those Sea Dragon boys don't play."

"Neither does Palinki."

Riley protested, but Ernie bulled his way to the right and let Palinki out of the jeep. He watched in the side mirror as the big man ran toward the fish market.

"Why didn't you order him to stay with us?" Riley asked.

"Why didn't *you* order him? You have the rank."

"I'm not in law enforcement."

"About time you admitted that," Ernie replied. "Anyway, maybe that was Sueño."

"Carrying a body around?"

"Yeah," Ernie replied, pulling back into traffic. From the main road, they went up an alley and stopped amidst the crowd of police cars and ambulances in front of the Eros Nightclub. As Ernie climbed out of the jeep, he took out his nightstick.

"How do you say in Greek," Ernie asked, "'I'm gonna knock me some son-of-a-bitch out'?"

"You don't say it," Riley growled. "You just *do* it."

But as Ernie charged into the melee, Riley stayed behind in the jeep.

Palinki knew better than to march down the market's central pathway. A huge man in a US Army uniform, MP helmet balanced atop his head, and a nightstick swinging at his side, was too much advance warning for the bad guys. Instead, he stayed in the shadows on the delivery side of the food stalls, dancing between the three-wheeled delivery trucks and the motorbikes piled high with plastic delivery crates. After a while, he caught up with the man carrying the body. He appeared to be wearing only flimsy pantaloons, and was perhaps shirtless. From behind, Palinki could tell the body belonged to another, smaller man in a faded military uniform. But with only the occasional glare of a naked light bulb or the flash of distant floodlight, it was hard to make out whether or not the man carrying the other was American or Korean. It looked like he was heading for the huge fish tanks at the end of the pier, where the wharf widened and there were more eateries. And more milling crowds scarfing down the wriggling tentacles of freshly sliced squid and guzzling glassfuls of bubbling rice beer.

The smell of the sea and the light glistening off the scales of live fish reminded Palinki of home, but he pushed such thoughts out of his mind. He had a job to do.

And then Palinki saw the group of thugs. At least five or six, he figured. One was on a moped, leading the way through the surging crowd. The others were arrayed behind him, warily checking each stall, their faces grim and slathered in perspiration. As they passed, Palinki ducked behind a large booth offering vast assortments of shellfish. A middle-aged proprietress turned to him in shock, but Palinki smiled and pressed his forefinger to his lips. The old woman nodded and couldn't help but smile back.

The men passed.

Palinki saw one of them elbow the guy on the moped and point toward the end of the wharf. And then the men were sprinting, the moped leading the rest like the sharpened tip of Neptune's trident.

I plopped Shirkey behind one of the huge tanks of mackerel swirling in green brine. Exhausted, he sat on the wooden planks of the pier, his head leaning against the glass. Suckers appeared as a red octopus attempted in vain to entangle his curly locks from its watery inner world.

"Did we lose 'em?" Shirkey asked.

I peered around the edge of the tank. In the distance, a man on a moped made his way through the crowd of revelers below the strands of glittering lights. A determined squad of soldiers followed closely behind.

"No," I replied.

Shirkey sat up. "They're here?"

"Almost," I said.

"What are we going to do?"

I glanced toward the end of the pier. It was a dead end, completely surrounded by the Yellow Sea. No place left to run.

"Whatever we have to," I said. "Fight."

I peered beneath the tank and found a short wooden plank. Not much heft to it, but it would have to do. "Here," I said, handing it to Shirkey.

"What am I going to do with this?"

"Jab them in the eyes," I said, "or in the crotch, like in bayonet training. When they reach for you, use your legs. Kick."

"Why in Christ's name do you think you were carrying me? My legs don't work."

"Well, figure out what you can do. These guys aren't going to let us off alive."

"What do you mean?"

"The guy before you, Werkowski. What do you think they did with him?"

"I don't know. I figured they collected a ransom, returned him to his unit?"

"No."

"What? What happened to him?"

"We found his body," I told him, "floating on the edge of the Yellow Sea."

Shirkey's eyes widened in panic. I didn't regret frightening him—he needed to understand that the situation was dire. And I'd given him the only potential weapon at our disposal.

Then I looked up at the tank, with my friend the octopus and five or six dozen mackerel swimming inside. I stood, pressing my hands against the glass and praying that the Sea Dragon thugs hadn't fanned out. I figured they'd stay fairly close together, trying to look like a group of friends out for a night of *mokkolli* and seafood.

Through the prism of swirling water, I saw them approach, their bodies constantly changing shape and their faces nothing more than undulating blue blobs. The tank was almost my height, half filled with seawater. When the Sea Dragons were within a few feet of the tank, I crouched slightly, placed my hands just above its center of gravity, and shoved forward with all the strength in my legs. It didn't budge. I lowered the purchase of my hands and redoubled my effort. The wooden edge at the tank's base groaned as I continued to push. It eventually lifted, and the water inside sloshed forward until its sheer weight became my ally, soon hurtling toward them so quickly that no power on earth could stop it.

As the tank fell, I pulled Shirkey backward and covered us as best as I could. Customers screamed when the glass broke with a thunderous noise and released a small tidal wave of water and sea life. I pulled Shirkey to his feet; he was so frightened now that he managed to take a few faltering steps, and with me supporting him, we made our way toward the back of a nearby line of stalls. The owners had stopped their cooking and rushed outside, and the people who'd been sitting on chairs and stools on the deck were now on their feet, some wading ankle-deep in the squirming mackerel.

The leader on the moped had U-turned at the last moment when the tank began to fall, and was the only one who hadn't been completely drenched. He jumped off his bike and forged through the mess, cursing as he ripped a small red squid from his arm and tossed it toward the edge of the pier. He spotted us just before we reached the end of the line of stalls and shouted to his men. The rest of the group spotted us as I glanced back, and began wading toward us like zombies.

After the first fish stand, there was less water, and what did remain flowed quickly over the edge of the pier. We had to get back to the main causeway, where there were more people and we might find help. Pulling Shirkey after me, I squeezed through a narrow partition between stands and stumbled over some stools next to a serving counter. The customers were at the far end of the pier gawking at the remnants of the fallen fish tank. Up ahead, we shoved through the crowd, some of the men cursing me for my rudeness. Shirkey had managed to maintain his footing, knowing it would slow us down if I had to carry him. Still, it wasn't long before the Sea Dragons had spotted us again.

They were much more aggressive than I'd been, shoving their way through the crowd so quickly that they knocked a few people down. But they got away with it, because no one wanted to get in the way of a half dozen enraged men.

They were only ten yards away now. I searched the seafood stands on either side of us for weapons. Finally, I saw something.

Shirkey and I staggered up to a man cooking at a stove. Startled, he turned just as I reached him and the band of thugs wrestled their way beneath the canvas overhang, Shirkey crouched, and the Sea Dragons ran straight toward us. I grabbed a wok filled with sizzling peanut oil, burning my hand on the metal handle, and tossed it into the face of the first man.

He screamed, clutching his eyes.

Shirkey, I believe, bit another of them in the leg.

I leapt over the counter and landed atop two of the men, who went down under my weight but then began squirming like eels. Someone else kicked my side, and another person was pounding my back. I jumped up, regained my footing, and started jabbing with my left and winging roundhouse rights, mostly into the air.

There was no way we'd win, but I wasn't about to go down without taking a few of them out first.

A grizzly bear entered the eatery. He swung a nightstick and knocked one of the Sea Dragons down, then another. The three gangsters still on their feet stared at him, wide-eyed. And then I realized who the human grizzly was: Palinki. He began brandishing the nightstick indiscriminately, at which point the last three thugs ran back out through the entrance.

Palinki turned to me. "You okay, bro?"

"Yeah." I pointed at Shirkey. "Would you take a look at him?"

Palinki nodded and knelt down to examine Specialist Shirkey.

The man who'd received the full brunt of the peanut oil writhed on the ground, still clutching his eyes. I felt guilty about possibly blinding him, but it had been a last resort. I crouched beside him and tried to get him to pull his hands away from his eyes. When he wouldn't, I poked around behind the counter and found a bottle of *mokkolli*. I poured the milky rice beer between his fingers, gradually coaxing him to open his eyelids, and when he did, I tilted the bottle carefully and dribbled a little of the rice beer directly into his eyes. I managed to wash out most of the oil that had collected there.

When the KNPs arrived, I tried to wave them off. The last thing I wanted to do was to be locked up by a corrupt Inchon police force. I didn't speak to them in Korean, but instead listened to them talk. They helped the half-blind thug to sit up, and seemed more solicitous of him than anyone else who'd been hurt in the cluster.

Ernie and Riley entered the stand. The place was getting crowded.

"About time you two showed up," I said.

"Where the hell you been?" Riley growled.

More KNPs arrived and conferred amongst themselves in whispers. Ernie glared at them, hand on the hilt of his .45.

I translated the snippets I could hear. "They want to take us all in to the Inchon Police Station," I said. "Sort this out."

Just then, Chief Homicide Detective Gil Kwon-up entered, followed by Officer Oh. The highest-ranking KNP on the scene bowed to Mr. Kill, and the two held a quiet conversation. Seconds later, Kill motioned for us to follow him. The sign outside above the stall read DAEWANG SEI-U TUIKIM, Great King Fried Shrimp. Revelers and workers stood gawking as we walked down the middle of the pier, a line of handcuffed Sea Dragon thugs being pulled along behind us by the KNPs. Several of the observers cheered, and the braver ones taunted the gangsters.

I was surprised that they applauded even us, American MPs. Staff Sergeant Riley hooked his thumbs in front of his canvas web belt, stuck out his bony chest, and strutted smugly in front of us, waving to the cute girls in the crowd. If they'd had flowers, he certainly would've been the one to receive them.

-21-

Several of the Greek sailors involved in the Eros Nightclub melee had been arrested by the KNPs, but were later released without charges. A dozen or so of the Sea Dragons who'd been involved were being held in custody, pending a conspiracy investigation headed by Mr. Kill and buttressed by the expert interrogation techniques of Mr. Bam.

Most of the Sea Dragons had stayed behind at the estate and had managed to slip away, as had Gui-mul, not to mention the *gumiho* herself.

"Like a fox," Ernie said.

Under Mr. Kill's close supervision, the Inchon KNPs remained on the lookout at nearby hospitals, waiting for more Sea Dragons to check in for treatment of injuries. But none sought medical attention, at least locally.

The next morning, Ernie, Riley, and I returned to 8th Army compound. After washing up in the barracks and putting on clean clothes, we returned to the CID Admin Office. I sat at the field table, typing up my report on an Olivetti manual. Miss Kim brought me a cup of oolong tea and patted me gently on the back.

I took out *Korean Folk Tales* and offered the book to her.

"No, Georgie," she said. "You keep. You need to know these things."

I supposed I did. I thanked her and shoved it back into my jacket pocket.

I'd heard that she'd been the one who'd forced Ernie and Riley to search for me. If they hadn't shown up in Inchon with Mr. Kill, Officer Oh, and Palinki, the Sea Dragon Triad would almost have certainly made me and Shirkey disappear.

Luckily, we were okay, and the Inchon KNPs were still undergoing their top-to-bottom overhaul, approved by officials at the head of the ROK government.

Led by Mr. Kill, a KNP detachment from Seoul located the *gumiho*'s estate and performed a thorough search. The place had been hastily abandoned, its furniture and household items left untouched but not a soul on the entire property. When I asked about the *komungo*, Mr. Kill gave me a strange look.

"You saw someone playing one?" he asked.

I nodded. Apparently, the long-stringed zither had also disappeared.

Corporal Albert Shirkey of the cold storage unit on Hialeah Compound was being treated at the 121st Evacuation Hospital here in Seoul, and was expected to make a full recovery. As soon as his doctor deemed him well enough, Ernie and I went to interview him. He was more lucid this time, and we weren't under nearly as much stress.

I asked him about Werkowski.

"He was still there when I arrived," Shirkey told us. "But when they brought me into the tomb and chained me to the platform, Werkowski attacked the bodyguard." He shook his head. "It was a mistake."

"The guard stabbed him?" I asked.

Shirkey nodded. "Ran him through, like in an Errol Flynn movie. But he was still alive and screaming, so I figured the blade had missed his vital organs. Then they dragged him outside, and that's the last I saw of him. I was hoping they'd taken him to the hospital."

"They tossed him in the ocean," I said.

This all fit with the autopsy report from Camp Zama, which had established drowning as Werkowski's cause of death. Though Werkowski had been severely malnourished and grievously wounded by the *gumiho*'s guard, he'd been alive when they tossed him into the Yellow Sea.

"What about Corporal Holdren?" I asked.

"He was definitely alive when they took him away," Shirkey replied. "They left the door open, and I could hear him struggling. They dragged him toward the cliff, and awhile later, I heard a boat engine from far off."

"So they transported him somewhere."

"Pusan," Shirkey said. "I think they took him to Pusan. It was the only word they repeated that I could understand."

This was the lead Mr. Kill needed. After I relayed the information to him, he passed it on to his chief interrogator, Inspector Bam.

Mr. Kill called me back in short order. One of the Sea Dragons had broken down and confirmed that Corporal Kenneth P. Holdren had been transported down the western coast of the Korean Peninsula to the southern port city of Pusan. But he had no idea why.

"Apparently, he's still alive," Mr. Kill told me. "But to save him, we have to move fast."

"Pusan is massive. How are we going to find one person in two million?"

"Bam will continue to request cooperation from the Sea Dragon men," Kill said over screaming in the background. "If we find out something new, I'll call you."

Early the next morning, Miss Kim called me to her desk and handed me the phone. It was Inspector Kill. "Have you ever heard of Oruyk-do?" he asked.

"No."

"It's an island, just outside the Bay of Pusan."

"Are you going to send the Pusan KNPs there?"

"No," he said emphatically.

So he didn't trust them any more than he trusted the Inchon KNPs. I didn't press him on the issue.

"Then who?" I asked.

"You. Holdren is an American. My superiors don't want to be accused of handling the case incorrectly if something goes wrong."

Politics as usual. There was no time to argue about it.

"I'll schedule a chopper," I said.

Within an hour, Ernie, Officer Oh, and I were in a helicopter heading toward Hialeah Compound on the outskirts of Pusan. What worried me most, as I explained to Ernie, was that the Sea Dragons were planning to exchange Corporal Holdren as a commodity.

"What do you mean?" Ernie asked.

"He's a product to be sold," I said.

"That's nuts. Who'd want to buy a GI?"

"Someone who needs one."

"Who the hell needs a GI?"

"Maybe the Reds."

"Huh?"

"Communist China. An American soldier would be a hell of a bargaining chip."

"For Christ's sake, Sueño. You've been reading too many spy novels."

"Maybe. But I can't think of any other reason they'd bother to transport him down there."

When we arrived at Hialeah Compound, we checked in with the local MPs and caught a kimchi cab to the US Army

Port of Pusan, a small compound on the seaward side of town. Sergeant Freeline, the NCO in charge at the operations desk, thought he was dreaming: Standing before him were two law enforcement agents in coat and tie and a uniformed female officer of the Korean National Police.

"This is like one of those cop programs on AFKN," he said. The Armed Forces Korean Network. "Maybe *The Mod Squad*."

"Cut the crap, Freeline," Ernie told him. "We need a boat. Now."

Freeline swallowed as he pushed his horn-rimmed glasses higher onto the bridge of his nose. I slapped my CID badge onto the counter; I'd had a new one issued in Seoul, along with a new military ID card. Freeline swallowed again, picked up a heavy black phone, and dialed five numbers. It rang for a second before someone on the other end picked up.

"Lieutenant Cochoran?" Freeline said. "Sir, you're not going to believe this."

"Tell him we need a boat," Ernie said, "*and* a driver."

I turned to him. "You don't *drive* a boat."

"Then what do you do with it?"

"You steer it. Or sail it. Or navigate it, or something."

"'Drive' is good enough for me," Ernie said.

A half hour later, we were chugging in a small craft across choppy seas, leaving the curved spit of headland on the southern edge of Pusan. All three of us—Officer Oh, Ernie, and myself—checked our weapons, keeping the barrels pointed toward the sky as we made sure they were loaded and ready to fire.

The sun was high overhead when we landed on the island of Oryuk-do. According to Mr. Kill's informant in Seoul, the Sea Dragon Triad had a warehouse near the fishing village of Sangmul-ri. Boats traveled in and out regularly, and from there transferred goods either to other islands south of the Korean peninsula or—if they didn't run into interference from the Korean coast guard—turned right and continued across the Yellow Sea to the coast of China. I suspected Corporal Holdren was one of the items awaiting transport.

"They're haggling over price," I told Ernie. "What with all the trouble up in Inchon, the Sea Dragons have fallen behind on their income projections. Mr. Kill agrees that an American soldier would help to make up the deficit."

"How much are they demanding?" he asked.

"According to what Mr. Bam beat out of the informant, *sipman bul.*" A hundred thousand US dollars.

"Damn," Ernie said. "Do they want me instead?"

Officer Oh apparently understood what we were saying. She stared at Ernie as if he'd lost his mind.

"What about the gummy whore?" Ernie asked.

Bam had pursued the topic repeatedly, trying every trick

he could think of, but not one of the captured Sea Dragons budged. There was no reaction whatsoever to the word
gumiho or the name Moon Guang-song.

The warehouse sat on a small hill overlooking the fishing village of Sangmul-ri. Down by the quay below us, men
secured boats to wooden stanchions.

"Fishermen," Officer Oh said. Returning, apparently, from
their morning foray.

The warehouse appeared completely dark, even abandoned.
We approached from the rear. There was no back door—only
a window, high up on the second floor.

Before we'd left the Port of Pusan, Officer Oh had contacted
the ROK Coast Guard, who promised to have one of their
ships stop by Oryuk Island as they made their way out to regular patrol. They hadn't arrived yet, but none of us wanted to
wait. We walked around to the front of the warehouse, where
the big double door for trucks was closed. A small side door
that presumably led to an office was shut. I tried the knob—
locked. Ernie motioned for me to move out of his way and
then stepped back, took a deep breath, and bounded forward,
kicking with his right foot. The door burst inward. Officer Oh
entered first, weapon drawn. Ernie and I followed, separating
to flank her. She switched on lights, and all that moved was
a mouse scurrying into its hole in the corner. A forklift sat
idle, and only a half dozen or so boxed electronics lined the
wooden shelves. We searched the building meticulously, from

the front loading platform to the *byonso* out back. No sign of Holdren or other life.

"The informant in Seoul lied to us," Ernie said.

"Officer Bam will be angry," Officer Oh responded grimly.

Disappointed, we emerged from the warehouse. Ernie started wandering downhill. Officer Oh and I followed until we reached the quay. An old man sat on a wooden stump there, deftly unknotting a tangled net. In front of him sat a box full of wriggling sardines. When he smiled up at Ernie, his entire sunburnt face seemed composed of wrinkles, like an intricate map of the surface of the moon.

"*Anyonghaseiyo, halaboji*," Ernie said. Are you at peace, Grandfather?

The old man nodded, still smiling. When Officer Oh and I arrived, he spoke to her in Korean. "The warehouse up there is empty," he said. "I could've told you that."

"What we're looking for," she said, "is an American soldier." She used the word *migun*.

"Why didn't you tell me? Don't you think I know everything that goes on in this village? I've lived here all my life."

I wanted to ask him about his career on the ocean and what life had been like before the Korean War, during Japanese colonization, but there wasn't time. Instead, I turned to Officer Oh and told her to ask him about the soldier.

So she did.

"I saw three Sea Dragon men drag him up to the peak

yesterday." He pointed a gnarled old finger toward the top of Mount Oryuk. "They came back without him."

"So the American's up there?" she asked.

"Must be."

I prodded Officer Oh to ask one more question before we left. "I thought the Sea Dragons were going to sell him to the Chinese government. Why would they take him up there?"

The old man shook his head. "The Chinese aren't interested in him."

"Why not?"

"What would they do with an ugly American? One more mouth to feed. Don't they have enough?"

Apparently, the deal had fallen through. The Chicoms had thought twice about poking the American eagle, and the Sea Dragons were left with a white elephant by the name of Holdren. We thanked the old man and hurried off.

As might be expected, the view from the top of Mount Oryuk was beautiful. The thatched roof homes of the quaint village sat like an artist's panorama, and the sea spread endlessly in all directions. A mist rose slowly in the distance, and I could just make out the dark hulls of fishing boats.

"There," Ernie said, "the coast guard's coming."

A couple of miles away, the sleek ship, red lettering elegantly detailed onto its white body, glided through the waves.

We all turned and looked once again at what we'd found up on the peak.

Corporal Alfred P. Holdren, late of the 44th Engineer Battalion, Army Support Command, was nailed to a tree by his hands, his throat slit open. I hoisted Ernie up to listen for a heartbeat, though we already knew any remaining pulse had long since faded away. There wasn't much blood, but the man had been so starved, his body almost seemed to blend into the wood.

Officer Oh was sick and crying. When we were sure Holdren was dead, Ernie and I managed to unhook his body and lower his corpse to the ground, then proceeded to react in kind. Ernie threw up, and I curled up on the edge of the mountain, holding my face in my hands.

The Sea Dragon Triad's message was unmistakable. When we messed with them, they messed with us. But what bothered me most was the talisman stuck in Holdren's belt. I plucked it delicately from him and held it in my hands. It was long and furry, an animal's tail. I wasn't sure, but I was willing to bet this had once belonged to a fox.

One down, eight more to go.

Back in Seoul, there was talk of dropping Shirkey's SOFA charge, since he'd "suffered enough." That is, until I made a call to Katie Allsworthy. After sputtering and calling me three kinds of a sonofabitch, she finally listened as I explained what was in motion with Shirkey, which spurred her to action. She proceeded to raise hell in the hallowed halls of the 8th United States Army, and a day later, the JAG office announced that, despite his injuries, Shirkey's SOFA case would move forward as normal.

He'd shown no mercy to his ex-girlfriend Soon-hui when he'd beaten her so badly that she'd lost a child; it was fitting that none be shown to him.

Mr. Kill called and told me that the Pusan KNPs' investigation into Soon-hui's death had stalled. There was a loaded pause as I absorbed with his unspoken words—her murder would never officially be solved.

"We already know it was them," I said. "Punishing her for talking to me."

"Yes," Mr. Kill replied, his voice low and steady. He paused for me to recover and finally said, "We can't save everyone."

"No." I sighed. "We can't."

Staff Sergeant Palinki received a letter of commendation for his actions at the Port of Inchon. Everyone stood at attention as Riley read off the citation, and Colonel Brace shook Palinki's hand before a couple dozen of us MPs and CID agents filed past to offer our congratulations.

That letter would be placed into his personnel file, and would go a long way toward counterbalancing the letter of reprimand he'd received for beating the hell out of those would-be rapists in Itaewon. The best part, as far as Palinki was concerned, was that he was now officially out of the arms room and back on the street.

His big face beamed as he shook my hand. "Busting heads again, bro."

I slapped him heartily on the shoulder.

-22-

"**M**andatory," Staff Sergeant Riley said.

"What are you talking about?" Ernie said. "They can't *force* us to go on sick call."

"Says here they can." He pointed to the memorandum. "And Colonel Brace has chopped off on it." Meaning he'd approved it.

"This makes no sense," Ernie said.

"Sense or not," Riley replied. "You and Sueño are to report to the One-Two-One psych ward at zero nine hundred this morning."

"They think we're *crazy*?"

"If they don't, I do," Riley said. "New rule. After every incidence of violence, you're required to be evaluated by a mental health professional. For traumatic stress."

"How about you? You were there."

"I'm perfectly sane," Riley said. "Besides, this memorandum doesn't mention me. Just you two."

I glanced over at Miss Kim, who studiously avoided my gaze.

In the end, Ernie relented. Fifteen minutes before the appointment, we walked outside to the jeep. He switched on the ignition and silently drove us over to the 121st Evac. After we checked in at the psych ward, Ernie was taken into an examination room by a nurse. Five minutes later, I was called into the doctor's office. Behind a small gray desk, looking sharp in her dress-green uniform and white lab coat, was Captain Leah Prevault, MD.

"Who told you?" I asked.

"It's a secret," she said, grinning.

"It was Miss Kim, wasn't it?"

She laughed. "I knew I couldn't hide it from the Great Detective."

I shuffled in my seat. "She worries about us."

"So do I," she replied, looking up from my records.

"I'm glad to hear it. Why didn't you write?"

"I did."

"Not often."

"No." She looked down for a moment, then back at me. "It's a poor excuse, but Tripler's psych ward has been backlogged for so long that we've been working triple shifts trying to catch up. I'd planned to write more, but I missed you, and wanted to talk things over in person instead."

"You took TDY?" I asked. Temporary Duty.

"Yes. My commander's been planning on sending me back to the One-Two-One for some time. They don't have anyone assigned to the psych department here anymore. But he kept on putting it off because of the caseload in Honolulu. When Miss Kim called and told me what you'd been going through, I told him I couldn't wait any longer."

"How long are you here for?"

"Two weeks."

"Tonight," I said. "Will you have dinner with me?"

"Of course."

"Do you still remember how to use chopsticks?"

"I was taught by the best."

We set a time and place. Far from the compound, away from the prying eyes of the 8th United States Army. Then someone knocked on the door. Leah called for them to enter and a medic hustled in, carrying a bundle of paperwork. "Sorry to interrupt."

"No problem, Jerry. We're done here, anyway."

I stood up from my chair and saluted Doctor Prevault. She smiled and returned my salute.

Ernie was waiting outside in the lobby. "Did you pass?"

"Yeah," I said as we started walking toward the exit. "Clean bill of health."

"Me, too. The medic said I didn't even have to see the doctor."

"Nope. No point."

"Just answered a few questions, is all. No headaches, no bad dreams, no loss of appetite. Nice to know I'm not nuts." Ernie thought it over. "Nobody's going to believe it, though."

"That you're not nuts?"

"Yeah."

"I wouldn't," I answered.

I must have been silent for a while after that, because Ernie asked, "Something wrong?"

"Nothing. But I saw Leah."

Ernie blinked. "You mean . . . ?"

I nodded.

"How is she?"

"In fine form."

He grinned. "Better be careful, messing around with an officer."

"Don't worry, I will. How about you and Captain Retzleff?"

"Good news on that front."

"Yeah? What?"

"Her fiancé got promoted."

"Her *fiancé*?"

"Yep. Stationed up at Division. Just found out he made the list for major."

As we walked toward the jeep, I stared at Ernie, dumbfounded.

"We're both very proud of him," he said.

■ ■ ■

Before she left Korea, Doctor Leah Prevault and I discussed Moon Guang-song. Based on as full a description as I could give of her past and behavior, Doctor Prevault speculated that her violent acts might not only repeat themselves, but could grow worse after the successive displacements she'd suffered—the loss of her child, then her father, and now her home. She couldn't make a final diagnosis without a direct examination, but thought long-term psychological analysis and care, possibly even in an institution, might very well be required.

"In other words, she's nuts," Ernie said.

"I guess so."

"And she's obsessed with you."

I shifted uncomfortably in my seat.

Ernie looked at me. "Well, she is, isn't she?"

"How would I know?"

We were driving toward Itaewon, chasing after a PX taxi whose customer was a dependent wife whom we suspected was headed to sell a load of PX-purchased goods on the black market. Back to mundane life.

"You think Mr. Kill will ever catch her?" Ernie asked me.

"If he doesn't, we will," I said.

"How?" Ernie glanced at me, momentarily taking his eyes off the road. "The Provost Marshal has taken us off the case, and we're back to black market detail. Werkowski's and

Holdren's bodies have been shipped back to the States, the bugle has sounded, and their families have been paid thirty-thousand dollars each in Servicemen's Group Life Insurance."

"Watch out," I said, pointing to a kimchi cab swerving between lanes.

Ernie turned back to the wheel, but he was still upset. "We're not assigned to the case—nobody is. How the hell do you imagine we'd catch somebody with that much money and that much mobility, plus an incredibly powerful Chinese gang to protect her?"

I was silent for a moment. Ernie came to a stop at a red light. "I'll think of something," I said.

"You're nuts, Sueño. The honchos at Eighth Army don't want to hear it anymore. It's an embarrassment. GIs murdered by a mythical creature and a gang leader. They just want to bury the whole thing. So do the Koreans."

"They *can't* forget it," I said. "Neither can I. We saw Werkowski's and Holdren's bodies. We know what she did."

Behind us, horns blared. Startled, Ernie shoved the jeep into gear and rolled forward.

"Okay, I saw it," he said. "But I'm not like you. I don't want to keep hitting my head against a brick wall for a thankless job that nobody wants done."

"She'll do it again," I said.

"Where? When?"

"Where we least expect it, and when it's most inconvenient."

Ernie hung a right at the road leading to Itaewon. "How do you know?"

"I know her."

Ernie pulled the jeep over, wrapped the chain welded to the floorboard around the steering wheel, and padlocked it securely. He peered at me. "What the hell happened to you when you were with that broad?"

"Staying with her—it was kind of like being given a gift."

"Some gift," Ernie said.

Together we walked up the narrow lane, ready to bust an unsuspecting woman for selling six cans of Spam and two jars of soluble creamer on the Korean black market.